Murder on Nestor
- Race to Death -

Space Detective - A Skip Brown Adventure

by Pj Belanger

Cover Art by RB

Murder on Nestor
- Race to Death –

Space Detective

A Skip Brown Adventure

Copyright 2013
BRP Publishing

This book is distributed in the United States by BRP Publishing

First Edition 2014

Printed in the United State of America
ISBN 978-0-9826481-6-2

BRP PUBLISHING

Dedicated to:

Donna

A Sister,

a best friend,

always there for me.

Table of Contents

PROLOG

What was that god awful smell, I thought as my head tried to clear. The realization that it was coming from *me* made my mind attempt to focus through the haze. I made an effort to sit up, but my body was not cooperating as I slunk back on the table. My head hit the hard wood with a "thunk". The harsh overhead fluorescent lights glared down bringing my nauseousness into the fore. *Where the hell am I?* My brain wouldn't work, it was stuck on the smell; my other senses were dulled, my brain was just paying attention to my nose.

"You all right, mister?" came from somewhere. "You dun have a fit of some kind."

Then the night's events came flooding back, my brain decided to awake, then shut down again. I picked up my head, trying to see who was talking. Through my mental cloud, I let my eyes adjust enough to get a blurred vision of a man in bright orange overalls holding a large broom. The colors hurt my eyes causing me to close them again. "Where am I?" I somehow managed to get out of my dry mouth. I had an acid taste that flowed out with the words. My words came out as a bunch of slurs, but the man answered me. Again the smell hit me.

"You're in the janitor's building. It was the closest to the stands where you was sittin.'"

His foreign off-sector accent didn't hide how leery he was of me and he backed up as I managed to get myself into a sitting position, my feet dangling off the table's edge. My shoes felt heavy, a rather strange feeling, but then my whole body was having trouble responding. "They say not to call an ambulance, you want an ambulance?" I could tell he'd like nothing better than to be rid of me.

"No!" was all I could manage as my hands cradled my head. I lifted my eyes trying to focus, but no go. My hand automatically reached into my jacket pocket feeling for my packet of pills. I somehow managed to squeeze one of the little blue tablets out of its packet and pop it into my mouth, swallowing it dry. My hands were shaking badly. The pills, I'd feel better in about ten minutes. At least I hoped I did.

"Who brought me here?" I tried to once again to concentrate on what must be a janitor, trying to get the words out with some clarity.

"A lady had two of dem track attendants bring you in here." He had backed up to the door, probably anticipating a quick retreat if he had to.

Then a memory came flooding back, *Ah, Hill had dumped me here*. My mind was now beginning to get organized. I looked down at my clothes. I had thrown up all over myself. It hadn't been the first time, although each time I hoped it would be the last.

I managed to crawl off the table, holding on to the edge, swaying a little as I tried to steady my over six foot body. "Where's the bathroom?"

The man just pointed and I followed his direction to a tiny corner dingy john. I washed up as much as I could. There was a half used roll of paper towels wedged on the handles of the sink. Cold water brought my eyes into focus as I looked into the small cracked mirror above the rusted stained sink. Two brown bloodshot eyes looked back at me, accusingly. *I know, I told them, I know I shouldn't be here.* I thought I could handle it. The eyes coldly criticized my stupidity; staring unblinking back at me. My own eyes blaming me for being a fool. A damn stupid fool.

I stumbled back out of the bathroom. The orange covered man was gone, his broom leaning against the wall. I looked around at the gray hanger-type building, made more grungy by the swinging overhead lights. It didn't help my concentration as everything seemed to sway with them. Mops, buckets, rakes, wheel barrows lay in all directions. The walls were covered in gardening tools. The floor glared gray cement, dotted with round red rusted barrels.

The smell of disinfectants made my nose crunch; it wasn't a pleasant mixture with the smells emanating from my own body. I crossed over to a metal door, wrenching it open, letting the outside air wash over me. The night's lack of light was a welcomed difference. Although it was mixed with the smell of fuel and oil type lubricants, I welcomed the change. Outside I leaned against the metal building, trying to get a hold of my emotions. The metallic walls seemed warm from absorbing the sun's heat all day. Which sun? Where was I? I tried to calm myself, I didn't need another episode.

I tried to focus my mashed-up brain. Then it hit me, where I was. I wasn't on Fulton, I was on Nestor! At least we shared a sun, I remembered that. Strange the memories that come out of a damaged brain. Then more memories as I looked out over the deserted racetrack and the deserted Midway outside the enormous grandstands. I knew exactly where I was and why. I felt the bile trying to come back up as the memories of the horrible accident forced its way forward. I fought it, taking out another pill, quickly swallowing it. Ten minutes later I was calmer, my stomach under control. I could see Nestor's two moons even though they were on the wane. Their soft light somehow brought my mind in order as their images filtered through the huge iron work supporting the grandstands.

The race track lay in front of me. I could barely see it through the tiers of seats. All was quiet. It must be late, I thought, as I looked around the empty walkways. No roaring of engines, no fans hurrying with their popcorn and hotdogs. I touched my cellbutton on my jacket collar, listening to its chromatic voice in my ear, "12:12am, Saturday, 3rd month, 6th day, Federation standard time, location Strom Super Track on ...."

I slapped it off. I knew where I was, I grimaced. Had it only been yesterday that I was lamenting being at the oppressively hot office, only yesterday.........

MAPS

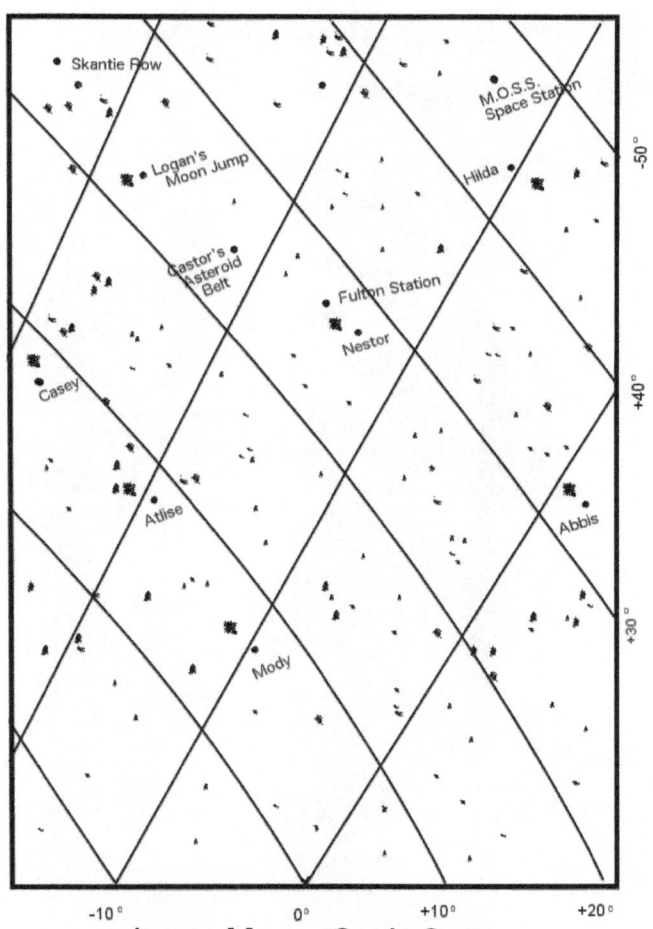

Jump Map - Crab Sector

Planet Fulton Station
Land Mass Map

Pryte Ocean

Thork Island

Windset Island

Muler Island

Jump Station

Crow Bay

Fulton City

Dome
Police Station

Diamond Island

Aston Ocean

Dot Islands

Chapter 1

Fulton Station isn't a large land planet but it is a damn hot one. From what little documentation exists, I know it was done quickly as it was the first planet the engineers put in the sector with the idea that it was to be used only for further sector construction. Thus they spent little time on it and planned only the small land mass which became the few clusters of islands we now inhabit. It was originally a place to store equipment and house the construction workers but a little consideration on climate control would have been nice. The temperature can get as high as 115 degrees during the summer season and get as reasonable as the low 90's during what the residents call balmy winter weather. It is only saved for habitation by its low humidity; go figure with 96/4 percent water/land ratio but it is what makes most of the year bearable. The trade winds from the oceans keep the humidity off shore giving us a dry, slow roasting heat.

Fulton City, being its capital, is the epitome of its name. Like the whole planet it is named after, the city radiates heat. Everyone lives in air conditioning. That is for those lucky enough to have a central air system that works.

The Police Station isn't one of them. That's the problem with having an "old" planet, too many old buildings and they have stuck us in one. "Us" being the headquarters for the local Fulton police with the top fifth floor for the sector detectives. Oh, the station has an AC system all right, but 99 percent of the time it doesn't function properly. I couldn't blame the maintenance crew, although I'd been known to swear at them, it wasn't their fault that the antiquated system can't be fixed. Gum and duct tape can only do so much. It is the sector's stingy lack of funds that is the culprit. We, meaning the Crab Sector police force, live with fans rotating loudly in every space possible and lots of underarm deodorant. Every one of my detectives has stains under their shirts' arms, hazard of the job. You'd think our illustrious city fathers would at least pay for the deodorant. But I'm being facetious, something I'm constantly being accused of along with my impatience and temper, a typical overworked Chief of Police attitude. I attended the yearly "Chiefs" Federation convention for all the sectors; the attitude prevails among the other head honchos. They all feel overused and understaffed. At least it's an excuse I often use - it's a demanding, frustrating job. A job I love despite complaining about it a lot.

It was Saturday, supposedly a day off for me, which meant I still went into the office but instead of a suit, I wore my khaki shorts and the lightest t-shirt I had with light beach sandals on my feet. It was a day to clear off my desk, chairs, tables and filing cabinets of all the week's work I'd thrown on them. A day with only a few people around to bother me; mostly my detectives that were trying to get their reports in before deadline.

I pushed the first floor main door open, one of those antiquated glass rotating traps, leading with my one hand as the other had a hot cup of Java - I know, despite the heat, I was addicted to the black liquid before my stint in torrid Fulton. I was introduced to the caffeine rich drink by my Uncle Jack when I was just eleven years old when I moved in with him. I'm sure my parents, who were doctors, would not have approved, but Uncle Jack was all my brother and I had after they'd died and he had no idea what was appropriate for adolescents, being an old bachelor himself. He was the perfect Uncle, not the perfect parent. Yet I had no complaints, neither did my younger brother. All in all we were lucky to survive such a tragedy intact as my parents were our whole world and it was a testament to the man how we never felt unloved or unwanted.

As the door turned opened, to my astonishment, I was pushed back by a cold puff of air. When I stepped in, I couldn't believe the AC was working. I should have guessed as the glass doors were all ice covered. My joy was quickly squelched as I looked over past the deserted foyer to the weekend receptionist, Maggie, who was wearing a heavy coat with earmuffs on her ears and mittens on her hands. It was so cold I thought I'd see icicles dripping from her nose, but that was covered by a scarf.

"Hello, Chief Brown," I heard from under the scarf wrapped several times around her neck. "They fixed the air conditioning but they can't control the temperature."

"Where'd you get the winter outfit?" I asked, walking over the worn linoleum floor whose original color was long gone to the long drab olive-green greeting counter. "I didn't think winter clothes existed in Fulton."

"Ski trip to Holka Mountain resort on Hilda," came the muffled reply. "Ran home and got them. Maybe you should get some too? At least it is keeping everyone away. They don't stay long."

She had a point. Despite the early hour, the lobby is usually full of Fulton inhabitants, everything from derelicts to ticketed complaining citizens. Today, all had fled, freezing temperatures are like the plague to

Fultonites. I imagined the receptionist was smiling under that heavy scarf. I didn't envy her citizen orientated job. Not that I didn't love Fulton's inhabitants but they could be real pains in the asses, especially the angry ones that came tramping into the police department. It's amazing how many things get blamed on the police. They usually don't make it to me but a few do - like irate politicians who feel that their speeding ticket was just plain "wrong". It's right - just pay it!

I'd never been to Hilda on a ski trip, hadn't taken a vacation in several years. Had only gone off planet for business, so the closest I had to appropriate freezing winter attire was a parka. I shivered all the way to the elevator, my breath leading the way with white fog. My shaking, freezing finger punched the button for the top floor. I swear I heard it crack. The doors slowly slid closed as if complaining of the freezing temperatures. I heard the creaking of the elevator's components, not filling me with great confidence that I'd make it. The elevator slowly ground upwards, I watched each floor light up then it seemed to tackle the next floor. "Come on, baby, come on." I encouraged it. The elevator was probably from the original building. Finally number 5 lit up, the doors creaked opened and I jumped out. The stairs next time!

Hopefully the fifth floor would be warmer. Didn't heat rise? To my dismay it seemed even colder. I quickly walked around shutting off all the rotating fans, shivering as the goose bumps on my arms quickly rose. I went over to the windows. Tall factory type panes of glass left over from being a warehouse. I pushed and shoved but they wouldn't budge. Several of my bulky detectives came over to try, but no deal! Old age had painted them shut. The thought of accidentally breaking one did enter my head but the place already looked a dump and who knew how long before it would get fixed.

I didn't need to add the smell and the noise of the city to the office decor. It was already depressing enough.

I wove my way through the cubicles to my back office. I passed several shivering detective bodies. I got only half hand waves as they hunkered down trying to get their reports in on time. That'll teach them to wait until last minute. The thought of heading home crossed my mind but one look at the tab notes strewed across my small office put that out of my head. I sat despondently in my desk chair and quickly sprang up as the cold metal seat sent shock waves through my legs and up my body. I swore, a string of curses leaving my cold lips! Another budget fallout - cheap metal furniture probably left over from Fulton's early days. I put my spare suit coat that I leave for emergencies in the office across the seat, sitting on it.

"Little cold?" I heard from my doorway. Captain Issam, my lead detective, dressed in a fur coat, a pulled down knitted hat and leather gloves, stood blowing cold fog into my office.

"What's, everyone got winter clothes but me?"

"Ski trip to Hilda," he remarked. Issam, an already short guy, looked like a Hilda penguin as he waddled his way into my office.

A ski trip, well that explained it. Everyone had been on vacation but me! I made a mental note that the next time I had a meeting on Hilda, I'd go shopping. Heavens knows I wouldn't be there on a holiday. Most of the time I spent on the cold resort planet was in the police headquarters checking on my staff there as I went from heated cab to heated office. It wasn't one of my favorite trips. Next time I'd spend the money for a winter coat and all that went with it; scarves, mittens and boots!

"Where the hell is the maintenance crew? Get them on the line." I sharply demanded although it came out more like a cold croak. I swear the words hung in the air frozen stiff like me.

"Day off." I think he was smiling under that scarf, knowing damn well there wasn't anything I could do about it. The monetary resources didn't include maintenance on the weekend either. Hell, we had to dump our own trash even during the week. I'd had to argue for the bathrooms to be cleaned more than once a month!

I picked up my cup of java, cold. I sat there glowering, something I do very well. I heard a few of my detectives in the outer office, loud complaints reaching my ears. No one confronted me directly, I'm not easy to confront especially when I'm in a bad mood. The best they could do was complain loudly, knowing I'd hear it come drifting into my office.

"Damn it! Let's go get a cup of java." Issam followed me, waddling after me in his heavy winter outfit, but at least he was warm in his bright red ski outfit. This time I took the stairs, which somehow seemed even colder, a raw cold that hurt the bones. We passed Maggie, the hunkered down receptionist, and headed out the door. It was like getting hit with a hot brick wall. When my body hit the hundred degree heat, I gasped for air, the hot intake of breath seared my throat and lungs. I heard Issam choking so I grabbed him by the fur and I walked quickly next door to "Danny's Café" and hurried in. The cooler air let me breathe again. Issam gasped for breath as he tried to get the scarf off his face. It only got tangled and he almost strangled himself.

The small café, like the police station, was an eyesore in the whole modern government complex which surrounds us. The small restaurant was right next door to the police station, like our building it was one of the "leftovers" from earlier days. It was officially billed as "quaint" in the city brochures. *Danny's Java Shop,* the sign behind the counter announced its intent of providing a good cup of strong dark brew. Despite the run down appearance it was one of the most popular places for breakfast and lunch for the government workers that populated the surrounding government offices' area. Even the Senators and Representatives of the Dome could be seen eating there.

"Hi, Boys," Sasha raised her hand in greeting. "Regular, Chief?" Then she spied Issam and looked askance at the Captain. "That you in there Cap?" She peered closely at the short puffed out man who looked almost alien and at least three times his small size.

He started peeling off his layers of clothes. "Air conditioning on too high," I told her as she handed me my cup of java, black. Sasha and her husband, whose name was Boris, where *Danny* came from I have no idea, owned the small restaurant. They were from off sector, I guessed near the Sol sector from their deep guttural accent and by the way they decorated their café. Unlike the soft pastels that were favored by Fulton's long time conservative prudish inhabitants, their restaurant sported loud greens, yellows and purples. Another hint was the lively music that filtered down from overhead; definitely not the more subdued melodies on the popular music stations of the City. In other words, Fultonites were rather drab, serious people, full of self-important governing responsibilities. Boring! It was probably a left over from when they were ruled by the non-human Bassodians, the reptiles had no sense of humor. They had originally engineered this hell hole and even after all this time their influence showed!

"Muffin? Got some good chocolate ones, gooey centers," Sasha teased me, holding one up for inspection. The pastry's enticing aroma drifted to my nose, making what little resistance I had quickly disappear.

"Ok, just this once." Of course it had been '*just this once*' once too many times as the tight waist on my shorts proved. Tomorrow I'd cut back and take those long exercising walks. Maybe I'd hit the gym. Yeah, sure! I remember when they had finally built us a gym down in the basement, probably from all the old equipment left over when they built the new Dome's gym. Most of the equipment half worked. Still, I'd run out and gotten expensive sneakers with every good intention of getting up early and hitting the gym. So now I had a pair of costly shoes that had sat in my closet all year, lonely and unused. Oh well. Do good intentions mean anything? My tight pants said no.

Issam grabbed his black tea and nothing else. I think his religion doesn't allow sweets or some such nonsense. His trim waistline fit his short stature. It hadn't done much for his hairline though, as he was losing the battle to baldness. My Captain blamed it on his kids, his teenaged girls. He was from Castor's Asteroid Belt. They grow them small there; known more for their intellectual brains. The one asteroid they could engineer into a planet was still smaller than most and bred smaller humans. But it was a sore point and no one dared to bring it up to a Castorian. They're rather sensitive about it and Martial Arts are big there. My lead detective had several degrees in the discipline. Castorians' shortness, some blamed it on the planet being a tad smaller and having to slow its rotation to match the rest of the sector's time but more likely it was their vegetarian diet. Who knew? It didn't matter, Issam was the best detective I had.

"Not good for you." He said in his heavy off Castor brisk accent eyeing my muffin. "It will clog your arteries."

I laughed, "I can think of worse ways of going. This damn planet is goin' to kill me first." We sat in the corner wall booth over near the window that overlooked Hyde Street, a habit that comes from watching my back too many times. It was quiet outside. Not much traffic, it being Saturday. Hyde Street ended just a few feet from our offices and the huge circular mall of the government offices began. A huge water fountain lay in the middle with the Dome building at the far side. Heaven forbid that our government high officials work on the weekends. Most probably had transited out to their home planets mid-week. The Dome, our official Sector Center of the Crab Nebula Government looked deserted, its bright new shiny golden top was empty inside but then I doubted if it made any different if it was full. It was a given that their air conditioning worked. They probably had high tech bathrooms too and nice lush offices with cushioned seats.

I had learned to deal with the bureaucracy of the government officials but it didn't mean I liked it. The Consulate was my boss, Lauren Borger, an honest man who did put the law first, often handling corruption as it should be handled - firmly and incorruptibly. Although I often didn't agree with him on his political views and his budgetary stinginess, I appreciated his support. The law came first for him. How he had stayed in his position as long as he had was a testament on his shrewd political nature. I didn't envy him.

I sat sipping on my java, dreading returning to the office. Issam was doing a crossword puzzle in the local paper. I was reading the back of his newspaper page; a quaint feature of the café, actual paper! Another sign they were from the Sol sector. Sol was an old fashioned sector with strange archaic traditions. Some said they actually had paper books. I'd never seen one so I doubted it. Although I looked across at Issam's newspaper, laughing, who knew!

One of the headlines announced in bold letters that more hot weather was predicted, no surprise there. The big sector race was next week. Of course, Nestor was hosting it at their two mile super track. Tickets were already sold out, probably had been for most of the Federation year. No flight Jumps available going to Nestor. No rooms available anywhere near the track. Their capital City, Nes, would be bulging with racing tourists. I couldn't help smile, Nestor was my home planet. Since age eleven, I'd grown up there, my life had been based there. The whole planet lives for the races. The population is a bunch of fanatic racing fans, my Uncle Jack had been one of them. He had worked for the Attenson Racing Team all his adult life.

I heard the doorbell jingle. Looking up, I saw a female police officer in the standard Fulton uniform. My street cops wore light blue fabric apparel that let the body breathe, convenient for the hot weather and comfortable for the patrolling they had to do. Her black regulation shoes were shining on the dingy café floor. Her laser stick fit nicely into the brown belt that encircled a trim waist. Everything was in order. She must be a rookie. Give her a couple of years on Fulton and she'd wither on the heated vine. Hell, give her a couple of months.

I had my muffin half way to my mouth when I realized I knew her. She saw me and nodded. "Lieutenant Hill!" I managed to get out despite my mouth being full of chocolate goo. I felt some of the syrup drip down my chin.

"Yes, sir." She stood almost at attention, a typical rookie reaction, catching herself and relaxing a little. She looked at my muffin and disapproval filled her face. Hill was a health freak. Exercise and good eating habits are her mantra. I should know, her desk was right down from Issam's office. I passed it every day on my way to my office. She was my newest detective, Lieutenant Hill, just out of the academy, top of her class, pain in the ass.

"What the hell..." I started to say but Issam interrupted me.

"The lieutenant is doing patrol duty on her days off. She thinks she needs the experience, having come right out of the academy into the detective division." He eyed me over his crossword puzzle. His slanted yellow eyes had a leery look, waiting for my well known temper to expose itself. His pointed ears twitched upward, a very Castorian trait. He was getting ready for my barrage.

I did not disappoint him, "What the hell," I repeated, my voice hitting the ceiling with its intensity. "Are you crazy, what about her work load..." First the air conditioning malfunctioning, then this! Not a good day.

It was Hill, my newest pain in the ass, that answered taking a defensive tone, "You were the one, **Sir**, that told me I was inexperienced and only got the detective job because the budget was so tight."

I sputtered, accidentally dropping my muffin onto the floor as I started pointing my finger at her, "I said no such thing."

Unfortunately Issam had to interrupt, "I'm afraid you did, Chief. That's why I didn't see any harm in her patrolling on her days off."

I felt the blood rush to my face, stinging my cheeks. "Whatever, it's not what I meant," I waved my hand dismissively at my Captain, "it doesn't mean to let your detective duties go to chase speeders and hand out traffic tickets to supplement the mayor's budget! It's not like we get any of it!" I knew Hill wasn't one of my detectives that waited until last minute for her reports. Hers were, of course, on time and precise. It still didn't stop me from thinking this was the stupidest idea since miniature file tabs were invented and became the most lost item ever sold.

I could see the reaction fill Hill's face, indignation coming into her dark blue eyes, "Is that all you did when you were on the regular force?" She stood her fingers hooked into her standard regulation belt, her head cocked to one side. She could have been a "looker" but her severe bun style hair and most of the time disapproving scowl rather ruined the effect. But then I hadn't hired her for her looks but for her brain. She'd been the first in her academy class and had graduated cum laude from Orion Law University. My rookie was also a stickler for regulations thus a constant thorn in my side as I am not big on sticking to rules, not to mention she came cheap due to our budgetary restrictions.

I felt myself stand, anger getting the better of me. My finger pointed at her again. "No, I was assigned the docks, the worst section of town!"

"Well isn't that strange, that's where my partner and I are heading in just a few minutes. Want to give me some pointers?" She had said it without the sarcasm that would have been insubordination otherwise. I just stood there, mouth opened, feeling like an ass with the whole Café staring at me. With nothing else to do I glared at Issam who ignored me and pretended to go back to his crossword puzzle.

I looked back to see Hill joining another blue uniformed police officer heading out the door. I yelled over, "I'll see you in the office!" Trying to recapture some of my dignity as the rest of the restaurant looked the other way.

She nodded as she closed the Café's door. Issam started to say something "I think...

"Don't say it. I know I just made an ass of myself."

"No, I was going to say I think you better wipe that chocolate off your shirt before it stains." He grinned trying to hide it with his newspaper.

I grabbed my cup of java and left for the wintry cold of my office.

It was close to noon. My hands were numb. I swear my java cup had a slim layer of ice on it. At least the cold had made me work faster trying to keep warm, almost all my backlog tabs had been done and in the outward computer files to be sorted. Maybe someday I'd have the budget to get modern equipment. Only my homicide detectives had miniature tabloids and not the latest models either. My regular force used their own personal cellbuttons to check in. Their police crafts were not the latest model. Although those that patrolled near the Dome did indeed have the latest security, being part of the "elite guard" for our illustrious sector representatives.

Fred Stoshingburg dropped in to tell me he'd filed his case report. The big man was shivering and complaining, a blanket trying to cover his upper body. He was born and raised on Fulton. Freezing temperatures were not in his repertoire. He was a large man taking up a third of my office, yet he was also as stubborn as he was big. He was persistent and relentless in his pursuit of criminals, especially druggers. Most importantly, those that trafficked the dangerous suffline drug. He maybe was a bull in a china stop but he was worth every inch of his big body. "You'd better go home," I told him. "Your blood's going to freeze."

"Son of a bitch," he loudly complained. "This dump needs to be burned to the ground."

"Until we have a budget that will build a new one, we'll have to make due." I laughed as he stomped out of the office, shivering from big head to his big toe.

Issam squeezed into my office, he had a towel wrapped around his face. "I'm heading home. I'll see you Monday." His words were muffled, sounding like he had cotton stuffed in his mouth.

"What's Hill working on?" I asked, remembering this morning's incident.

"Got her scheduled for Nestor, she has an early Jump Wednesday. Earliest Jump I could get her. It's hell getting to that planet this time of year."

"What's the problem on Nestor? It's race week." I knew the planet's obsession with the entire week heading up to the big race. It was wild place but I had a decent sized, well trained police force there.

"Got a suicide that the brother is claiming isn't. They don't want any troubles there, very sensitive about press coverage this week. So she'll investigate, show them we care, then get home."

What's the chance the brother's right and it's not suicide?" I asked my warm captain while I shivered away.

"Not much. Has something to do with a woman getting killed in a hover accident. Guess the guy took it hard. I gather the suicide was having an affair with her. They claim he'd been depressed over it. So suicide probably, brother can't accept it."

I nodded, we get over three hundred investigations a year referred to home base. All unpleasant, most easy to solve, a few real bad ones. "She ready for that?" I looked up at the bundled blob blocking my entire door.

"Oleg is going with her." When I looked questioningly at him, he said, "She's okay, she's over the nauseousness of the first three months. Oleg is not happy about going with a rookie but she'll do it."

"No trouble with the Jump, won't bother her?" I shuddered, I did not like spatial travel, or I should say my stomach didn't.

"Nope, it's a short ride, less than two hours." He turned to leave. He knew it burned my ass that a pregnant woman had no trouble with Jump travel while I hated every second of it.

I stopped him, one last question. "Why aren't Nestor's police handling it? Stan Holden is pretty capable." I hadn't hired him, he'd been head of the Nestor force for quite a number of years but he seemed a more than capable superintendent. I couldn't ever recall a complaint about him.

"It's complicated. They don't want the local police involved. I guess they're stretched out, it being their big race week, tight championship this year." He looked at me to see if I'd respond. Issam was one of the few that knew my background, my closeness to Nestor's racing. When I didn't respond, he continued, "The request actually came from the FIO. The agency is there on another investigation, not related and you know how demanding they can be! Guess they don't want the local police distracted. Acting the big shots again!"

"The Federals are there?" Now it made sense why Hill got the assignment, no one wanted to deal with the FIOs, give it to the rookie. The Federal Investigative Operatives were pompous asses who flaunted their connections, running right over us 'locals'. "Think Hill will be alright with them?"

"Yeah, be good for her. Oleg will be with her. She'll be there just a few days at the most."

I nodded, still stinging from this morning's exchange with Hill. Serves her right. The Federation Investigative Operatives were a bunch of prima donnas that couldn't get out of their own way and made everyone's lives miserable. No one wanted anything to do with them. It was part of being a rookie, getting stuck dealing with them. With any luck she'd not even see them. Too bad! *Serves her right*, I thought. Hill had a way of being a complainer, everything had to be done to regulations! She was always pointing to the rule book, give her a few years - it would be sweated out of her. At least I could hope, couldn't I?

Issam seemed to read my mind, "She probably won't even see them." He looked at me and we both laughed. Neither one of us wanted to bet on who would come out the better from the exchange. We weren't sure it would be the FIO.

Issam stepped back as Fred Stoshingburg came stomping back into the office. In his hand was a huge iron wrench. He threw it on my desk, "Problem solved!" Then stomped back out.

I then realized no cold air was coming out of the vents. As a matter of fact, no air was coming out at all. I looked down at the wrench. I had a bad feeling the wrench was the reason.

"I'm heading home!" Issam quickly disappeared from my doorway, leaving me alone with the wrench.

Chapter 2

Wednesday brought rain, pouring rain. We usually get rain almost every day but it only lasts a few hours; early morning, usually ending before I even leave for work. Then before breakfast the old intense heat comes roaring back as the warm spirited winds pick up, drying everything up quickly, returning rapidly to our low, at least livable humidity. This rain, however, was continuing, something about a rare front stalled over Fulton Island, which is our biggest central land mass.

The inhabitants of the capital city depend on the normally blowing trade winds coming off our large ocean, which keep the storms moving and our sweat glands down. Livable land, the little there is of it on all of Fulton Station, is broken into several good sized islands. They are all bunched together, Fulton Island being the largest measuring 2500 sq. miles. It is mostly taken up by the capital city of Fulton. Like all engineered planets, keeping us on Federation Time, the population lives on one side of the planet. There are a few stragglers, hearty foolish folk that try to live on the small islands on the backside but the backside has extremely erratic weather and they usually don't last for long; some rescued, most not. We call them Nofros, which is short for Nonconformists.

Most every humanoid planet, of course, has its Nofros. We even have a police statistic on how many make it every year. Sadly less than ten percent but that doesn't stop them from trying. It's a human thing. The non-humanoid parts of the Federation Galaxies don't have their inhabitants trying to beat the odds by living where they are not supposed to. We humans point to it as our spirit of adventurism, the rest of the known inhabited universe calls it dumb. Oh well, we are the youngest of the "discovered species" which is often pointed out by the outer worlds as they make up excuses for us. They just shake their heads or whatever they possess and try their damnedest to ignore the humanoid sectors. We reply by annoying them further. I digress.

Fulton Station was originally, as its name implies, a hub planet for construction and trading in this sector. It was quickly put here and haphazardly engineered in this part of the Crab Nebula multi centuries ago. The planet was used to store and supply the sphere contractor's workers and their families as they were developing the rest of the sector. When more accessible Jump routes were found, Fulton was almost left abandoned, half forgotten. A few adventurous people remained but mostly the warehouses became deserted and the then small undeveloped towns were left to ruin.

What saved the planet was that it ended up conveniently centered, thus it became the focal point for the local government when the sector had progressed to needing one. After the various planets were developed the Federation decided the Crab Sector needed a central governing body and applied to the Alliance Assembly for its official approval. Fulton was the natural choice as there weren't enough inhabitants to displace or to piss off any of the voting public as favoring another planet. The Crab planets could populate a new capital with multi sector government workers with the least amount of problems. The planet Fulton Station does have representatives but they don't get to vote, only scream their heads off, which of course is ignored.

Fulton Station now contains the Dome, or I should say the New Dome as it was just rebuilt with all the modern amenities that tax dollars can build. It is the meeting center where all the representatives meet for both the Senate and Parley. The Senate consists of three reps from each Crab sector planet and the Parley is one Judge from each planet keeping our politicians honest, making sure that they are sticking to our Federation Charter. Then there are those two reps from Fulton. They get to sit and listen and yell about how they should get a vote.

Fulton also contains the centralized police station for the planets, although each planet also has its own local police force and tends to look to Fulton for sector supervision. The planets also depend on our advanced forensic and detective expertise. Thus I was in the "Chief" position expected to overall supervise the policing of the Crab Nebula Sector and also to help on complicated cases when called upon which was often enough to keep twenty of my detectives hopping.

To maintain a uniform transportation system throughout the Crab, the Jumps are coordinated and regulated from our new updated transportation center. Also, central planetary news comes out of Fulton's News Bureau, beamed throughout the Crab sector day and night. A high speed Connected Jump is designated just for the news bureau's use, so data is never interrupted and can be beamed quickly from the Federation to all our local worlds. I say "never" but the Federation does, on occasion, commandeer all our lines and we get shut down. It is especially annoying when the Bassodians, hogging our Jumps, come through with a designated sphere on its way for engineering somewhere else. We can be held up for days, travelers are stranded, inter sector communications disrupted, until those damn pompous reptilians pass through. It is especially irritating when they give us no warning.

Again I digress but I must say, we may aggravate the rest of the universe's species, but shit, they can really aggravate us too. The worse thing about it, there is nothing we can do about it but let our blood pressure go up! It's not that our human Fed Reps don't holler and scream, we're just ignored. Humans are thought of as unsophisticated and tend to be snubbed. That's really not true, to be snubbed it has to be somewhat consciously done, the rest of the Federation isn't really conscious of us at all.

In any case, my detectives are kept busy servicing the Crab sector and since all the planets were engineered to have about the same properties, with these sectors catering to humanoids, it all works fairly well. We only need minor adaptability kits to function wherever we are needed.

I kept looking out the dust covered windows wondering when the rain was going to finally end. It was again hot and now unusually humid inside my office. I had my fan pointed directly at me, blowing hot air around with little effect. The unusual humidity was making it quite uncomfortable and making me irritable. My wrinkled limp sport coat was hung up and my tie already loosened, my collar open, deodorant in full use when Hill appeared in my doorway.

"What's up?" I grumbled at her and got a terse cocked nod in return. She was still irritated with me over the incident in the café. "Are you set for Nestor?" I wanted to ask her how her off duty patrolling had gone and if she liked the dock area, but decided not to go down that road which would lead to more explosive dialogue.

"Yes. I'm all set to go." She stepped aside letting Issam slip in. His bald head was glistening from sweat. He had to keep wiping his face with a handkerchief to keep the sweat from his eyes. I don't know which one of us looked more crumbled, especially near the neat and trim Lieutenant Hill.

Issam fingered his tab note then handed the file to Hill, who efficiently added it to her own tabloid. "I've posted your tickets to the transportation center, you'll just need your police I.D." My captain was very thorough. Unlike me he was very organized, a typical Castorian. He half smiled at Hill. "You've lucked out. You'll be staying at the Checkered Flag Hotel. You're fortunate, the Feds are paying for your stay at one of the best hotels since everything is full. I gather FIO keeps regular rooms for themselves there. It'll be a zoo this week but they don't want any bad publicity, so don't act like a detective or the damn press will smell you out! No publicity! I've already received several urgent memos from the Nestor senate representatives at the Dome stressing no publicity!" Issam pointed his finger at her, "Watch yourself, listen to Oleg, she knows what she's doing."

"I understand." She curtly said. "I'll keep a low profile."

I hadn't said anything, Issam was covering it pretty well. My rookie wore a black pair of slacks with regulation pumps, also black, and a starched white blouse with our orthodox issued gray tie. Her standardized issued sports coat, which my detectives themselves had to pay for of course, looked wrinkle free despite the heat and her auburn hair was tied back in a tight bun. No sweat for our Lieutenant Hill, it wasn't in her regulations. I couldn't help it, I had to say something. "How about losing the tie, jacket and hair, everything about you screams government employed. It's a laid back atmosphere during the Championship race and trust me, the sports news hounds will be everywhere looking for a scoop. They take over most of the reporter's news Jump lines during this week's races. They'd love nothing better than to put a Fulton detective on the front cover."

She frowned at me but nodded that she understood. "I heard you're from Nestor. Could you fill me in on what to expect?"

I saw the alarm in Issam's face, his slanted eyes going wide, his ears twitching. "He hasn't time right now, let's go." And then he rolled his big angled amber eyes at Hill. When she didn't seem to get it and was about to say something, he mouthed, *"He doesn't like to talk about it."*

She said, *"oh"* just as softly.

"I'm not deaf, either of you!" I grumbled quite loudly, making both of them jump. It wasn't that I couldn't talk about Nestor, I just preferred not to. Sounding like a recording, I gave her a quick synopsis. "It's full of racing fanatics. You sleep, eat and breathe racing. The place smells of gasline fuel from the cars, that's what they call the racing vehicles, by the way. The roar of their engines can be heard all over the capital city and probably beyond because everywhere you go they'll be playing the races on humongous floating screens. You'll get racing news from their skies, from the retail stores, on the trains, in the elevators, from the bathrooms. You haven't met dedicated fanatic fans until you've experienced Nestor."

"Oh, well I heard you used to be a driver, of some notoriety they say..."

Issam grabbed her arm, "We really have to go."

Hill looked back at me with a question mark written all over her face.

I just replied as she was pulled out by Issam, "That was a long time ago." At least it seemed like a long time ago, maybe I just wanted to put it way back in my mind. I felt my blood pressure rising. I reached into my pocket taking a small blue pill, downing it with my hot java. Ten minutes later I felt better and the anxiety was pretty much gone. My neck muscles relaxed, my shoulders softened, and I slouched back in my chair, feeling better, relieved. I hadn't had an episode in over two years but still I didn't take any chances.

It couldn't have been maybe five minutes later that my monitor rang. I saw it was Daisy, our administrative assistant with her "please answer" on the screen. "**What!**" I barked. I'd get interrupted all day if I let the ditsy secretary bother me, so I didn't encourage it.

"Sorry Chief, but this woman says she's your sister-in-law?" I guess the thought I might actually be human and have a family was out of her realm of imagination. "Her name is Julie. It's an off planet call."

I immediately snapped the connection. "Julie?"

"Hi Skip." I could hardly hear her, her voice was muffled.

"Is something wrong?" I didn't hear from my brother often, although I tried to call him at least once a common cycle. He was always between planets, mostly out of sector. Unless it was off season, he was racing and that took him all over the Federation. There were 23 official tracks and 32 actual races. So he was gone three quarters of the standard cycle. They lived on Nestor only during off season like all the other drivers. The racing circuit was more home than home was.

"Well," she seemed hesitant.

"Just tell me!" I was getting worried, Julie was a competent, strong willed woman, this was not like her. Her silence alarmed me more.

"I shouldn't be calling you," she stammered. "I'm in the den, I have to be quiet. I don't want Ray to hear me. I'm sorry to call you at work but I couldn't remember your cell without getting it off mine and he'd notice."

"It's fine. Just tell me!" I exploded, my police cop voice forcing itself forward automatically.

"I was wondering if you could come, he's not telling me something." Her voice was so low I had to turn up the enhancement on my monitor.

"What do you mean '*something*'?" I asked.

"I don't know. He's leaving Ralph and making the switch to Rosluke."

"Why would he do that, Ralph's been good to him? He's got the best autos on the circuit. Why would he do that to Ralph?" My brother had been with Ralph Attenson Racing since we were kids working with my Uncle Jack. It was inconceivable he'd go elsewhere.

"I don't know, I'm..., I'm afraid he's gotten himself into something. He's even saying that he doesn't need me to service the cars. That I can stay with Ralph until he gets settled into the new organization."

Now I was worried. Julie was one of the best racing mechanics in the league. My brother Ray was indeed lucky. She was also pregnant with their first child. This was not good.

"Maybe I shouldn't have called you, I know you have trouble dealing with this..." her hesitant voice grated on my nerves. It was so alien to her. This was not the confident Julie I knew and greatly admired.

"I'll be there as soon as I can!" I told her even though my brain was screaming *NO!*

"Thanks Skip," she sobbed. Julie never cries, never.

"I'll see you soon. Please take care of yourself, it's two of you now."

"I know," was all she said before the call went dead.

I sat for a good three minutes before I could get my hands to stop shaking. I had trouble getting another blue pill out. I had to go to Nestor. Ray would be racing there, it was also his home planet as it was for most of the drivers. They were all home-based there. It had been for me too. I had to go home. My hands started shaking again but I calmed myself. I would handle it. I had to handle it. Ray was the only sibling I had. Our parents were killed when we were young. We were raised by my Uncle Jack, who had lived on Nestor. Racing had become our lives, had been our salvation after the crush of our parents' deaths. Well, our salvation until my accident. With Uncle Jack having died a couple of years ago, there was no other family there. Julie's family was out in the Sol Sector, over a day's Jump. I had to go back. I would go home.

I pressed Daisy's button. Before she even had a chance to say anything, I snapped, "Get me a ticket to Nestor, ASAP!"

"You have to be kidding Chief, there's nothing until after racing week is over. The Jumps are filled."

"This is an emergency!" I almost yelled at the monitor.

Silence. A timid voice finally came on, "I'm sorry Chief, I'll try but I know when I was getting Oleg and Hill scheduled I had a hell of a time."

Oleg and Hill, I thought. "All right, never mind, I'll take it from here." I left my office, hoping that Hill hadn't left yet. I passed Issam's office to the cubicles just beyond. Hill was on her monitor, talking to someone when I rudely interrupted. She glared at me as she disconnected. I was not her favorite person today. I rarely was. I probably was everything she had been taught not to be. Oh well.

"I'm going with you to Nestor." I told her.

With an astounded look, she blurted, "Why? Is Oleg sick?"

"Something like that." I wasn't going to explain. "When are you leaving?"

"Our Jump is in a little over two hours." She nodded to her packed bag, lying next to her on the floor.

"Ok, I'll meet you at the station. I have to go home and grab a few things."

"Well, you can give me a ride, I left my craft at home, Oleg was driving. Let's go." She stood up, grabbing her bag. I noticed she had a much more casual look. White slacks, a yellowish blouse minus the tie and a short tan jacket had replaced her uniformed look and she'd tied her light auburn hair back with a colorful tie-back. She actually looked relaxed and rather fetching. Then she gave me that severe disapproving face as she took in my disheveled appearance and the image quickly dissipated. Whoof, gone!

I just looked at her not finding the words to disagree. I wasn't going to take time arguing with her, so I accepted the inevitable. I stopped in Issam's office, abruptly spitting out words. "I'm heading to Nestor instead of Oleg. Explain to Oleg. There are problems. Take over. Have the Jump ticket switched to me."

He nodded but came around from his desk putting his arm on my shoulder. "Do you think this is wise, Chief? This is the first time back, isn't it?" Issam knew I'd been to every sector planet but Nestor, always avoiding it, letting others fill in for me. He knew of my little blue pills and my fear of going home. He was one of the few that did. "Do you want to talk to Lily?"

"If I had a choice, Carl, I wouldn't go but I really have no choice. Family problems." I quickly explained about Ray's strange behavior. "Just tell Lily if I run into problems I'll call her."

He nodded. Carl Issam had been my lead detective since I had become Chief four years ago. He'd also been a good friend, both he and his wife Lily. I was very fond of his family. His wife and two daughters were his life. His wife was my doctor/therapist. She was a damn good doctor and had been instrumental in my move to Fulton. They were one of the few that knew of my condition and had kept it to themselves, for which I was extremely grateful. Grabbing what I needed from my office I headed to the elevators, meeting an anxious Hill, tapping her finger with an impatient annoyed frown. Oh well.

Since it was raining, we headed down into the basement and went through the tunnel to the parking garage. Hill looked incredulously at my Ant. It was the small version being only a two-seater craft. I could almost read her mind as she looked at my heavy set body and then back at my small vehicle. I just ignored her. My 6' 1" body frame fit fine with my size 40 inch waist hardly touching the steering wheel.

She threw her small overnight bag in the cramped back and climbed in next to me. Her legs were long and she had to scrunch a little to get into the passenger side. "You're the one who invited yourself along." I commented and got only a short grunt for an answer.

I lived on the outskirts of Fulton City in one of the pre-government old industrial parks. The zoning committee had offered a great deal on the abandoned warehouse buildings left over from the city's trading hub days. The city council had rehabilitated the area adding parks and good roads and the property owners fixed up the buildings into apartments. The rents were kept reasonable and easily filled.

My building overlooked the edge of Crow Bay, an inlet that circled its way out to the Aston Ocean,

Fulton Station's biggest body of water. As a matter of fact, the ocean took up most of the planet. Because of the bay, the housing was protected from the worst trade winds that could cause rough seas but the harbored area still provided a good view of the open ocean from the top floors. I had lived there since I came to Fulton.

"I've never been here," she told me. "It's quite lovely. Do you ever use the parks? Looks like great jogging trails especially along the bay."

"Do I look like I jog?" I laughed.

She laughed too, "Frankly, no."

"Well I do walk the trails when I can. I have two dogs that like to be taken for walks."

"Oh, really?" She sounded surprised as if dog and I didn't belong in the same sentence.

There wasn't time to dispute her assumption as we pulled down into my parking garage which lay underneath the five story concrete building where I lived. I parked in my spot. I had two spots. The other spot held my turbocycle.

"Nice bike. Someone likes speed," she said, but I didn't tell her it was mine.

"I'll be right back." I informed her as I extricated myself from the Ant. I had to admit it wasn't a graceful exit but hell I hardly ever had to charge the damn thing and it was easy to park.

I didn't realize she had come with me until I was up the ramp and into my lobby. I entered the first floor's large open area. Killa was behind the reception counter, I could just make out the top of her head. She stood on her stool and peered over. "Hi Skipper." Her low alto voice didn't go with her 4' 4" tall body but her light purple eyes did. Her almost silver white hair with her pointed tiny delicate ears caught the sunshine coming in the large foyer windows causing her to look like she had a halo. She was looking behind me when I realized Hill was standing in back of me.

"What?" I stared at my rookie lieutenant. My stares usually melt butter but Hill just shrugged.

"I'm a little claustrophobic," she looked over at Killa as if it was her that needed the explanation not me. "The underground parking made me a little nervous."

Yeh, sure. It was more like she was too goddamned nosy. I decided to ignore my brazen detective and focused back on Killa. "I'm going to be gone a couple of days. Don't forget the dogs see the vet tomorrow?" Then as an afterthought I pointed to my rookie, "And this is Lieutenant Hill, this is Killa."

"How do you do Lieutenant." I could tell the purple eyes were scrutinizing Hill, trying to fit her into the picture. Her pupils went from light violet to dark mauve. Killa gave up and turned to me. "Of course I won't forget. The van just came back from the shop." The small woman stepped down and came walking from behind the counter. She hardly came up to my shoulders. "The generator will be here today, I'll make sure they test it out before they leave it." I nodded as she walked to the elevators with us at the other end of the lobby. "Also unit 4, Stacy Keller's apartment, is getting a new cooking unit today. That will make him happy."

"Any trouble, just call. I'm going to Nestor, the Jump takes about two hours our time, so you'll be able to reach me by tonight." I knew Killa was aware of the Jump's time but I was trying to sound as nonchalant as I could. Her worried rapidly changing eyes and her reddening ears showed me I wasn't succeeding.

"Nestor?" The small woman looked at me, her pupils went wide with concern but she didn't want to say anything in front of Hill. She just glanced from me to Hill and back again. "Skip..."

"I'll be fine." I waved my hand at her dismissing the fear in her face.

She shook her head, worried violet visual acuity scanned my face for answers but she didn't say anything else.

"Don't worry." I grabbed Hill into the elevator. I wasn't going to leave her with Killa, she'd have my superintendent fully debriefed before I got down. I watched the worried look on the tiny woman's face disappear as the doors closed and I entered my code.

"Is she?" Hill sounded not sure how to proceed with her question. She repeated her question, "Is she a..."

"She's the superintendent." I interrupted her, I was going to ignore her actual question at the same time wondering how Hill knew what Killa was.

"I figured that, is she a Ligi?" That was Lieutenant Hill, right to the point, no beating around the bush.

"You mean is she from the planet Ligithia? They do not like that word!" Hill heard the anger in my voice and unconsciously backed up, finding nowhere to go in the small elevator.

"I didn't mean to be disrespectful, I just never met one before in person outside the Orion Sector. Never! So is she?"

"Yes." I was surprised she'd known but I wasn't going to pursue the look she was giving me. Closed discussion. Before Hill could comment further the elevator door opened into my apartment and she gasped as my two dogs awaited me, all 352lbs of them. Anyone not use to them is rather startled, the lieutenant was no exception. At least she didn't go for her gun holster but I heard her intake of air and felt her grasp my arm, squeezing it quite hard. For once my rookie was speechless!

Chapter 3

"It's ok guys, she's ok." They immediately let their guard position down and bounced over to me, almost knocking me over. This was a familiar ritual every time I got off the elevator. I frisked their floppy ears and told them to sit, which they did, looking expectantly at me for their supper. Even sitting, their heads came up to my shoulders. Their black eyes showed an alertness that marked their breed and their intelligence, making them great guard dogs. No one would easily get access to my apartment without my permission and I pitied them if they did. The dogs weren't fierce in nature but that didn't mean they couldn't be. They could be big lap dogs but not until they knew you belonged. I had no doubts their protective instincts, if provoked, would kick in. The best thing was that no one wanted to find out.

"It's too early," I told them. I looked around for Hill, she was still frozen by the elevator, a look of sheer terror on her normally calm analytical face.

"What are they?" she squeaked out still not moving a muscle from the elevator.

"Great Hybernian Hounds." I proudly told her. "They are still puppies really, not quite two years old yet. They'll grow some more, put on some bulk and a few more pounds."

"They don't look like them, I've seen pictures. The ones I've read about have pointed ears and are usually all black or gray. I've never seen a spotted one."

She took one step into the apartment, still keeping her distance. "I knew that hounds were big but to see them for real..."

"They were bred to kill the boars on Hybernia. Breeders usually crop their ears so the boars can't grab onto them but since I don't think they'll be chasing boars around in Fulton I left their ears floppy. You are right, they are usually all one color but every once in a while they are born spotted. Although Bear and Hoover are purebreds, their black spots on grey prevent them from being professionally presented at shows held by the breeders. I gather that to be show quality, the hounds must be a single color. Still they are fine purebred hounds. They're brothers. From what I was told their mother is over 200lbs. The females tend to be bigger."

For the first time, she looked around, noticing that my apartment took up the entire top floor. "I bought this building when I moved to Fulton City. I got a great deal on it and renovated it for 16 smaller apartments." I explained as she did a 360 circle of the apartment, her head staring up at the tall immense ceiling. The dogs trotted behind me into the kitchen. The ceilings were so high that outside the remodeled area my voice echoed.

Her eyes took in the mostly undone apartment. Most of it lay opened, ceiling to floor windows took up the outer walls and the cement floor that had not been carpeted, glared reflected gray light. It still looked and felt like a drab old storage factory. Where the dogs and I were was a partitioned finished kitchen with a table, next to it was a comfortable den and finally I had a bedroom done with a bed and bureau and a half-finished open closet. The one and only bathroom was on the far wall near the stairs heading to the roof. At least I had spent a little on a modern kitchen and a large luxurious bathroom. The rest wasn't anything to write home about.

It just looked massive and the view of the city and Crow Bay were breathtaking.

The rain had finally stopped. Hill went over to the ocean view, squinting in the sun. I heard her take a deep breath, the skyline had that calming an effect. The sail boats dotted the water, seagulls floated high above them. During a storm it was even more impressive. The views are what convinced me to buy the old dilapidated warehouse. It had taken almost a full year to get the apartments ready. I wasn't in a hurry for my apartment, such is the life of a busy cop and a bachelor to boot. I didn't have the time nor the money for someone else to finish it.

She looked at me, a strange look I read only too easily. If she wanted to be a good detective, Hill would have to learn to hide her feelings. Her look said I should not be able to afford this on a policeman's salary - even a Chief's salary. "I'm not on the take," I assured her. "After I finished my university law degree, I had a little left over from my racing winnings to buy this place. Not much, just enough and the rents keep it going." I didn't tell her my ex-wife got the bulk of my racing money. To my surprise, I found it still too raw to tell anyone that.

"Take her to the roof, guys," I told the two hounds. Her eyes went wide as Bear gently grabbed onto her wrist and led her to the stairs leading to the top of the building. She looked pleadingly at me but quickly realized if he wanted to take her arm off, he would already have done it. "Go ahead, they won't hurt you. I'll grab a few things." The three of them went thru the flaps that covered the doorway, keeping the apartment from the outside heat. I heard her footstep as she followed the dogs up and out onto the roof. It would be hot up there. I usually waited until evening when the roof blissfully lay in shadows and the cool ocean breezes felt refreshing. It made you appreciate the air conditioned apartment that cost me a bundle to keep cool with the high ceilings.

I grabbed my overnight suitcase and threw in a few clothes including my disguise kit and took my extra gun including its charger and threw it in with my underwear. I placed my bag by the elevator and headed up the stairs. Hill was laughing as she watched the two dogs race around the gravel track I'd made them. "This is great. What's this, half the roof?" She took in the park-like roof top I had made for the dogs. In the middle was a picnic area with a large hot tub that I kept cool. It was a luxury I had indulged in for myself. I had a place for the dogs to go to the bathroom and an automatic cleaning unit that dumped down into the outside dumpster. I pointed to the 10ft. cement wall dividing the roof, "The other side is made up for the residents, it contains a grilling area with picnic tables and sunning chairs. The residents like it."

As the two dogs raced by she asked, "How do you tell them apart?"

"Well, Bear is the faster one and is slightly bigger weighing in at 184 lbs of sheer muscle. There is not an ounce of fat on either one of them. Bear will always lead with Hoover always following behind. Yet Hoover is the smarter of the two. He thinks of things to get into and Bear then mimics him and trouble follows. They are best of pals. They sleep together, complain together - when one whines the other is in harmony with him. Most of all they get into things together. Hoover figured how to open one of my kitchen cabinets and then Bear dragged five pound bags of flour all over the place. I came home to two dogs that looked like ghosts and a hell of a mess." Hill laughed as the dogs wandered up to her, rubbing up against her vying for attention. 'They flirt together too. They have made me realize how 'human' dogs can be."

She looked at me strangely. "You sound like a proud parent. How'd you name them?"

"I didn't, got them from the pound when they were nine months old. They were already named. They had called me to help put them down, the breeder didn't want 'unshowable' dogs. The pound was afraid of them. It was one of the few times I'm glad they called the 'Chief' as it was an unusual request. I fell in love with them instead and took them home. Come on let's get going if we're going to make that Jump."

She nodded. The dogs followed down the stairs, the cool air of my working AC was a relief from the heat of the roof. Killa was waiting, she must have had someone covering the front desk. She had my bags open adding more clothes. "You never pack right." She shook her finger at me. Hill looked amused that someone could actually lecture me and I not bark back.

"I'm fine." I frowned at her. Killa was getting on in years but she refused to slow down. I swear she still thinks she's my nursemaid. She was probably the closest I had come to a mother after my parents died.

"Have you got your Jump disorient pills?" The small woman asked. "And don't forget your other medicine." Having been an integral part of my life since childbirth, she also knew me well.

"Yeh, all set, stop worrying. Already took one," I assured her. "Just call if anything goes wrong."

Killa went over to the far window. I followed her over knowing she wanted to talk out of earshot of Hill. When I did, she whispered, "Why are you doing this?"

"I got a call from Julie, she's worried about Ray." I softly explained what Julie had told me. Killa was also close to my brother Ray and his actions alarmed her as much as it did me. Being from Ligithia she was hypersensitive to human feelings and a worry wort.

Killa's eyes went deep purple, her ears twitched rapidly, then she nodded, it all made sense to her now. My brother would be the only reason I'd go to Nestor. She'd been with Ray and me all our lives, had been with my mother at our births. "Do you need me to go with you?"

"You'd never get a Jump ticket, you know what it's like during racing week. I'll let you know if anything is wrong plus I need you to keep everything sane here."

She nodded but I could tell from her face she would be worrying the whole time I was away. There was nothing I could do. "She's from my sector." Killa remarked nodding in Hill's direction. "She smells like she's from Orbo."

"How do you know? How can you tell?" Ligithians always astounded me. Their intuition and senses outmatched most normal humans.

"I smell it in her blood." Killa's violet eyes sparkled. "If I'm not mistaken she's from Orbo City itself, her accent matches their dialect, though she tries to hide it. It is an honorable planet, they fought to save us. I remember the smell of their soldiers. I like her."

I gave her a hug and went looking to gather Hill, who'd disappeared with the dogs into my den. My big screens covered most of the walls, with one wall a shelf full of my racing accolades. I had made up my mind several times to throw all of it out but somehow I never had.

My newest detective was looking at all my trophies. "I should just get rid of those. Old history," I said.

"No. You were named 'Rookie of the Year'. Look how young you look?" Her mouth went into a smirk, pointing at the picture on the wall. "How old were you? You look like a kid! You look trim and fit."

"Seventeen. Racing keeps you trim, especially all the traveling. No time to eat. You're gone most of the time, I did my secondary schooling from the road."

Her eyes took in everything, I got the feeling she didn't approve of someone so young being on the road. The dogs sat on either side of her, trying to get her attention. She'd definitely lost the fear of them as each hand was scratching ears. "What..." Hill hesitated. I knew the questions she wanted to ask. Questions I didn't want to answer.

"It's a long story Hill. Let's save it for another day," or not at all. I had no intention of letting Hill know anything else. I resisted the pull of putting another blue pill in my mouth and grabbed my suitcase. I gave the dogs a treat on my way out, getting a loud deep "*Woof*" as a thank you. Then the two dogs started whining realizing that I was leaving them behind, bouncing around me, blocking me from the elevator. "Come on guys, don't make me feel bad." I pulled on their tails. It was Killa that gathered them, holding both, letting me get around them to the elevator.

The lieutenant nodded her goodbye to my superintendent, following me out to the elevator. As the doors shut, I saw Killa with each dog standing on either side of the small woman, bookends of strength. I sighed as we headed down.

"Who's she bonded to?" Hill asked. Damn, no wonder she wanted to be a detective, the woman was just full of questions, too many questions. Had she always been this nosey, probably born that way I thought sarcastically.

"My mother originally," I answered her question but quickly added, "she's free to go where she wants."

"But she can't." Hill pushed, "So are you her keeper? You must have Laositian high blood." The disdain she held in her voice was so evident it made me cringe. Hatred of human slavery could do that, had done it. It had almost caused a rebellion in the Orion sector. That debacle is still a black mark to the human sectors, so much so no one talks about it.

"It's not that simple and yes my Grandfather was from Ligithia, but my Grandmother, who died when my Uncle Jack was born, was from Sol. I wish it was simple," I repeated. I wasn't proud of my Laositian heritage; the high blood ruling class of the slave planet. It wasn't like I had a choice in it. My mother had been running from her heritage all her life and Killa had only complicated her guilt. The Federation tried to do something about it. Troops were even sent but the dying of the Laositian masters also killed their slaves through some type of blood bond. No cure has been found yet, despite the work of scientists like my parents. It ended up an awful embarrassment to the Federation and a disaster for the Ligithian slaves. It was not talked about, written about, Orion was far enough away to be forgotten by most and the Assembly made sure it was a forgotten embarrassment.

"No, it never is simple," Hill said as we got into the Ant and headed to the station. The rain had started again and was pounding on my little car. I couldn't help think this downpour was not a good omen.

The Jump station was always busy, day or night. Fulton's Jump Station had traffic coming in from all over the sector. Government business was around the clock. We found our Jump terminal and upon showing our badges were sent directly to await the boarding. Seeing the long lines, especially those heading to Nestor, I was for once glad of police privileges. I was well known by security and got nods from all the guards patrolling the area. This brought the head of station security hurrying out. "Is everything alright, Chief? No one made me aware of you coming down."

Like Issam, the security supervisor was from the Casteroid Astroid Belt. His short stature, however, was enhanced by more than a few pounds. Unlike Issam, I guess Fulton had not been a good influence on him. His nervousness could be heard as he stumbled with his words, his off world accent making it worse. Like Issam he was losing his hair, nervous sweat was dripping into his slanted yellow eyes, his pointed thick ears were red with embarrassment. I probably would have felt sorry for him, but it's not in my nature, so I glared him into silence. He stood there huffing and puffing, pulling on his tie and shuffling his feet.

I felt like swatting him across his almost bald head as the other passengers turned in our direction, alarm showing on their faces. I was not an unknown entity in Fulton as my face had appeared in the news, as little as I could possibly manage but still I was recognizable to those paying attention to crime news, usually violent crime. Not reassuring to those around us.

From the look on my face he got the message, shutting up too late but none the less shutting up. "I'm going to Nestor," I half growled at him. Smiling I turned to the other waiting passengers, "It's race week, looking forward to the races."

They seemed to relax. One even said, "Is Ray Brown some relation?"

"My brother." I nodded and everyone went back to reading their newstabs. No emergency, just another racing fan heading to the Championship race.

"So sorry," the supervisor told me as he backed away from the glaring look I was giving him.

"Your brother, Uh?" Lt. Hill sat next to me. "Oleg isn't sick, is she?"

"No." I opened up a newstab that was on the seat next to me, opening it up wide enough to block her from view as I did so. It wasn't any good as she lowered the tab screen with her hand. Brazen!

"Wasn't it you that told me last year that personal business was not to interfere or get mixed with department business?" She eyed me with those big light green accusing eyes. "If I remember correctly..."

I broke her off, "It will not interfere with what you're investigating. Unlike last year," I saw her blush as I reminded her of the incident where I had to go chasing after her when I learned she was investigating a murder that was connected to her sister's death, "this is not related in any way."

"Still..."

I cut her off, "in ANY WAY!"

It shut her up and I went back to reading my news screen until our run was called.

"Chief," I guess she wasn't going to shut up after all, "I never really got to thank you for all you did, you took the blame and everything. I know you had a lot of explaining to do."

"Please, let it go Hill. We still got the Blithie family busted and in the end it turned out to be good." I had gone through a lot of high level questions and tough answering sessions but since we had found the drug family's corrupt drug trading records that had caused so much heartache which sent most of them to prison, it had turned out alright. The murdered girl had been from a prominent Fulton family and they had stepped in, thanking me and using their influence to stop any proceedings against me. I had successfully kept Hill out of it.

"I know I can be rather nosey." Nope she wasn't going to shut up. "I come from a large family, seven kids. We are all into each other's business and I guess it comes naturally."

I just nodded my head, realized she couldn't see it with my news screen open, lowered it and just nodded again. Guess she took that as meaning she could keep talking. I had to learn not to give her any encouragement.

"As you know, I'm off sector from Orion. That's how I know a Ligi," she quickly realized her mistake and changed. "I mean Ligithian. It's on Orion's outskirts. I know all about those damn slavers swine. I know what a bungle the Federation made of that war. Both my older brothers fought in it."

So Killa had been right. I had forgotten that little bit of knowledge about where Hill had come from but nodded as if I had remembered her personnel file. That explained how she knew who Killa was. Very few in our part of the cosmos knew of the Ligithians or their enslavement. The war had been far away and only a conflict technically. I only knew of it because of my parent's research. The news bureau had made it sound like it was this small local Orion conflict. I knew better, my parents were deeply involved in the research after the war to find the cure for the blood bond that kept the slaves from freedom. My mother and father had lost their lives because of it. Murdered because it was rumored they were close to finding a solution.

I did not say anything to Hill, it was something not to be discussed. Our Uncle had drilled it into us that the only way for us to stay alive was to hide. Killa, however, was a constant reminder. We hid her first on Nestor then now here on Fulton Station. "Ligis" as Hill so crudely called her were rare in the Crab and their plight unknown. Most that knew her thought her a dwarf from the Sol sector. Since my apartment complex was designated for the disabled, Killa promoted the midget idea and fit right in. Hill was the first to know. Damn!

We headed into the ship to make the Jump, taking our seats. I felt the white gel-filled seat conform to my body but I knew it wouldn't do much good. My body still tensed. I'd taken two disorient pills but they never did too much good. My mother use to ply me with the medicine for Jump sickness even as a child and it hadn't done any good way back then. While my brother stuffed himself with pizza, I spent the trip in the lav.

"We are next in line." Our female pilot announced. "Two hours ten minutes we'll have you on Nestor. Nes City has great weather, of course. The city is busy busy. You'll have quite a wait, I'm afraid, getting into the city as it's packed for the races. Just be patient. Have a good time. Close race this year." The pilot laughed, then added, "Go Sonny Jistin!"

Everyone laughed as Sonny was a favorite racer although the guy behind me said, "No way, Lilianst has it won." I grinned, Lilianst was a racer from my era, nice to hear he was still contending with the younger ones. Professional Federation Racing tended to favor the younger racers as it took a lot of stamina to keep up. The racing circuit schedule was brutal. I felt my stomach tightened, not sure if it was the anticipation of the Jump or the memories. Either way I popped another disorient pill followed by one of my little blue pills into my mouth. Hill looked questioningly at me. I just ignored her.

We got into orbit and then the ship hit the Jump. Hill took out her video pad, catching up on the sector news. Her eyes followed me as three times I made for the lavatory, throwing up my guts. Usually I don't eat anything for a couple of days in anticipation of the effects of the spatial traveling but this happened too quickly.

"You have it bad," she said once as I slipped back into the chair, letting it caress my body to no avail.

"Yeah, I never take the Jumps well. Had it rough when I was racing and had to travel a lot. But I manage." At least it had kept me slim and trim as I didn't eat much while on the circuit with all the inter sector travel it involved. I grumped at her hoping to end the conversation. It did as she went back to eating her pretzels. Damn woman!

Hill skipped off the ship as I staggered behind her. My head felt like a bowling ball. I'd feel better, short Jump sickness usually wears off pretty quickly. The terminal was busy and loud. As I predicted, huge screens filled with racing news were everywhere. The racing motif carried throughout the building. We were surrounded by checkered flags, racing posters, fake engine roars that came from the various shops, all announcing their favorite drivers and their teams. Everyone was wearing racing T-shirts - some fluorescent, some pulsating names. I was pleased to see my brother had his share of fans. Hill noticed too as she pointed to them. *RAY BROWN with Ralph Attenson - Racing for the Championship* decorated several of the stores, selling all sorts of racing gadgets. Team banners had their share of the enthusiasm. The excitement was high as only Nestor could produce for their racing. Everywhere there were huge holographs that pulsated **START YOUR ENGINES**.

We hadn't gone too far when we saw some of the racing cars being displayed in a large lobby, a few colorfully dressed drivers were doing autographs. I was glad my brother wasn't among them, I wanted to see him alone first. Enthusiastic fans were screaming for their signatures. There were all kinds from flamboyant to conservative dressed fans, from young to old.

"This is unbelievable." Hill shouted in my ear. I had warned her.

"Hey, isn't that Skip Brown!" came from a bunch of reporters covering the event.

DAMN!!

Chapter 4

I shuddered as a rather rotund man was hurrying over. I barely recognized him as one of the reporters that had covered me years ago. He had been younger and slimmer then and his hair was now thinner and peppered with gray.

"Is that you Skip?" he squinted, as if perhaps he wasn't sure it was me. When he was sure he mumbled, "Well, I never thought ..."

"Hi, Merv," I said, amazed at myself that I remembered his name, although my good memory was one of my better assets for my police work. I rarely forgot a face, even in disguise. I find something that I know to connect with a past recollection. I also rarely forgot the particulars of a case. Evidently Merv didn't either. I tried to brush him off, "Just visiting. Gotta get going."

"I can't remember you at any of the races since ..."

I cut him off, "Here to see my brother, he has a chance at the championship this year. He's the one you want."

"Well, aren't you in some security business? Your brother wasn't too specific when I tried to ask him about you." He looked over at Hill, I suppose expecting me to introduce her but of course I had no intention of doing so. My brother, knowing my feelings, kept any knowledge of me as quiet as he could just giving a terse "security business" as a quick answer to my whereabouts. I didn't need reporters hounding me about my former life in Nestor, not in the job I was in. I'd been lucky that all focus had been on my brother. Ray kept the spotlight on himself with the success he was having.

My job was hard enough. Fortunately, after my accident I had never come back and it had taken a long time to recuperate at the space station hospital, thus I was forgotten when I had begun my police career on Fulton. I suppose it was the last place anyone would come looking for me, in the police department in Fulton Station. After all, Fulton had all those famous politicians, more than enough sunlight for me to hide in the shadows.

Merv, with an excited expectant look, had his cellmike out waiting for my reply. I gave him a vague answer, "Something like that, nice seeing you ..." I grabbed Hill's arm then quickly headed off. Several other reporters had come up. Damn, didn't they have better things to do? I gave them my back before they could think of getting pictures and we hurriedly made for the front lobby of the station. Holding on to Hill's hand, I dragged her quickly along, weaving around all the racing activities and crowds loaded down with everything they needed for the races. We dodged waving colorful flags announcing which driver they favored. We careened around a woman who had ten suitcases. Two Skycaps were juggling her huge packages, a third had already dropped most of his load. It slowed the reporters down as they dodged the flying suitcases, giving us a chance to beat them out the door.

"Hey, isn't he the one, the driver that had that bad accident. The one that caused all the questions, wasn't he arrested ..." I heard from behind me. "Hey, Skip, you gonna visit Lonarer's widow?" one of the young reporters yelled after me. Heads were turning, even the drivers signing autographs looked over, stretching their necks to see who was stealing their thunder.

I kept going quickening my pace, looking for the way out. I heard Merv chastise the pushy rude newsman, "Leave him alone, you don't know how great he was, he's a legend, show some respect. He went through a hard time and it wasn't even his fault!"

I pulled Hill through the huge glass doors that led to sidewalks outside of the terminal looking for transportation out of here. It was packed. The limousine and buses were stuffed, with even more people waiting to board. There were long lines waiting for the taxis. I saw one of the yellow vehicles over in the corner, out of the line. I rushed her over to the idling craft hearing the reporters coming through the doors, yelling at me. The driver looked like he was eating his lunch and wasn't paying attention to his surroundings.

I opened the back doors, thankful he hadn't locked them. I shoved in the two overnight bags and pushed in Hill beside them.

"Sorry mister, on my break," came from the front, a thick croaking type accent matched up with an olive sharp angled face and light green eyes with dark green pupils. Most of the cab drivers were from Vesti in the nearby Pinwheel Sector. Their planet rivaled Nestor's enthusiasm for racing. The Federation Cup Race was held there. Many Vestians came to Nestor with ideas of getting into racing and a few had made it. They were small muscular people that fit nicely in a racing car with the stamina to outlast everyone else. Marina Kikak was the most famous. She'd won the championship two years ago for the Williamson team and was in fifth place this year.

Most of the multitudes of Vestians, however, don't end up making the circuit but end up being cab drivers instead of race car drivers. Vestians always smiled, were always cheerful and were known for their polite manners. They were also hard workers and reliable. That's why the cab companies recruited them. It wasn't a pleasant job, Nestor locals were notorious skin flints, giving poor tips. They saved their money for the races. So the Vesti cab drivers' good nature was sorely tested. That Vesti smile greeted us as he said, "Sorry, off duty, right now. Have to stand in line."

I shoved my badge in his face startling that smile right off his face. "Get us out of here, NOW!" My voice boomed over his intercom speakers that had the racing news blasting us in the back seat. Typical racing fan, typical Nestor.

He looked at the badge and started to say something, took one look at my threatening face and started the car, leaving the reporters yelling after us.

Hill frowned at me, "So much for trying to keep a low profile! You were worried about me!" She accusingly pointed her finger in my face. "Wait until they do some research and find out who you are!"

"Damn, I didn't think anyone would recognize me, I should have disguised myself." I had thought that they'd have forgotten me. I thought the years would hide my familiarity. I should have known, mentally kicking myself. Everyone was a racing historical buff on this damn planet.

"They're crazy here. Is everyone a racing fanatic?" She sat back sinking into the seat, looking back at the receding reporters waving their arms at us.

It was the driver that answered her, "There ain't nothin else lady." He smiles and in his rear view mirror we can see his teeth spell "Hank Sims" in bright orange and purple - Hank's team colors. Good god! I could tell Hill wanted to ask him how he did it. I pointedly told her, "Don't ask!" Her mouth closed but she kept looking at his face in the mirror fascinated.

I gave him instructions to take us to the Checkered Flag. He looked appropriately impressed, thinking wrongly he'd get a good tip.

He stepped on it, weaving around the other cabs, getting honks. Giving Hill the eye, he asked, "You some kind of celebrity?" Looking in his center wide back view camera mirror at her, he almost ran over several racing reporters in their pursuit of knowledge.

Both of us yelled, "NO! WATCH OUT!" Our words only got us one of those "sure" knowing looks. He had us pegged - her as a rich celebrity important enough to have a police escort.

"Your badge said 'Brown', any relationship to Ray?" I didn't answer. Observant bastard.

He wasn't done, "He's also one of my favorites, got the best cars and knows how to drive them. See him last race? Even in heavier gravity he came in second." Well maybe not a bastard.

As we came into the city proper, racing took over the landscape. Every building was decorated in colorful banners promoting one racing team over another. Loud blaring speakers competed with each other to be heard yelling out driver's names, giving announcements on upcoming events. Even with the windows up I noticed Hill cover her ears, shaking her head in dismay. "How can you hear anything, it's just mixed noise!"

"Nestorites get use to it, believe me. They can sort it out; what sounds like mumbo jumbo to you is clear as a bell to them." Banners floated high in the air announcing the minute to minute points accumulations. When we got into downtown Nes, Hill made the mistake of putting down her window, roaring engines could be heard filling the air with even more tempestuous noises.

"What's that stink?" She scrounged up her nose. Gasline, especially to Nestor inhabitants, is called *sweet, heady and intoxicating to the nose.* Those not use to the smell call it nauseating.

There used to be an uproar about the pollution it caused, even some blaming it for brain tumors and birth defects. This set in motion a multi sector government panel. Whether because of the gas lobby or because of scientific fact, the report proved it had no bad health effects because it was from made from nature's natural plants. I believe I remember reading "it is no worse than smelling baking bread, probably better." Whatever, everyone was happy and the issue was dropped, to the relief of Nestor's gasline industry.

It was the driver, his indignant voice booming over the noise so he could be heard, "That ain't stink, that's the smell of money lady. That's gasline. It wouldn't be Nestor if it didn't smell like that!"

"It's the fuel that runs the racing cars throughout the Federation Circuit, pro and amateurs," I explained to her. When you lived on Nestor, especially near the track, it was normal, you didn't even notice it unless you made an effort. "It's harmless, or so they claim, it's made from the thick growing Halka grass. *All natural ingredients, good for the environment,*" my voice sounding like the popular commercials. "Most of Nestor's middle plains are covered in it. That's why, I suppose, professional racing is based here. Big money crop, huge tankers leave daily headed for all the sectors. It's Nestor's biggest export."

Our cab driver even scared me as he turned around taking his eyes off the road, "That's putting it mildly. Where you from?" His picture over his visor told me his name was Ni Li. It was bright neon blue coded, all off sector workers had to have them. He pointed to one of the Rosluke Racing banners, "I'm trying to join their team." It was just like I thought, a wanna be racer dreaming of a racing career and never would make to anything but the team's car washer.

"I'm from Orbo," Hill told him, so she could lie, just a little. Orbo was her home planet.

"Orbo, don't know it, far off sector?"

She nodded, "Three day Jump. In the center of Orion. This kind of racing isn't real popular there."

He shook his head, his eyes darting to me in the rear view mirror, "You from Fulton Station, ain't you?" One look from me and he shut up and turned again to Hill. "Racing is a popular sport, always growing, we get all kinds from all over when the big race is on. Can't imagine not having it. Must be pretty boring place."

He pulled up to the Checker Flag entrance. The luxurious fifteen story yellow brick building loomed over a big circle driveway decorated like a race track with holographic bleachers with an actual man waving a checkered flag at the doorway. Of course huge screens lay all along that now held pictures of all the top drivers but would be showing the speed trials once they began later this afternoon. Long lines of limousines and other taxis were unloading incoming visitors. Bell hops dressed in the different team colors were loading up luggage and escorting everyone in.

The loud noise of engines was not far away as the racetrack itself was close by. They even had their own track entranceway in the back. It was amazing how memories could come flowing back, even unwelcomed memories. I had given press conferences here. The end of the year racing banquet was held here where I'd received my awards. The restaurant had been a favorite of my ex-wife, probably more for its expensive menu and the prestige of eating there than for the food. She was like that. Status over quality, they did not always go hand in hand.

A bellboy dressed as a track official opened our door, taking Hill's bag. I gave the correct fare plus a little more, the driver scowled at me. Hill reached around and gave him a lot more. "Thanks Lady."

"He gave up his break for us." She looked accusingly at me.

"He'll now go back and get a lot more from those reporters. Especially now that you confirmed we're someone!"

She ignored me but I saw in her eyes I'd made my point. The lobby was packed, the excited buzz of human conversation overwhelmingly annoying. It was the constant buzzing of bees. We went right up to the counter, at least fifteen counter people were keeping the room registrations flowing. Money brought service and this hotel was on the top of the bill. With so much going on, I was glad we were just blending in. Hill gave her name. To my surprise, she was given a suite door fob on the top floor. I could tell questions were going to come out of her mouth. I didn't want to ask any questions and draw any attention to us so I quickly grabbed the fob from the attendant and shoved it in her hand. Taking her arm, we were heading towards the elevators quickly.

Hill looked around soaking up the atmosphere. Everyone was dressed in the various team colors. Slogans flashed on the walls, describing the different teams, giving statistics and the odds from moment to moment. On the screens I saw a few of my former racing opponents but most were new. The sponsors of the teams were familiar however. Those never changed, only who was talking them up. An ad with Steve Allis holding a popular laundry detergent, smiling at the bottle - like he ever did the wash! Casey Mills was drinking from a ColaMola bottle, which I'd bet was full of his favorite whiskey. Yeah, you did what you needed to do, those racing cars cost a lot to keep running. Sponsors were golden and it was highly competitive to get and keep one.

I half dragged Hill to the elevator that was for the suites. I suppose to someone who'd never grown up with this racing fanaticism, the overwhelming promotion was fascinating but I'd seen it most my life. I knew the ins and outs, and it had a whole different perspective to me. Hill turned round and round trying to grab it all in. Even when we were in the elevator she kept watching the screen on the wall as we rode up the fifteen floors, listening to the non-stop announcements of the racing news. In the background was the faint roaring of the engines, reminding everyone what Nestor was all about.

"Wow! They are really serious about this upcoming championship," she remarked, awed by the intenseness after one of the drivers had appeared on the screen, exclaiming in almost barbaric terms his determination to beat all his opponents. You'd think he was a Hyberian hunter out for the barbaric kill.

"Yeah, we're a bunch of great actors! Part of the job," I sputtered.

"That's the first time you've included yourself," she remarked.

I shook my head, "Guess it never leaves the blood." I grabbed her bag and headed down the hall to the suites. The hallway rug looked like a paved raceway, the walls were three dimensional screens of bleachers full of screaming fans. Hill's eyes glossed over taking it all in. Already she was a typical fan.

Each suite of rooms was named after a famous past driver. From the names I glimpsed I gathered you had to be dead to qualify for a suite named after you. We finally came to "Johnny Peterson" suite, printed over the door of room 1522. I took the key fob from her hand, as she kept looking down the hallway forgetting where she was. I opened and heard the door give an engine roar as it opened up. I pressed "quiet" on the fob and it shut off. Blessed quiet followed. I dragged her into the room.

"That is amazing," she said looking back over her shoulder. "How do they do that?"

"Why do they do that is a more appropriate question," I snapped at her, bringing her back to the here and now.

The suite was a set of three good sized rooms, a large living area/kitchenette with two bedrooms off to the side. The whole room's motif was, of course, racing but it was "old fashioned" racing as Johnny Peterson was one of the original drivers, over a century back. A large picture of him in his racing outfit graced one wall. No fancy uniform, no fancy helmet just him standing next to his car, his outfit was semi-fireproofed but nothing else. No air tubes, no crash foam. That was true racing, I thought then chastised myself for being "old". When I had been racing I used to scorn the "old timers" for their attitude to return to "pure" racing. Now look at me!

"Did you know him?" Hill asked, going up to the wall and touching the image, thinking it was a virtual wall but it didn't move.

"How old do you think I am?" I half laughed, half growled. "He was one of the original drivers back when racing was primitive compared to today. Of course, she wasn't familiar with today, where the uniforms interacted with the drivers and the helmets were DNA compatible.

"Oh, sorry." She looked goggled eyed around the room. The rug was checkered but not overpowering, the furniture was made to look like old fashioned cars, with victory flags covering the cocktail tables. The small yet complete kitchenette was more modern than my own kitchen back home. It was all done in Peterson's colors, with all pictures of his trophies and other accolades decorating the walls.

The bedrooms were done in the same vein; the beds were mock duplicates of his cars. The windows were shades of his colors with his number 22 appearing when they were closed. On the bureaus were push button holograms with slides of his life. Hill watched one documentary as I checked out the bathroom, situated between the two bedrooms. The screens were everywhere showing upcoming events, even in the shower. All consuming, that was Nestor, all-consuming fervor for their favorite sport.

"I can't believe we got this suite. They must really want to keep this under wraps, no one would suspect a Fulton police investigator with these digs."

"Really nice." Hill said, still engrossed by the story of Peterson. He had a friendly smile and even from his still life pictures his easy going nature came through. He didn't have to worry about sponsors, fanatical fans or pushy owners. Racing had been sheer fun then.

I wandered into the main living area. I shut everything off with the fob and walked over to the balcony and pressed the fob button for the doors. As they slid open the roaring of engines could be plainly heard. Although this room didn't face the entrance to the race track, the sound of the cars pounding around the raceway was plainly heard. The sound surrounded me, I felt the sweat on my brow as memories flooded into my brain. I dug into my pocket taking out a blue pill and popped one into my mouth followed by a swig of expensive bottled water that had been left on the table. I breathed deeply, stepping back into room, welcoming the quiet as the doors slid shut.

I went over to the couch, slipping down into the thick cushions. I was already feeling better as the pill took the edge off my nerves. I reminded myself that it had been over two years since I'd had an episode and I felt my hands unclinch and calm return. I silently thanked Dr. Lily for making me take relaxing exercise classes. My body naturally now breathed deeply, my mind automatically started thinking of pleasant memories overriding the ugly ones.

Hill was in the kitchenette getting herself a drink from the refrig. Her tabloid was sitting on the cocktail table. "What's your plans?" I asked her.

"Well, I have to check into local headquarters. I've already read the file, so I just have to see the brother afterwards. I'll call and see if I can set up a time to see him tonight. Perhaps we can wrap it up and be back in Fulton tomorrow?"

"I have to visit my brother and straighten a few family matters out. Hopefully we can leave early tomorrow." The championship race was late tomorrow afternoon. Part of me wanted to stay, part of me knew I shouldn't. My hand automatically reached into my pocket for a pill. I stopped, I could handle this. My hand went to the fob instead. I turned on one of the screens. It was showing the practice sessions going on. My brother was listed for early afternoon. "I'll leave pretty shortly. He should be home right after his practice run."

I picked up her tabloid and immediately the file came on. A picture of a man came on the screen and life froze for me. I stared at the face and the world went a blur.

"Chief, Chief!!" Hill was yelling at me. I tried to focus on her but her voice sounded distant. "Chief, what's the matter? You're pale as a ghost."

I came back, getting a hold of myself. She was standing near me. I looked up and then back down to the picture. "Is this the man who committed suicide?" I knew my voice quivered despite my great effort to keep it calm. I had years of dealing with horrible experiences as Chief of Police yet my voice still sounded weak.

"Yes, did you know him?" She stood over me, her hand shook my shoulder as if trying to shake me out of my shock. It worked. Hill put a cup of hot java in my hand. My hand was quivering as I put it on the table next to the picture. I wasn't sure the cup would make it to my mouth.

I just nodded. Pressing the screen, another picture came in focus of another man who was slightly younger. "This is his brother Tonikikut or Tony."

"Yes, how did you know?"

I went back to the first picture. I pointed to the face, "Monicutticu or Monty as most knew him, was my crew chief." I looked up at her, "He didn't commit suicide. He was a Tohegian."

She sat next to me, taking her tablet. Looking closely at the picture, "Tohegian ..." she thought a minute, "from the plains on Casey?" Despite being from off sector, Hill obviously had studied the Crab Sector, no wonder she had been first in her academy class, she did her homework. Casey was one of our biggest land planets, engineered for farming where a good portion of our local sector food is grown. It was home to the Tohegians.

"Yes." I explained further, "They are tribesmen, make up about ten percent of the planet's population, one of the first to populate the planet. Small clan villages dot the plains. They believe in reincarnation and the sanctity of the soul. Very religious, very against certain sins. They don't believe in alcohol, coveting wealth, lying, and certainly not suicide."

"Perhaps this one wasn't as religious, after all don't most stay on the plains, not many go off planet."

"No, he hadn't been changed by Nestor, he was every inch of him a Tohegian. He practically raised me along with my Uncle Jack."

"I think you owe me an explanation," she calmly said in her most interrogative voice, crossing her legs, leaning back into the cushions. "I need you to explain. I'm meeting Tony soon, I don't like going in blind."

"I'll give you a slight overview." I suppose I owed it to Monty. I didn't tell many anything about myself. As chief, the less known the better, but I owed my old friend something so I told her what I knew. "After my parents died, Uncle Jack, who was my mother's brother, took us in. I was eleven, Ray was just six."

She nodded, "I'm sorry ..."

"It's old history now, I'm just setting the stage, so to speak." I put my hand up, sympathy was the last thing I needed. "Uncle Jack was a racing fanatic, more than even most. He was crew chief of one of the racing teams owned by the Attenson family. He taught us to be mechanics, how to be part of a crew and eventually at fourteen I started practice racing. Monty was his young side kick along with his brother Tony. They were like family."

"It's rare one of the Tohegians leaves, but both left?"

"Yes, both brothers had great mechanical skills and there is a racetrack on Casey. As a matter of fact the Tohegians are known as machinist, great with mechanical things. Highly intelligent, the plainsmen tend to work on all the complicated farm equipment that Casey so depends upon. Monty caught the racing bug and where better than to come to than Nestor? Where Monty went Tony followed. I gathered my Uncle had a great deal to do with them coming." She nodded then pointed to the large screen I had turned on. My brother was on the track, racing his big *orange bird* as he called his car. I watched for a few minutes, then shut it off.

The quiet room seemed strange, no roaring engines. I continued, "Monty became my mentor. He showed me how to set up my car and he spotted for me. Most of all he was my friend. He would fascinate me with his stories of the Tohegian rituals and the wild plains of Casey."

"Spotted? Did he lend you money?" she looked totally confused, it was hard to remember that someone who didn't know about racing how foreign it could seem.

"Spotting for a racer is when someone acts like a coach during the race. Despite all the data coming off your helmet, it is hard to see all around you. A spotter sits high in the small grandstand near the first turn of the track, in your team's box and helps you know what's going on. Tells you when someone is coming up on your blind side. Reminds you to watch your fuel intake. Things of that sort. A second brain so to speak."

She nodded, seemingly understanding the best she could. "You must have to have great deal of trust in that person."

"Absolute trust." The pain must have shown on my face, the grief of his death hitting me. She put her hand on my arm.

"Do you want to take a break?" she quietly asked.

"No. Anyways, I turned pro on my seventeenth birthday. Despite my Uncle's objections, Monty convinced him I was ready. The youngest ever to do so. It was in great part due to Monty's tutoring. I was rookie of the year but more importantly I took the championship, first ever rookie to do that. The second year I was headed toward another championship, as a matter of fact I got the trophy in the hospital. I had so many points that even not finishing the last race I still won. It was the Championship race of the year, here on Nestor that everything fell apart. There was a horrible crash. A driver was killed and I was hurt real bad. I had almost a year of recovering."

"You were so young!" She remarked. "What happened, why didn't you go back?"

"I had some brain damage. I'm now an epileptic, under certain conditions I have seizures."

I had gotten up and was pacing in front of her. She looked shocked. "Is that why?...."

She didn't get to finish her question as someone knocked once and then the door handle started turning. We both looked at each other, both grabbing our holstered guns and pointed them at the door.

Chapter 5

"Hey, Judy," the door slowly opened setting off the roaring engines and a loud "You here?" was yelled over it.

Judy? Then it hit me, that was Hill. I looked over at her, she was putting her gun back in her holster, I followed suit as a blonde haired man poked his head around the door. His flashing blue eyes went to Hill and his mouth broke into a large grin. Then they focused on me and a frown graced his boyishly handsome face. Hill reached into her pocket retrieving the room fob and finally quieted the roaring engine sound. Relief!

"Chief Brown?" he said stepping into the room, putting a room fob in his pant pockets. So he had a key to the room, interesting. Well he knew who I was but I hadn't a clue who he was, although I had an idea. He was maybe a little younger than I was, maybe. He just wore the years better. Impeccably dressed in an expensive tailored casual dark suit made for him, minus a tie, he looked very much a Federal Investigative Operative agent. I'd met so many of them, they stood out like a sore thumb to me.

"Hi Phil." Hill dryly remarked, "What are you doing here?"

He ignored her question, focusing on me instead, "Didn't know you'd be here Chief. Although, I'm not surprised, figured you'd show up sometime." I kept my temper in check, I'd dealt with these pompous bastards often. The FIO, I swear, breeds them or maybe it's the only kind that joins them.

Hill interrupted him, "This is Phil Ober, he's an agent for FIO. Why are you here?" She stepped right up to him, causing him to take his attention from me to her. He smiled down at her. It was too warm a smile for my liking. I automatically took a step toward him but Hill glared at me and I stopped and just stared fiercely back.

He didn't seem to notice, his eyes were all on Hill now, with a familiarity that I was uncomfortable with. He put his hand on her arm but she shook it off and took on that disapproving look I knew only too well. I'd seen that look often enough in the office. It could kill flies at fifty paces. I noticed Phil backed up, now not so sure of himself. Hill could have that effect.

"We're here on an investigation. Heard you were being sent. How do you like the digs?" He swept his arms around the suite looking quite satisfied with himself.

"I like the rooms very much. You're not responsible for these rooms?" She didn't sound happy and he took on a sheepish grin. I was taking a deep dislike for agent Phil.

"Yeah. We're here. We keep rooms here at our disposal. It's like this wherever we are. We need to have a base. We even have apartments on Fulton Station." His eye brows went up, eyeing my reaction. He got nothing, he wasn't going to get me on that point. Could care less where they hang their useless hats. "Thought you should be close by, to help us. See the difference when you work for the Feds?"

Now, that did it. Now it was my turn, my temper thermometer heading to hot. "She's here on a routine investigation. She's not here at your disposal!"

Lt. Judy Hill turned to me, eyes blaring. "Chief!"

Back out came the smile, he raised his arms as if placating children. "No, no. Please let's not get all ruffled." He turned his smirk on me, "Routine investigation, you say? Why are you here? Surely a suicide investigation doesn't warrant the Chief?"

"I don't know where you got your information but it's none of your business why I'm here, get the hell out and leave your key!"

"Sure, as soon as I get my expensive surveillance apparatus if you don't mind." He turned to Hill and put his hand out.

"No," she emphatically stated. "If you put anymore in here I'll beat your ass 'til you can't sit down. You're getting sloppy it took me all of four seconds to find them. I should have guessed it was you."

"Now that's the Hill I know....and love," he laughed.

I was ready to wipe the smirk right off his face but Hill walked over to the kitchenette's sink, turning on the disposal and threw something into it. The loud crunching hurt the ears. The look on Phil's face was one of horror, then annoyance.

"That's not playing nice, Judy. I came here to help you, not you help me, although mutual cooperation will be appreciated."

"We don't need..." I started to say, I wanted to wipe his smart aleck smirk right off his face with a few of his designer teeth with it.

"Oh, I think you do." He turned his six foot trim physique, the type of body that works out everyday, in other words opposite of my own, then headed toward the door. His expensive Guiccil pants and matching white fitted shirt also reminded me how much the Feds got paid. "Your brother? Willing to throw him overboard?" he shot back from the doorway. "Or can the big Sector Chief handle it all himself?" The agent didn't do sarcasm well I doubted it was from lack of practice, just lack of smarts.

"Wait!" I growled at him, his hand dropped off the door and he turned to me. "What do you know about my brother?" My hands were clenched trying to keep my temper in check. I wouldn't give him the satisfaction of reaching for one of my blue pills. I put myself in "calm mode", something Dr. Lily had been practicing over and over with me. I felt it work as my hands unclenched. My mind became focused not angry.

"You mean do I know he's being blackmailed?"

I felt like I'd been sucker punched. It must have shown on my face because he looked surprised, "You mean that's not why you're here? You didn't know?"

"No, I knew something was wrong but that's the last thing I would have thought of. Tell me more." He must have seen the fire in my eyes because he took a wide berth of me as he came back into the room taking a seat at the small round dining table that flashed Peterson's 22 when he sat down. An old fashioned racing car holograph lite up on one side and began racing around the table top.

Hill shut it off with her fob, shaking her head, "cute".

"No," I replied, "overkill!" But that was Nestor.

"Know the Rosluke's?" Phil spoke up, crossing his legs under the table putting his arms crossed behind his head slouching comfortably in his chair. I suppose he thought to show his relaxed side, "your brother is switching to them."

"Yeah, that I do know, they're an old Nestor racing family. Wealthy because of their immense halka grass farms and gasline refineries. More into racing for the prestige of it. They've won a few championships by just throwing money on getting the best of anything money will buy or some say they cheat. They been caught a few times, fined, suspended. Although lately, don't know. I haven't kept up with the fine details of the professional racing world. Other than my brother's career, and that comes from my sister-in-law.

I don't know much else. I know that Walt Rosluke runs the family, he dumped his first wife after two kids. He's never remarried but he's a known womanizer. His two sons, one older than me and one younger, went to off sector private schools and had little to do with us. Those that did know them, don't like them, but that could just be jealousy."

"Yeah, well Walt has gotten a few big names lately to switch to their team. I'm talking big names. Threw lots of money at the drivers. Your brother can't be bought." He paced over to the large sliders looking not out but at his own reflection. Narcissistic asshole. He actually straightened his hair.

Going over to the sliders but avoiding my reflection, I pointed out an obvious conclusion, "My brother is more concerned with racing. Outside of Julie, it's everything to him. He's been with Ralph Attenson all his life. My Uncle Jack, who raised us, was one of Ralph's top crew chiefs. If there is anything Jack taught us was a love for the sport and loyalty to Ralph. That is why I came here to find out why Ray is switching. I can't imagine what could convince him to switch, especially to Rosluke." I hated admitting all this private information to him but I needed info and I wasn't going to get any if I didn't give some.

"Well, Rosluke got your brother or I should say got *to* your brother. They have a very embarrassing video of him cheating on his wife with a woman of ill repute. It's true, I have a copy." He held up his hands, knowing I'd be angry, "Don't get mad at the messenger."

"What!" I must have yelled it as Hill stepped between me and the agent. "I don't believe it!" My hands clenched tighter. "What are you trying to pull?"

He shrugged, "It's not my tape, it belongs to Rosluke. Whatever you'd like to believe, they got one. Here's the copy of it." He handed me his tabcell. "Just touch the screen and your brother's name." I grabbed his tab from his outstretched arm, cursing as I did so.

"He adores Julie, besides being his wife, she's his top mechanic for god's sake! She's expecting their first kid." I couldn't believe it and with a prostitute! Now I did reach in and take a blue pill. His eyebrows went up but he didn't say anything about it.

"He's not the first, won't be the last." He shrugged then stepped back as my rage was very obvious.

It was Hill that interceded, "Phil, the Feds are here to investigate a simple blackmail problem?" She sounded skeptical and she was right as Phil sarcastically grinned. He was good at that probably practiced it in the mirror.

"Of course not! We are here investigating illegal weapons laundering. We've been trying to find the link the rebels are using to transmit drops. We have all the bases covered. We got all the transmit lines, all Jump lines, even all non-conventional ships covered. We can't find how they are getting the information to the renegade leaders on where to pick up the arms and how they are receiving payment for the weapons. Our inside contacts can't find out either. They have only had hints of the operation. A few names have surfaced."

"Rebels, here in this sector? In the Crab Sector?" I asked but quickly forgot it as the video of my brother came on the tablet he'd given me to view. It showed a beautiful naked girl approaching my brother who was getting undressed. He smiled at her as she put her arms around him. It panned out, he was butt naked! It wasn't a long video but it was enough.

I felt sick to my stomach. What a fool! Wait until I got a hold of him! I'm not saying my brother was an angel. We both had our foolish youthful pranks. Heavens, me more than him. He'd always been too busy with racing to get into trouble. We both were. I had been foolish enough to get married at seventeen. He had waited until he was twenty four. Unlike me, he'd found a perfect woman. What had happened? My heart ached at the thought of what this would do to Julie. They were just starting a family! No wonder my brother had caved into the blackmail. What Ray didn't realize is the wives mostly always find out anyway. He should have told her. It would only get worse, I knew from my police experience. Blackmail always bites in the end, better to confront it right up front.

Hill had been watching the video from the side. She quickly looked away when I noticed her. I ignored her blushing perhaps because I was flustered myself. It's something when you are close to the people involved, all of a sudden police training goes right out the window. My police training however did forge forward as I wanted more information. "This is a high quality well put together video, not some amateur trying to make a quick buck." In my police work I'd seen a lot worse quality but none much better than this.

"Yes," he took his tab back, "Rosluke paid good money for that. Although he claims that he found out about it and purchased it to save your brother from embarrassment. Of course that is a crock of shit. He planned it and paid to have it made."

"How does that connect my brother with the arms deal? Obviously it does or you wouldn't bring it up. You wouldn't even care." The welfare of one driver was not FOI business.

"Well," he paced over to the window sliders, opening the doors to the patio, letting the sounds of the car racing filter in. He pointed out the window at the sound obviously trying to make a point. "We've traced the arms' connection to the Rosluke family. Not conclusive, mind you, but enough to ask ourselves why their name keeps seeping into the picture. The youngest son, Emanuel, cocky rich bastard, is friends with the son of one of the arms' dealers. That led to taking a look at the professional racing circuit. As you know, the racing contests take place in most of the Federation humanoid worlds, almost every sector. It's a popular old fashioned sport that commands that its participants travel extensively." He looked over at us to see if we were getting his point.

I did. I knew enough of their travel schedules. It was the most painful part of the job for me. The constant Jump schedule was brutal to my stomach. "So you think they are using the traveling between sectors to pass the info on the drops."

"You got it. But what and how? We tried secretly scanning the crafts. Plus we know the racetrack officials check the vehicles. Rosluke's been caught a few times on supping up his vehicles. No dice in that direction but we might be missing something. Those damn transports are complicated machines, unlike regular crafts. No regular mechanic knows them. The drivers themselves have to go through security scanning before boarding the Jumps like everyone else. We put agents at the station scanners. Again, no dice, they come out clean. The owners and staff travel to the race tracks but same deal; to Jump you go through security. We're at a standstill, a frustrating standstill."

I could tell all his racing knowledge came from reports, he had no idea about the ins and outs of the sport. "Those complicated crafts are called autos or cars.

They are indeed complicated, some might even call them antiquated technology out of ignorance. You'd not know what you're looking at if you got regular hover craft mechanics. They both move, that's about it. They are different beasts." Damn I didn't want to be talking about this, my hand went to reach for a pill but I stopped myself. I'd become less dependent on them lately, using my calming techniques, I wanted to keep it that way.

"Well, now, that's where you might be able to help Chief Brown." His well-shaped eyebrows went up, the conniving smile returned.

"So now we get to it," I spat. From the side I saw Hill grimace. She knew I was about to explode. "What, did you think Hill would be able to get me here? Plan to wine and dine her in this fancy dig?" I asked sarcastically but cursing myself for making it easy for the FIO. I'd come on my own. I felt like a goddamn fool. They were blackmailing me using my brother, they were just being coy about it.

"Well, I looked forward to seeing her, mind you," he said getting a pained angry frown from Hill, "but yes I did have something like that in mind. She's worked for you before if I recall what you two did on Skantie Row, nice piece of work by the way. Helped us a lot to crack the Blithie family's drug ring."

Helping them! They hadn't done a thing. Their asses hadn't been shot at. They hadn't been almost killed. If I remembered correctly they hadn't even been on planet. Skantie Row was too violent even for them. I couldn't help it, pompous fool, I ironically laughed, "Well, you overshot smart conniving ass. It's been a long time since I worked on 'those damn vehicles', they've changed quite a bit. I'm little help to you." I felt a sense of satisfaction, he'd over stepped his plans, ignorance will do that. But I was wrong.

"We weren't thinking of you, we were thinking of Julie." He backed up waiting for my reaction.

He didn't have to wait long, as my temper exploded, "You leave her alone! She's pregnant and will soon have enough on her plate!" I pointed my finger at him, "You Feds think you can ruin everyone's life at any whim you want but you can't! You son of a bitch! You're no different than those Roslukes."

"Whoa," he walked over to the door, "no pressure, only if she wants to help. Think about it. At least ask her." He slipped out the door.

I shut the sliders bringing quiet, which lasted quite a while. I needed to calm down. I finally looked crossly at Hill, "J-U-D-Y!"

She had the sense to at least blush a little, "I knew him in Law School. He used to teach Federation Law. I happened to take his class."

"Just how well did you know him? Did he give you an 'A'?" I spit it between my teeth.

"It's none of your business," she glared at me and of course she had every right to do so. It really wasn't any of my business. She told me anyway. "Last year when I was at the academy I bumped into him again. He was lecturing on the role of the Federation Investigative Operation. He'd become an agent. He tried to recruit me but I wanted to be a cop not an agent. After my sister was killed, I wanted to something more substantial."

"Well isn't that comforting," I rudely said to her back as she went to the sink, retrieving something in her hand. I was taking out on her my frustration with the FIO and my brother. Realizing it, I shut up. I actually had a few moments of remorse but just a few.

Hill didn't seem to notice however, "Don't underestimate him, Phil is quite good, especially in technology surveillance." She handed me a small round disk, "These are new bugs, I didn't flush them all down there. They are undetectable unless you carry one of these." She showed me a small electronic bug detector that I didn't recognize. "So I learned something from him. I always check for bugs where ever I stay. You'd be surprised how many places do surveillance." She put a gel type wrapper around it, neutralizing it, then pocketed the bug. "I think Issam can get this analyzed. We need to keep ahead of them."

She could tell by the look on my face that I wondered how much she'd learned from agent Phil and she turned red again. I went and sat on the couch, putting my head in my hands, frustration getting the better of me. How stupid could my brother be? What had he been thinking of?

"We all make mistakes," She commented as if reading my thoughts. "What are we going to do?"

"We?" I looked up at her, "I think you're heading home on the next Jump. This is way beyond your pay grade. I'll need a top operative here now."

"No!" She almost shouted at me. "You need me, I can handle the Feds, especially Phil, unless you want your brother to be implicated. Trust me, he can be quite ruthless and if it means flushing your brother down the toilet, he won't think twice."

She had a point and worse she knew it. I thought it over and reluctantly agreed, "We need to make everyone think we are just investigating a suicide. If Rosluke suspects, he'll shut it down. I want to get to him before he implicates my brother further. I sure hope Ray isn't involved in the arms fiasco. Hopefully it's too early for him to be involved." I had no doubt that was what Rosluke intended. Ray had no idea what he was signing up for. "Do what you came to do, report to the local police and then we'll see about Monty's brother Tony. Then we'll go from there. I'll meet you back here before dinner. We'll make plans then. Be careful, the FOI will have ears and eyes everywhere and don't underestimate what influence Walt Rosluke has on this planet. It's formidable. The least they both know, the better chance we'll have before they shut us off the case."

"You going to see your brother?" she asked.

"Yep."

"That's not going to be pretty." She shook her head at me.

"Nope."

I took a long hot shower but it didn't wash off the disgust I was feeling. I watched my brother finish his practice through the hazy steam on the shower's monitor screen. I wasn't sure how I was going to approach him. I'd always been the "protective" older brother. I hadn't done a real good job lately. I shouldn't have cut all the ties with Nestor or I wouldn't be surprised at his troubles. I should have come home earlier. I changed into casual clothes taking a hat with a blonde haired wig, I added dark sunglasses. I would slouch down, making me look a lot older and shorter.

Ray lived on the far side of Nes City in an area called Racing Alley. I'd take the underground until I was in the outskirts then I'd grab a cab. It was the safest way around the reporters. I just hoped they weren't out stalking the drivers' homes. Every one of the drivers had mansions with walls protecting their property. It was the only privacy they had. Hopefully, the reporters would mostly be at the track and not wasting time at the mansions.

From experience I knew the walls were there to keep fanatical fans at bay more than the reporters. I shuddered at the memories of the au-natural female fan whose body was painted in my team colors or the drunk man yelling at the top of his lungs, pounding on my door with his fist, angry that I'd lost. Those were only some that had scaled the walls and shown up at my door. It keeps most of them away, anyways. I laughed remembering the time my naked ex-wife was at our pool and a bunch of skydivers floated down to her, carrying a banner of "Go Skip Go." She had screamed her head off at them, gone, not for clothes, but had gotten a gun and scared the living daylights out of them. She'd fired several times searing their clothing as they ran as fast as they could. Yep, that was Charlene. Life had been interesting sometimes.

As I was dressing, Hill had gone out and came back carrying a couple of packages. "I got some local clothes, I don't want to stand out." She had a bus boy with her, helping her carry the packages. I went to leave. "Wait!" she yelled at me then casually walked over reaching into my jacket pocket and retrieving a tiny object. She handed it to the man and mouthed softly, "Take a ride." at the same time handing him some money. "And don't forget to leave that in the cab."

He nodded and left.

"What the hell!" I exclaimed, they had bugged me. This must be an important case, they wouldn't have chanced it otherwise. You don't bug the Chief of Police with impunity! Obviously the FOI did.

"Told you Phil was good. Give that guy a few minutes so they think you're leaving. Told you, you need me."

For once we were in total agreement.

Chapter 6

I stole out of the busting at the seams hotel, weaving my way through the packed lobby. The last of the guests were registering and chaos was threatening to overwhelm the front desk. No one even looked at me as I headed out the front door. I took a short walk to the underground station that was located nearby for the convenience of the guests of the neighboring hotels. Just as it was easy to slip through the crowded lobby, I easily mingled with the sizeable crowds in the underground train station. Many were coming inbound, heading in to the positioning time trials. Still, it was busy going out too, the trains were packed to the gills with standing room only most of the way.

The city was full and on holiday; many workers had time off. It was estimated that during the big races, there were two majors a year, the capital swelled to three times its normal population. Every hotel was full, the streets jammed with traffic, the restaurants full. The retailers loved the influx from all over the human federation as money flowed on racing memorabilia. I knew the police were stretched thin, trying to keep the hoard of off-planet visitors safe from pickpockets, scam artists and ticket scalpers.

No one on the platforms paid attention to anything but the race news. People were bumping into each other as they were intent on their tabcells or were hurrying over to the nearest screen as some announcement was being made. Many passengers missed their trains as they were so intensely focused on the huge screens that were showing the ending of the practice runs. Tonight would bring the actual time trials for the starting positions. The excitement was contagious, with fans yelling at the screens each time a driver took a turn. During the actual race it would be wild. Bars and pubs had to put on extra security to keep the enthusiasm from getting out of hand. The hospitals were gearing up as every year their emergency rooms overflowed with fans that had forgotten it was *only a race* and had slugged someone who disagreed with them.

I looked at the underground map. I'd get off at Harlington Square, the next to last stop, which I knew would be less crowded and easier to catch a taxi. Even inside the actual underground trains the fans were watching the small wall screens which were broadcasting the latest updates. Every man, woman and child had an opinion, there were plenty of favorite drivers. Heated debates abounded over every aspect from drivers to owners to even the color scheme of the cars. "Why isn't she driving her red car today!", "What the hell is he doing, doesn't he know enough to hit the track high on that end?"

My head was swimming from all the yelling. I'd be glad when the train ride was over. One lady kept poking me in the ribs every time Tammy Walshik's number 77 car took a corner. "Go girl, go girl, go girl," she'd yell then poke me again. The thought of arresting her for battery did enter my head, glad when she got out at the Steele Park stop; at least my ribs were.

I had trouble keeping my mouth shut when it came to my brother's criticisms but I did, biting my tongue. Amateurs guessing, pretending to be the drivers, but it's what made the sport. Without them it was rather a futile exercise. Some drivers and owners forget that. Thanks to my Uncle Jack, we never did. I could hear him in my head, *"Remember son, no fans, no racing."* I missed him. I hadn't come back for his memorial service, I was in early therapy and it was recommended I not go. I'd regret that the rest of my life. He had done a great job raising us with Killa's help. I suppose that is why I couldn't fathom Ray's behavior but then I certainly had made my mistakes, as Charlene came soaring into my mind. Oh well!

As the trains got further out it was a relief as fewer and fewer passengers were left to argue. My head hurt from all the excited chatter. I had forgotten how Nestor's overwhelming passion of living, breathing and eating racing could at times be too much. In some ways I had missed it. I popped a blue pill in my mouth. The memories always took their toll but it didn't matter, I still didn't want to lose them, even if I had been given the chance.

At the square I hailed a cab and took it to the city's suburbs onto what is known as "Racing Row". The cab passed one mansion after another, all racing related inhabitants; owners, drivers, racing families, crew chiefs. There was some big money in racing, I ought to know, or least my ex-wife did. I had owned one of these mansions, it seemed another life, that part distant and inconsequential. I'd been too busy traveling to pay attention to where I actually lived. My big house seemed more like a vacation home. Though Charlene had traveled with me, she just loved the racing circuit life, she also loved her mansion. I'd make the money, she'd spend it. I wondered how Julie would handle their hectic life once the baby came? Others had managed. I just hoped the kid had a family once Julie learned what Ray had done.

The cab left me at the driveway entrance to my brother's house. It used to be my Uncle Jack's. We'd grown up here. I could barely see the huge brick structure at the end of the long driveway. I entered the code that opened the door near the gates. I was right, he used the same code we'd always used as kids; our mother's birth date. I walked down the driveway that was surrounded by a well-manicured but simple lawn. Despite my travel sickness, we went everywhere with Jack, so most of our lives were spent following the circuit. Our schooling was done with the other kids in makeshift classrooms with tutors paid by the owners.

Still, off season was spent here; fond memories of pool parties and friendships with other driver's kids romping on these lawns. Memories of driving our turbocycles that we had souped up. Taking long cycle trips around Nestor with Uncle Jack, Ray racing me for the lead. Sometimes Killa, who would pack a picnic lunch, even came riding on the back of Uncle Jack's old antique Trooper cycle. We had helped him fix the old machine up, polishing it to a fine sheen. We'd also spend hours at the Nestor track practicing. Good old fashioned memories. I hoped Ray's kids had the same. I hope my brother hadn't ruined it.

My eyes searched for any activity around the huge brick house but I didn't see any, not even a gardener. Of course, it was just before the trials, Ray probably wanted it quiet. I remembered I needed to concentrate before I got in the car. Charlene hated it, as she hated being ignored. She'd often take off, going shopping. It was important to go over the track in your mind, to think of the strategy that Monty and Tony had laid out for me. Each time, each track had different problems.

I knocked at the door, I could hear the roaring of the doorbell announcing me. After a minute a maid answered, an older lady with a severe look of black everything. Black hair, black dress, black socks and shoes with no color relief what so ever. Her hair was drawn back in a tight bun. Only her pale face contrasted with the rest of her, which made her severe grimace stand right out. Her frown could kill a dog. For a moment I almost asked her if she knew Hill.

"Yes, what do you want!" the all in black dressed maid voice loudly snapped. It came out like a whip. She looked skeptically at me, peering out the door, looking down the way I come and wondering how I'd gotten in. I had already removed the disguises but I guess I still didn't look quite respectable. I gathered she couldn't see the resemblance I had with my brother, of course he was 25 lbs lighter and five years younger.

"I'd like to talk to Julie. I'm her brother-in-law." I smiled, hoping it would do miracles and change her attitude but it didn't. Guess I need to practice, I'm not known as a friendly face- but still I did make an effort.

Her eyes squinted, her nose huffed and the door slammed in my face. Alright, she hadn't heard of me. After a few minutes, I was just thinking of ringing again when Julie, herself, came to the door. "Oh, I'm so sorry Skip. I haven't said anything about you coming. Marthie should have let you in but you know how fans can be. She thought you were a fan that came up with a new story. We had one show up the other day, completely naked with Ray's number 15 tattooed all over his body. The tattoos were even Attenson's team color scheme!"

"You don't have to explain, I still remember," I told her, hugging her tight. Despite being pregnant, she was awful thin. She was a beautiful girl, dark long silky black hair, dark brown eyes with skin an almost olive complexion that only enhanced her exotic nature. Ray had met her off sector, she was a saleswoman for her father's auto hobby franchise. Her father specialized in helping the public duplicate the racing cars and selling other racing memorabilia. Her father had done well in part because Julie was a great sales person.

Ray had fallen in love with her on the spot when he gone to an autograph session at the hobby store. It still took him three years to get her to marry him but he'd been persistent, visiting her in the off season and anytime he could. After they were married she then turned into one hell of a mechanic, not content to just sit home on Nestor or follow him around like the other spouses. That was Julie.

"You look great," I told her.

"Don't lie, you never were good at lying. Guess it's against the principals of being a good cop." She laughed, "I haven't been sleeping good."

I'd guess not eating either, I thought but didn't voice. She didn't need me making things worse. I'm sure her doctor was telling her to eat. "Where's Ray?"

"He's in the den watching the practice runs end, going over how he'll attack the trial. I've set up the car to run high. The shocks are tight. The track was paved last year. Going high will make a smoother ride, they didn't do the lower rim as well. In practice, he had a good run with this set up. He'll be fifth tonight in the trials. I've got the car all ready. I find Nestor's course easy to set up for, there are no surprises. Now on Casey, that's a different story. It's older and much too banked and sometimes they oil it a couple of weeks before the race filling in the cracks. You have to be careful there. I actually walk the entire two mile stretch before that race."

I had to laugh and hugged her again. She was one smart crew chief. One hell of a mechanic to boot! She hugged me back.

"We'll head to the track in a couple of hours. He's trying to relax." she nodded towards the den.

"It's hard not to get all wound up, have to keep loose." I smiled at her. Although she smiled back, her sad eyes betrayed her.

"I want to thank you Skip, I know this is hard on you." I went to tell her it wasn't but she put her hand up, "Don't deny it. If I wasn't so worried. So worried ..." tears welled up. She shook herself and half smiled, "there I go again. It must be the pregnancy, my hormones are going crazy. It's just we've always been so open with each other, this is hard to take, his silence."

"Hey, don't worry. I'll take care of it." I hugged her shoulders, she was a couple of inches shorter. Her hair smelled like flowers, a freshness that reminded me of the spring mornings I remembered from my days on Nestor. Fulton Station hadn't any seasons, only one season, hot with wilted flowers trying to survive the climate. It's hard to smell a cactus, our national flower.

She led me out of their foyer down a hall to a small comfy room that held a big curved screen and lots of couches. Ray was sitting on one. His racing trophies graced a whole wall. He'd won a lot of races. I'd not seen one of them, I guiltily thought, not one. Julie and Ray had always visited me. I'd been at their wedding that was held at her home on Sinna in the Sol sector but other than that I couldn't manage the races. I hadn't even watched them televised, although Killa did and always filled me in. She also got all the professional circuit magazines, leaving the tabs where I could conveniently find them, hoping I'd read them. I usually didn't.

"Look whose here?" She announced bringing Ray to his feet, surprise written all over his face.

"Skipper?" His voice ringing with astonishment. He came over and grabbed me, hugging me hard. "Well, I'll be, what brings you here?" Then he looked at Julie, a dark expression coming over his face, "Did you call him? I told you there was nothing to worry him about."

"What do you mean?" I reached over grabbing him, squeezing his arm, "why would she call me? I'm here investigating Monty's suicide. Tony's contesting the ruling."

"Oh," understanding came on his face, then sadness, "I'm sorry, I couldn't bring myself to tell you. I didn't, didn't..."

It was Julie that finished his statement, "We didn't want to upset you and we didn't think you'd come for the memorial service, given your condition. We thought with the season so close to ending we'd come and tell you ourselves, like we did at Uncle Jack's death."

"How's Killa?" Ray asked. "Keeping her busy I hear." He glanced at Julie where all family information came from. It was Julie that kept in touch with me. My brother, like all professional racers, hadn't time for anything else but racing.

"She's fine. I keep her busy running the apartment building. As long as it's helping me, she's content. She sends her best. She wanted to come but it's impossible to get a ticket here. I'll call her later on one of the Jump lines."

"So you're here investigating Monty?" For the first time I noticed Ray's haggard looks. He looked much older than his twenty six years. His eyes had dark rings underneath and he'd lost weight. He had been lean and trim before, now he was gaunt. I would guess a lack of sleep and worrying had been having their effects, just like it had with Julie. What a mess, I thought as my stomach did flip flops. How was I going to fix this?

I reached down shutting off the screens. "Tony is complaining to the authorities that his brother didn't commit suicide, so we came out to investigate." Ray's frown told me all I needed to know, that he didn't believe it either. Ray was like Uncle Jack, all his emotions showed in his face, he could never hide much from me. When he had gotten into trouble as a kid, I'd caught him before he could even tell me, whether it was at school or if it was personal girl problems. He couldn't hide anything from me. Now would be no exception.

"I'll go make us some java. I know you'd never refuse a cup Skip." Julie headed out, conveniently leaving us alone.

"Well, how goes it Ray?" I asked, taking a seat, trying to keep my voice from showing the tightness of my nerves.

"Fine, I hope to win the Championship. It all depends on Stan Linkis. Only ten points separate us."

"That's great," I wasn't much for small talk, perhaps that's why I became a police detective, it fit my personality. "So tell me why you're leaving Ralph?"

"Is that why you're here?" Ray pressed the remote bringing up the shades, letting the afternoon sun filter in. In the natural light he looked even more pale, more gaunt, more worried. "Who told you?" he demanded sharply, his mouth going into a tight pout that I knew so well from our childhood. Ray could be stubbornly obstinate.

"Does it matter? What's the reason?" I stared at him, I could see the strain show even more. His eyes seemed dull, emphasizing the dark rings around them, his face looked even more drawn. I very much doubted he'd take the championship. It takes all you have and right now Ray hadn't half the spunk he usually had. You couldn't win if you couldn't think straight.

"You know don't you?" he asked. His eyes looked accusingly at me, somewhat defiant, somewhat scared.

"Yes." I looked him square on, not letting him retreat.

"Have you seen the video?" Now he did look down, he couldn't look me in the eyes.

"Yes, pretty bad." I stood up, going over to him. "What were you thinking?" I couldn't keep the anger from my voice. I saw him cringe and shrink even more from me. My heart ached, I'd never seen him like this. He'd been spunky as a kid, spunky as a driver. Full of endless energy, now he seemed drained of everything.

"Well, you wouldn't believe it, no one will believe me," his voice cracked. He went over looking outside as if trying to find answers that he couldn't find here inside. He repeated, "no one is going to believe me, especially Julie. I can't stand the thought of losing her."

"Believe me, I've seen and heard it all, try me. You're my brother, tell me the truth." I put my arm on his shoulder. He was slightly shorter than me, his eyes teared up. His body was shaking either from fear or rage, I wasn't sure.

"I was framed." He walked away from me. "I know you hear that a lot but it's the truth! It's the goddamn truth!" His voice cracked and he half sobbed. "I can't believe I was so duped, so used."

"Alright, explain, slowly." I could tell he was starting to hyperventilate, I'd seen it often in formal interrogations. "Slow down, tell me starting with the beginning. The very beginning and don't leave anything out, whether you think it's important or not!"

"I got this call from George. You know George Tesmor. His father was one of Williamson's drivers. We use to attend classes together. He told me he had a new type of racing outfit. Wanted me to come see it. A whole new concept that, like our helmets, was based on DNA. He was getting the franchise to sell them. He asked I not tell anyone, that it was top secret but he valued my opinion. I was to tell no one, including Julie or he could lose the contract."

"So you went over to see it." I already saw what was coming but let him tell it.

"Yeah. He showed it to me. It was made of a new type of material. I don't doubt it is something new, never felt material like that. He left me alone to try it on. You know, you don't wear anything under it, the tighter the fit the better. It has to blend in with your skin. I've seen some of the prototypes but none have been ready for marketing.

Well, no sooner did I have my clothes off and was starting to put on the outfit then this naked woman comes out and runs over and embraces me. I pushed her away. She was very persistent. I even yelled for help, lot of good that did me. Well, you know the rest. I got out of there quickly, even left my socks there. George had suddenly disappeared. Two days later I get this video. They doctored it to look like I was having an affair with her. Even have me smiling at her. You saw it! No one would believe me. I don't even know her goddamn name!"

"So which Rosluke got a hold of you?" I asked, keeping my anger from showing.

"The old man, Walt. He told me it had been sent to him. Said he was shocked at the video, that once Ralph saw it, I would be finished with Attenson racing and never mind what my wife would think. It would ruin us. He told me the girl was a prostitute. How awful it would look in the news. You know he's right, Ralph is a stickler for upstanding behavior. He'd never want a scandal. So Walt offered me a job with Rosluke racing. Said he had influence to cover it up. That no one need know. What could I do? No one's going to believe me."

"You should have called me," I admonished him. "Have you ever told anyone what I do for a living?"

"No. You didn't want me to, so I just tell people you're in a security business. I don't even tell them you're in sector. Even Ralph doesn't know. All anyone looks at Fulton for is what the government is doing.

Enough scandals with the politicians. No one notices the police."

"Perhaps you should have confided in your wife." Julie was standing in the doorway, she must have been listening from the hallway. "Have you so little trust in me, so little faith!" Julie was crying, her hands cringed in front of her in anger. "Doesn't our marriage have enough trust in it or is our love so shallow?"

"Julie, you don't know how many times I wanted to tell you. I was so afraid you'd leave me. You're pregnant, I didn't want to cause you any more stress." Ray was shaking, trembling from head to toe. I was afraid he'd pass out. He looked at Julie pleading with her to understand.

"You stupid man!" she yelled at him. "I've been worried sick. I haven't slept, I can't eat. You stupid man!" she screamed at him again and ran out the room.

"Go after her," I told him. "Beg on your hands and knees. Agree with her, you are stupid!"

He left. I sat on the couch, my head pounding from the emotion of it. At least this I was handling. My little blue pills stayed in my pocket. Strange I never knew what could trigger my brain into overdrive.

The woman in black came in carrying a tray with java. I smiled at her and to my surprise she smiled back. It completely changed her, her whole face lit up. "I'm sorry about what happened earlier Mr. Brown, we get some real kooks. I thought you were one of them."

"Perfectly understandable," I assured her. She'd even brought along some chocolate croissants. Julie knew they were my favorite.

"I'm glad you're here." She looked over her shoulder. "Very glad."

"Been kinda rough?" I asked her, seeing the tears forming at the corners of her eyes.

She just shook her head. "I think it'll be alright now. They are a lovely couple. They just needed to clear the air. I've been with Julie since she was a child, I'm a distant cousin. I was so glad she asked me to come and run their household. I have no one else. We were so excited about the baby. I'm very fond of both of them. Hopefully this will clear the air. Their bond is strong, they will survive this."

"Let's hope so," I told her as she left. I sure hoped so. Julie was the best thing that ever happened to Ray. Uncle Jack was great but he wasn't our parents. He had no idea how to raise two rambunctious boys, yet he did a great job of raising us, if a little unorthodox in his methods. Still, often it was only the two of us depending on each other as Jack was busy with his racing obsession. Killa did her best but she had problems of her own. My marriage at 17 was a disaster. I somehow thought that Charlene would fill the void of my parent's death. I wouldn't listen to anyone, married her against Uncle Jack's advice. Water over the dam, I told myself. Yet, if I had met someone like Julie perhaps things would have turned out different, perhaps.

It was Julie that walked back into the den. "Are you going to be alright?" I asked her. Her eyes were red from crying, her hair a mess. I was glad to see her wedding ring still on her finger.

"Yes, I think so." She sat across from me. Her eyes had more life in them. The indecision had been replaced by assurance. She had a handle on her life again. "Thank you. I had no idea. He's so stupid!" She threw up her hands in frustration repeating, "He's so stupid!"

"He's telling the truth." I told her, "He can't lie to me, never could."

"Yes, I know. If he'd told me I would have believed him. He caused himself more grief by not telling me the truth right when it happened."

"Did he already tell Ralph he was switching?" I asked.

"Yes. He's right, you know, Ralph is rather old fashioned and prudish. He runs a tight organization and takes pride that all his drivers are above reproach. He hates any type of scandal, thinks it reflects on the sponsors. Don't get me wrong, I'm not complaining. He treats his drivers really well. Treats our families like we are his own. Of course Ralph only has his daughter Cally, and she's a handful."

"I know Ralph's views, I use to race for him. It's probably one of the reasons I married Charlene so young. It was the proper thing to do or so I thought. He thinks of his drivers like they are his kids." Ralph Attenson had taken it hard when I had given up racing. I'd never told him about the brain damage. I couldn't face it then, I felt like a sub human. I only told Ray and later Julie. Uncle Jack had died before the diagnosis. I still had trouble facing it. I saw it as a weakness and later when I entered law enforcement I hid it well, as criminal enemies exploited weaknesses.

Julie already looked better, she pointed her finger at me, "Ralph was very angry when Ray told him he was switching. He almost wouldn't let Ray finish this season, even though it could be a championship for him. I think he never got over Ray refusing to marry his daughter, Callistie." She smiled, the first time I saw the old Julie coming through.

"You mean little Cally?" I remembered the child that he used to drag around the racetracks, especially since her mother had died when she'd been a baby. He doted on her, his only child. She had grown up at the racetrack. Cally Attenston, a little blonde doll, often sat in my car asking a hundred and one questions. She'd never been interested in actual racing though. She sat in my car asking me personal questions and telling me the latest gossip. Callistie hadn't gotten along with my ex, Charlene and visa versa. Too much alike I guess.

"She's not *young* Cally anymore." Julie explained. "She's grown up into a gorgeous long legged beauty. Has a modeling career but lacks the discipline and the need frankly to really be successful at it. Ralph's been trying to get her married to the right man and have the right grandson. Notice I said grandson. Callistie isn't what I called the perfect daughter for a traditional father and that's putting it mildly. He may be very strict with his drivers but he's lost total control of her."

"I'll go talk to him, explain everything." I wondered how he'd changed since I'd last seen him. He'd been a stubborn but fair man. A real moralist, but I'd seen a compassionate side to him once his temper had settled down. I was counting on it.

As if Julie had read my mind, she remarked, "Think he'll listen to you? He's rather unmovable when he gets something in his head. Ray is definitely in his dog house. Although Ralph always claimed you were his favorite racer."

"Oh he'll listen to me, not as a driver but as Sector Police Chief, he'll listen." She looked strangely at me perhaps seeing for the first time not Skip Brown racer or even as a brother-in-law but Chief Skip Brown, a tough cop.

Chapter 7

Julie agreed to call Ralph and have him meet me at his house. She handed me the fobkey to Ray's expensive sports craft which I'm sure he would not have agreed to, but he was getting ready to go to the track and hadn't been there to object. "Ralph's number two on the craft's screen," she told me as she handed me the fob. "He's moved since you've left. Had a new house built on part of the old Strom's property. I don't suppose I should warn you not to supercharge. There are a lot of police this week and the roads are loaded with them."

"Now that would make news, 'Chief of Police gets speeding ticket'." I'd be ribbed to death by my office, imagining the disapproving look on Issam's face when I returned home.

"The police know Ray's car so you might not be bothered but..." Julie started to say but then caught herself as she realized who she was talking to. "I don't mean the cops show him any favors...:

"Don't worry. I'm well aware of the awe in which the drivers are held here. I use to be one. You aren't revealing any secrets." I remembered only too well how much Nestor coddled their heroes. Free lunches, showered with gifts, the best tickets on the planet to any shows, even soldout shows and yes, the cops looked the other way when it came to speeding tickets. We paid for it with no privacy, our lives scrutinized, the spotlight could melt a driver if they hadn't the temperament. I wondered how I had managed it. It hadn't seemed such a high price to pay back then but at seventeen/eighteen, nothing daunted me. My ex-wife Charlene had basked in the adoration, had thrived in it. I went to reach for my blue pills but stopped, conscious of Julie's eyes watching me. I calmed myself throwing the memories to the back of my mind and left for Ralph's mansion.

In the garage were several vehicles. The Hundil stood right out from the more conservative family hovers. My brother had it made especially for him. It was bright silver and looked like a bullet. I slipped into the white leather velvety soft seat, feeling the seat conform to my body. The seat belts automatically wrapped me in straps. He had the car set for all his comforts. Fresh air came floating in at just the right temperature. The windows automatically tinted to allow less sunlight. Then the loud music came blaring on. I fumbled with the fob managing finally to shut it off by yelling at it. I guess it understood "shut up" as the volume diminished to bearable. Ray and I never did agree on his choice of music. It would take a while for my ears to stop ringing.

As I left the garage I could feel the smooth thrust of the engine. It made me sigh at the pleasure of it. Definitely not my Ant! As I drove down the long driveway, I could feel the power pushing me back into the seat. Despite it being completely different than my brother's race car where the power rumbles in the chest, this was just smooth quiet power. Power nevertheless and I let it wash over me. I hadn't felt anything like it in a long time, not even my turbocycle could match this pleasurable experience. I smiled from ear to ear and relaxed.

I got past the gates, again fumbling with the gate controls on the fob, and pressed Ralph's address on the dash's screen. It showed me exactly how to get to his house or it would get there for me. I chose manual controls. It wasn't far as he too was one of the Nestor's racing elite and owned one of the mansions. It felt so good to have a sleek fast vehicle under my touch, my Ant would seem drab now. Of course, my Ant needed charging once a week, this thing had to be charged every time you took it out of the garage. The thought of sending it into overdrive and seeing what she could do, it did enter my head but I kept my mouth shut. I wasn't sure of the command and was not willing to take the chance. My mind grumbled that I was getting cautious in my old age. Another part of my brain thought it was about time. I wasn't a race car driver anymore. I couldn't help let a little envy for my brother creep into my brain.

Ralph's house was twice the size of Ray's. Massive manicured lawns surrounded it. The wrought iron gates with a big "A" opened automatically. I was expected. The long circular drive went right up to the front door. Unlike Ray's house, this house was a buzz of activity. Gardeners potting plants, a groom was walking a horse, servants were brushing the walkways, golf carts designed to look like Attenson's racing cars were running between the several backyard buildings. My brother's number 15 duplicate cart was bumping along, its back filled with lawn chairs being moved. The backyard, I could see, had a huge garage with doors opened showing several expensive hover crafts. Ralph lived his racing. Like most of the owners, racing was not his main source of income, just his overwhelming passion. Ralph Attenson's Financial Services was one of the biggest commodity trading firms in the sector and kept his racing "hobby" in fine form and his daughter in fine designer clothes.

A neatly uniformed maid was waiting for my arrival, the huge double door was wide opened welcoming me. "Mr. Brown, please follow me. How nice to see you." We went through most of the massive house, you could hike in this palace. It was much larger than Ralph's last place. The maid finally pointed to a cupola-type atrium. I walked through and to my surprise a young beautiful half-clad woman greeted me.

"Welcome home, Mr. Skip Brown." She came and gave me a hug, "You probably don't remember me, but I fondly remember you."

"You're not Cally?" I innocently asked, knowing quite well she was. I saw her appropriately blush. I wondered how often she practiced that in front of her mirror.

"Yes, I am." She touched my arm in greeting. "I'm the one who use to follow you around like a little love sick puppy. You were the nicest of all the drivers and the best looking, I might add."

"That was a long time ago." I looked around but her father wasn't anywhere to be seen. It was a beautiful room. I didn't remember ever being in such a lavish room like this. Exotic plants filled the glass area, exquisitely carved wooden statues brought from off sector, probably from one of the far outland type planets that catered to well off tourists, were strategically placed giving it an out-of-world feel. Cally fit right in, it actually enhanced her beauty. I had a feeling this was her favorite room. A showcase for showing off her beauty! I had to admit, it worked. She looked absolutely gorgeous with an alluring innocence that she pulled off perfectly with her stance and carefully made up eyes.

"It wasn't that long ago. What was it, ten years ago?" she twirled around, giving me a good look at her perfectly shaped body.

"Something like that, don't age me," I laughed. It was more like 14 years but who was counting. I'm sure my out of shape body made a great impression. I hadn't aged as nicely as she had.

She moved over leaning backwards on a center glass table that had been set with java mugs and a carafe. Her dress had a skirt that was cut in slices, giving me a good look at her shapely legs, the top was low cut, giving me another good look. All in all, she was quite temptingly fetching. Her long blonde hair curled around her neck and her oval shaped face was professionally made up to accentuate her large blue eyes. The whole effect was ruined by her knowing she was appealing, there was no actual innocence. The woman was well orchestrated.

"Are you moving back to Nestor, coming back to racing finally?" she grinned showing a perfect made for public smile. Those teeth must have cost daddy a good bit. This was reminding me of a cat and mouse game with me being the poor rodent, but for what? Despite her growing up, she somehow managed to remind me of the young Cally - self-centered, always conniving to get whatever she wanted. But me? I'm sure there were lots of young virile men to keep her busy. Why did Phil come into my thoughts? Yes, agent Phil would fit her bill nicely.

I snapped out of my amusing thoughts to answer her, "No, I'm just visiting, I'm only here a couple of days." I shrugged my shoulders nonchalantly. I was hoping she'd get the idea I was not interested. I hadn't come here to play games with Cally. I like them a little bit older and a lot wiser. I'd learned my lesson on Charlene, had cut my baby teeth with pain. No, never again I thought, never again.

"Well, maybe my father can change your mind." Then she grinned again, "Maybe I can change your mind." She looked up, her big blue eyes flirting, making intimate promises. I had to admit my male hormones did pick up, but not for long. Someone else was in the room.

I became aware of another woman in the porch's doorway, standing at the edge of the glass enclosure. She was watching us from the archway, a disapproving frown gracing her entire face. She was young, perhaps just a little older than Cally and had intense staring eyes that were focused on Ralph's daughter. Where Ralph's daughter was passively alluring, this one was aggressively pretty; dark curly short hair, large brown eyes, slim athletic build. I would bet she lifted weights. She had an appeal all her own. Cally saw me looking and turned seeing the peeved off girl. It hit me, this young woman was extremely angry, it radiated right off her. I was the object of her anger, her eyes told me as she focused on me. Hate or something close to it was being directed at me. I knew exactly why, I'd seen it before when answering a heated domestic dispute. As a cop there was nothing worse, nothing more scary, nothing more uncontrollable.

"Marcie, you aren't supposed to be here!" Cally's voice was now cold, piercingly cold. All gone was the warmth that had been focusing on me. Ralph's daughter was now angry too.

"Oh, really. You shouldn't be here either. You don't have to do this!" Marcie's voice was pleading, her arms reached forward towards Cally.

"Shut up. Leave us alone, you're going to ruin everything!" Attenson's daughter was whining now, her voice shrill. She turned her back on Marcie, trying to pretend she wasn't there. She put her smile back on, walking toward me, ignoring the other woman.

I'd had enough. "And what exactly is she ruining?" I asked in my Chief's voice. It brought both of them staring at me, suddenly aware of this large irritated man's attention. Both seemed to step back. This was not the seventeen year old Skippy. I saw Cally's face become anxious, wondering exactly who I was. The boss's girl never was talked to that way and she wasn't sure how to handle it. Gone, to my satisfaction, was the haughty assurance replaced by uncertainty. This I could handle, time for answers.

After a few moments of silence, I said, "Well, speak up!" I boomed. I saw the intimidating fear that I saw when I was interrogating someone. It usually was very effective and it was now as both took on an alarming look, exchanging glances of worry.

It was Marcie sounding like a small pouting child that answered me. "She's seducing you to please her father. If you marry her, he'll leave her alone after you give her a child, it had better be a boy too! Think you're up to it old man."

"Marcie!" Cally yelled at her, Now you've done it. Father will be furious."

"And you are?" My tone left no doubt I wanted a full answer with no lies.

"I'm her lover, the one she belongs with." It came out softly but the determination was strong despite that. She stood there defying me to challenge her, which I had absolutely no intention of doing. This "old man" was no threat to her.

"Marcie!" Cally went over and sat down at the table, taking a delicate porcelain cup and throwing it. It shattered nearby, bringing in a maid who hurriedly started picking it up. I got the feeling this was a common occurrence.

I shook my head. Yep, this was little Cally, the spoiled child I knew at the track. The one who always got her way. "Where's Mr. Attenson?" I asked the maid.

"He's in the screening room, sir," pointing in a general direction.

I left figuring I'd find it myself. I found it by following the sounds of racing cars.

The room was a three hundred and sixty round screen. Several shots of the racing cars were showing. They were semi holographs giving an almost dizzying feeling. He turned, seeing me, it took him several seconds to recognize me. Then he widely grinned. He was a tall distinguished looking man, a proud man. He reached me in two strides, giving me a big bear hug. "Glad to see you Skip, mighty glad to see you." He held me at bay looking me over from head to toe. "A great sight for these tired old eyes, although you've aged and put on a few pounds. You need to get back to racing, while you still can, while you're young!" I didn't want to tell him, his daughter's friend had just called me old.

"I suppose civilian life will do that to you, Sir." I shook his extended hand. It was firm and confident yet his hair was now peppered in gray. An almost overwhelming feeling of loss flooded my brain. I had really missed this man, really missed Uncle Jack and Monty too. I almost reached into my pocket for a blue pill but stopped. I could handle this!

"We'll perhaps it's time to rejoin the ranks. You have time, you're still young!" He shut off the sound, bringing a much needed balance to the room. He also snapped it to regular screen projection. "Where's Cally? Thought she'd bring you in. Where are her manners?"

"She's back in the atrium with her friend," I told him. He frowned, realizing I knew about Cally's preference. Pain filled his face. I was again ready to reach into my pocket for my blue pills, sometimes emotions could do me in but again I seemed fine. Perhaps coming to Nestor wasn't such a bad idea. Perhaps.

"Damn," He sputtered. "You know I always thought of you as family, Skip. Thought maybe you'd marry my girl and take over my racing empire. It would make this old man a happy grandfather."

"Thank you for the compliment but I'm happy right where I am. I never told you Ralph, but I had a hard time recovering. It took me almost a year just to walk again, two years to fully regain my sight."

"Yeah, I do know that, I followed your progress. I know. It took half a year to clear your name. Lonarer's wife shouldn't have blamed you. The tapes finally vindicated you. Ray told me you wanted to be left alone. He wouldn't give me the details but I honored the wish. It was the least I could do for you. Had a hard time, didn't you? Ray just told me when you'd left the hospital. It took almost a year on MOSS, the medical ops space station, didn't it?"

"Water over the dam," I told him. "The accident, I blame myself some. I shouldn't have pushed it so hard. If I'd just let the car go in the wall I wouldn't have hit Lonarer and split his car in half."

"You can't fight natural instincts, you tried to save it. Lonarer turned right into you. It's like saying if only Markus had not hit you from behind. It's nobody's fault. I think you'd find Marian doesn't blame you anymore. She's gone on with her life. Married a doctor and has several more kids, I hear. I took good care of her, so did the William's Team."

"I'm glad to hear it," I told him. Perhaps I'd get the courage to see her, perhaps.

"By the way your ex, Charlene, married Hank Sims. Though rumors are she's ready to dump him. He's not winning enough, although Rosluke is paying him big bucks." As if the mention of Rosluke triggered something he frowned deeply. "I suppose you're over here to talk about that damn brother of yours. He's leaving me high and dry. He tells me Julie can stay awhile. She's the best, don't know what he's thinking, do you?"

"Yup," I answered . "I want you to forget he ever told you he was leaving."

"What!" He walked to the middle of the room and shut off the screens completely. "Getting cold feet is he? I don't forget so soon. After all I done for him. Treated you boys like my own and he just walks in here and dumps it on me."

"He was being blackmailed by Rosluke." The screens had rescinded into the ceiling, leaving the room all windows. The glass had automatically darkened keeping the sun dimmed. I looked out at the expansive lawns; extensive gardens, stables, even a small lake here in the back. *This could all be mine* entered my head, I just had to give him a grandson. My stomach turned and I almost reached for my blue pills. Then I realized it was a natural reaction, not something my pills could prevent. I couldn't go back, not ever, even if what he offered appealed to me. I looked over at him, he was absorbing what I had said.

Finally, "Blackmailed, how?" I could tell he hadn't digested it completely. The idea was so foreign to him. Racing was a clean sport for him, blackmail wasn't something that entered his world.

"They produced a tape of him that embarrassed him."

"Embarrassed him?" Again, he couldn't come to grips with anything to do with sex. I imagined he hadn't faced his daughter's reality yet.

He wasn't getting it, his puritanical mind didn't reach that far, so I'd have to explain more. "It made it look like he was having an affair. An affair with a prostitute."

"What! He knows I don't go for that! What the hell is wrong with him, Julie is the best thing that ever happened to him. He can't lose his best mechanic. Glad now he didn't have any interest in Cally!"

Spoken like a true race owner; racing first, family second.

"They couldn't buy him, so they framed him." I explained the whole thing, shocking him into realizing what had happened. Still, he looked at me like I was crazy. Things like that don't happen, not here, not on Nestor. I could see his mind working - how would the sponsors take this, what would the fans think?

"And you believe that? Framed him? Don't be a fool Skip." He laughed sarcastically. "He's not the first man to get caught with his pants down. I'll not take him back. He'll fit right in with that Rosluke bunch. His sponsors would drop him the minute they heard of it!"

"I believe him and not just because he's my brother. I'm not a fool, Ralph!" I went over to him and shoved my badge in his face. "I will find out how it was done and I'll see them jailed."

He looked at me and then back again at the badge. "You're a policeman?" He looked again at the badge possibly wondering if it was a fake. "It says Chief? And the Sector Chief?"

"I'm sector Police Chief. I supervise the entire sector police force and my team of detectives serve the entire Crab Nebula Sector. Like I said, I'm no fool. Ray's not lying. I'm here on what I thought was a routine investigation and I found out the Feds are here investigating the racing community." I didn't tell him they were focusing on Rosluke nor that it involved illegal arms dealing. I'd shocked him enough already.

"Oh my god." He sat down on the couch becoming very pale. "Has this something to do with Monty's death? Tony came to me, asked me to help."

"I don't know exactly what's going on with the FIO''s investigation," I lied. "Monty still worked for you, didn't he?" I sat on the couch's arm, looking up at him.

He turned ashen gray. Attenson Racing was being threatened. His fear was evident in his shaking hands. He voice also shook, "Yeah. I was shocked. It didn't make sense, not Monty. I knew he was upset over the death of Caroline Waser. They say he was having an affair with her but she was going out with Tip Stucksko. Tip races for Rosluke now, used to race for Al Summer's team. Anyway, she died in a fluke craft accident. She was speeding and drinking. Her craft went over Cannon Clift. It has a treacherous turn, she went right over the guard railing."

"We got word from the FIO that they wanted us to quietly investigate Monty's suicide." I could see he was stricken. I hated doing this to him. Monty had been with him a long time but I had no choice. "Tony complained, he doesn't believe his brother committed suicide. They didn't want a stink on race week so one of my Lieutenants came to investigate. I didn't know it was Monty 'til I also got here. The Feds were already here Ralph, what do you know about Rosluke?"

"I know they are a second rate team with great drivers that they swiped from other teams with offers of big money. I thought that's what they had done with Ray. They have a bad reputation of cheating. How many times have the officials caught them either souping up their cars with illegal chems or putting super chargers on their boosters? Lately though, nothing! They've been clean. But it goes to show if they don't cheat, they don't win. They hardly have made the top ten the last few years."

I didn't want him to know what the Feds were looking for so I wrapped it up. "Just keep quiet about the FIO being here, Ralph. Give Ray another chance but don't say anything until after the season's over, I don't want Rosluke to know yet. Let him think Rays is switching until I nail him."

Ralph nodded his head. "I'm sorry Skip, really sorry."

"Sorry for what, it was Ray's own fault, he should have trusted us more."

"No, I'm sorry you're still not racing. You were the best I ever had. You were the whole package. Fast, classy and well-liked by the fans. The sponsors couldn't get enough of you."

"I appreciate you saying that Ralph but my brother is better than I ever was, give him a chance and he'll bring home some championships for you."

"Sure you don't want to at least give Callistie a chance?"

"No! One failed marriage is quite enough, thank you. I'll see you at the track. I'll be at the trials tonight."

He handed me four VIP passes from off the table. I thanked him and followed another prim and properly attired maid out but took a detour to the atrium. Cally and her friend were still there. Cally was moping over what looked like a martini while her friend was smoking something. Best to ignore. I wanted some info and I'd bet Ralph's daughter was into the track's gossip big time. Some things never change.

They both looked up at me, Marcie with hate in her eyes, Cally with amusement, wondering what I wanted now. "Tell me, did you know Caroline Waser?"

"Yeah," they both answered but it was Cally that took it further. "She was Tip's girlfriend that died in a car accident over at Cannon Clift Road. They say she was really drunk."

"Did you know her personally?" I pulled a chair out and sat on it backwards facing both of them, trying to put them at ease. It worked with Ralph's daughter but not with Marcie, who glared at me. I was on her hate list and she was the type that kept you on it.

"Not really, too high folutin for me," Cally waved her hand. "Thought she was too intellectual for us. She went to University U. Local human sector schools not good enough for her. She looked her nose down at most of us. She dressed terrible, by the way."

That was Cally, shallow to the core. "What's she doing with Tip then?" I asked, knowing most of the drivers didn't have much more than secondary educations. Racing professionally didn't allow time for schooling, I knew that from my own experience. I had been on the road schooled until my accident. Although Uncle Jack had made us attend school during the off season, a rarity for racing kids but it got us to know the local children. Jack had really tried, he really did.

"Don't know. Some females find racing pro's irresistible." She laughed eyeing me with those big blue eyes. "Why did Charlene marry you?" I didn't respond knowing she was still hurt that I wouldn't consider her proposal. Her eyes batted at me, "You know she's married to pretty boy Hank Sims, couldn't give up those racing pants."

"So I heard." She was getting off the subject. "Do you think Caroline was cheating with Monty? They say that's why he committed suicide, he was despondent over her death"

"That old man? Come now," she laughed again, "Monty was helping her do some kind of research. She was into electrical something or other." She shrugged, it was all I was going to get out of her. "Intellectual stuff" didn't interest her.

I took my leave, time to get back and see how Hill had made out. I admit it - I supercharged the Hundil on the way back to my brother's. I handed Julie back the keys with a smile and told her I'd see her at the trials. Then, I put my wig and hat back on and found my way to the Checkered Flag Hotel.

Chapter 8

Hill let me in. She had every screen and sound effect on. The large screen was blaring the news from the track, soon the time trials were going to begin and all the announcers were scrambling to get a driver to interview. The table was roaring away with the holographic car racing around its perimeter. Peterson's life story was blaring from the bedrooms and the monitor screens from the bathroom were echoing the big living room screen. My eyes and ears winced but she motioned me to the patio. I followed her out.

"I'm not sure Phil hasn't come up with some new bug. I think it's safe out here on the patio. There's not much out here to hide a bug. I've scanned and searched. I found one and put it next to the blaring video screen inside. Let it stay there so he thinks I missed one." Now that we were outside we could hear the low thunder of the engines from the nearby track. It was loud but not enough to keep us from talking and certainly not as confusing as the cacophony of all the inside noises.

"What in god's name are you wearing?" I looked at her, my eyes blinking from the purples, pinks, oranges and lime greens. Her t-shirt was actually pulsating. I didn't stare too long, probably not good optics for an epileptic. "Please shut off some of it, you're screwing with my brain, you're giving me a headache!"

She touched her glowing bracelet and the lights went out. "Sorry, I got some local outfits," she exclaimed standing with her hands on her hips. She had a Tee shirt that glowed the number 15 on the front, my brother's number, with his name pulsating on the back. She had a bare mid drift with pants that hugged her low on the hips and flared out at the bottom. "These are the latest, they call them bell huggers." On her feet were thick cork high heeled shoes with number 15 on the sides, and I mean high heeled. They must have added four inches to her height. She looked like a bimbo racing fan from head to toe. Her auburn hair was half braided with the rest flowing down her back. Glowing different colored flowers were peeking out of her curls. Sparkles sprinkled in her hair finished it all off. She even had a glowing belly button with my brother's number in the middle. It was so alien to her nature that I wouldn't have even recognized her if I'd passed her on the street.

"You're gonna kill yourself in those shoes." I stared at them, her pants flaring above them like bells ringing. "At least the pants are aptly named. Please don't tell me they ring too."

"No they roar." She pushed a button on her waistline and swayed her hips and the damn pants sounded like an engine starting up. "I got you a pair too. One size fits all. They are the latest fashion, everyone is wearing them." She went over and handed me a bag. I looked inside to see a dark orange stripped shirt with my brother's numbers blaring and matching dark orange bell huggers. She'd gotten me dark orange sandals that matched. At least they weren't high heels. "You'll match his car!" she enthusiastically announced as she handed me the bag.

"No, I'm not wearing those." I put the bag down, very tempted to throw everything over the side of the balcony but I let common sense prevail, they might hit someone below or scare them to death. "What have you found out besides the local fads? I suppose you think I'm going to sign an expense report for the clothes?"

She frowned at me as she sat at the porch table and pulled a chair next to mine. When she drew near I smelled something strange. "What the hell have you got on?" My nose went into scrunch mode. "You smell like the race track, for heaven's sake!" My eyes watered.

"It's the latest perfume. The beautician called it *Gaslina Plus*." She shrugged, "Look and smell like a native. Lesson One at the academy." I couldn't tell if she was joking or was deadly serious. I hoped kidding. "They have one called *"Exhaust Exordiare"* but it was a little too pungent for me, though I was tempted to try it."

I looked at her like she was crazy. One day on Nestor and she was as bad as all the rest of the crazy racing fans. "Please don't tell me you're gonna smile and have 15 smiling back at me!"

She ignored my sarcastic remark and my incredulous look. She handed me a celltab, "Take a glimpse at these files. I went to the Nes police station. Nice modern place by the way. Makes *our* station look like dump."

"That's because it is a dump." I watched as she punched a few keys. A picture of a nice looking young girl filled the screen. I drew my chair closer, "That's Caroline Waser?" I asked her, my eyes seeing the intelligence in the face. Just from her picture I could see the alertness behind the eyes. If she had attended University U, she had to be smart, they took only the top academics and very few humans. She was a pretty girl, typical Tohegian; dark tanned skin, a flat but still attractive nose, big luscious lips and ears that slightly stick out. Her eyes were black, again a typical Tohegian. She wore her black hair up in a braid with the formal beaded ribbon woven in with it.

"Yes, read her obit." Hill pressed another key and the report came up.

"WASER, CAROLINE. Dead at age 24. Accident fatality. Graduate of University U cum laude with Biochemical concentration. Leaves behind a father, Heroticla Waser and mother Heleinoc Waser and brother Danolics Waser from Mt. Hiden, Casey. Memorial service to be held on Casey City third Wed. of sector month at Mt. Hiden Reservation Church.

"She was a Tohegian. The obituary confirmed what I saw in the picture." I sat back in my chair, stunned. No wonder she was with Monty so much. Tohegians were a tight knit group, they were rarely outside of Casey. That was why he was such close friends with her. It had nothing to do with an affair. I wondered who had thought that one up and I was betting on Walt Rosluke.

I went on to read the police report and autopsy. Multiple broken bones but died from a crushed skull presumably from the crash. Her craft had not gone through the guard rails but had been traveling so fast it actually catapulted over the guard rails right down the steep mountain sides, into the Canyon Clift ravine. It had taken the helicraft with jaws to get her hover out. Her alcoholic blood count was way over the limit, almost three times the allowed limit. I winced, that's a lot of alcohol. Something was wrong. Hadn't anyone investigated? Hadn't my superintendent Stan Holden realized something didn't smell right? With that much alcohol in her system she wouldn't be walking or driving but literally passed out.

"If she was a true Tohegian, she didn't drink." I commented. "Did you find out anything on that? What did the head of the accident investigation tell you?"

I should have known Hill would cover all the bases as she answered me. "Funny thing, it was signed by Stan Holden, the Superintendent. I guess he didn't feel any further investigation was necessary. I'll ask the brother Tony tonight. If you say he was close to Monty then he should know something. I have an appointment after the racing trials to interview him. He works for Ralph Attenson's driver, Bill Connors."

"I know. Both Tony and Monty switched to other Attentson drivers after I left racing. Recently it had been Bill Connors." Again I felt the pain of regret. I imagined my brother felt the same way. Ray had tried to get Monty, but my shadow kept the Tohegian brothers from accepting. Then Julie had stepped in but from what my brother had told me, my sister-in-law had been close to Monty and that meant Tony too, of course. They had trained her to be a top notch mechanic and crew chief.

Hill shut off the tab, "I'd like to ask Caroline Waser's boyfriend Tip Stucksko, who drives for Rosluke by the way, but he's busy with racing. I got turned down by a rather rude man who says he's their media director."

"That's understandable," I told her, "the drivers are going crazy right now but we'll see what we can do tonight. I got VIP passes and that'll get us into the pits. I think Tip can give us a few moments of his time. It they let us near him."

She looked up at me, "Pits." I could see her eyes widen with visions of what "pits" meant. I'm sure it wasn't a pleasant picture. I had to remember she was a racing novice.

"Pits are where the cars are kept before the race. It's an old expression." She nodded but I could tell she still thought it barbaric. "There are two pits. One is off track, they keep the car carriers there. They unload the vehicles and then take them out to the center island. The outside pits are where they go pre-racing time. Then there are the inner pits on the island that the track circles. The cars go there during the races. The mechanics have their trailers there with their mobile garages. The actual cars line up on what is known as pit road according to their time trials. It is here that their "crews" change their tires, give them gasline, get them back on the track after they take a 'pit stop' during the race." I could tell she was trying to understand. My lieutenant would understand when she saw an actual race.

My ever diligent rookie took out a map showing the entire track complex. I should have known, efficient to a fault, that was my newest detective. Her finger traced the track, going around the inner circle. "So they 'pit' and then race on the track." I couldn't help it, I

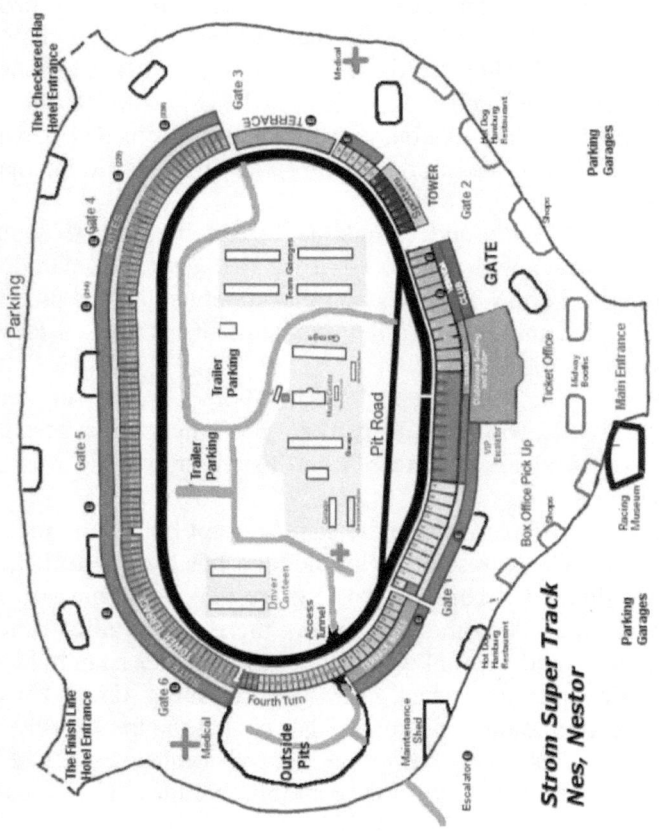

Strom Super Track
Nes, Nestor

laughed at the confused look on her face. I had to remember to a non-racer the terms were alien, some of it did sound pretty silly.

My cell rang, my call to Issam had finally connected. His "Issam here. That you Chief?" sounded haggard. He sounded hot, he looked hot, but maybe my picture of him sitting at his desk surrounded by fans was to blame for my conclusion. I hoped I didn't look too cool.

"How's things?" I asked him, feeling guilty for being on temperate weathered Nestor, of being outside with a slight breeze going through my hair.

"What's that noise?" he asked.

"It's the engines from the track." I spoke up realizing how used to the noise I'd already become. It was just background noise. "Is everything okay?" Despite a fuzzy connection, I could see Issam's grimace.

"Yeah, it's hot, over 110 today. What's new? How's your brother?" He wiped his bald head with his towel; we all kept sweat towels at our desks.

"Things are more complicated than I thought, but is anything ever simple?"

"Nope," he answered me. "Lily wants to know, how you're faring?"

"Tell her just fine. Better than I thought. Anything I should be concerned with."

"The Consulate called, wants you to call him when you get back." Issam seemed to be reading from his notes, as he paused, "He got a call from some guy name Phil Ober. Consulate Borger wants you to cooperate with the Feds. Knew that would thrill you."

"Son of a bitch." I grumbled, getting a look from Hill but I shook my head at her. She went back to reading her map. "He's a Federal agent. He's here investigating illegal arms dealing in our sector. Nestor especially."

"Well that explains it. Must be something important, watch your back Chief. Other than that, Stoshingburg crashed his hover while chasing a drug suspect. Chased him down on foot. The dealer is in the hospital after Stosh got through with him. I think he was mad, his hover is totaled. Lieutenant Oleg got the word, she's having a girl. Martin is over in Castor. Two murders. They think they're drug related."

"Tell him to be careful." I interrupted. "Send Stoshingburg if he needs backup." Fred Stoshingburg was our expert on the drug crime throughout our sector. He pursued the dealers relentlessly.

My Captain frowned, "Yeah, I already thought of that, although Fred doesn't want to go. Might be good to get his big ass off planet, let this latest accident die down." Issam was of course on top of it. "Everything else is pretty much routine. Got ten detectives off planet, but nothing serious, routine business."

I just shook my head at the cell. "I'll handle the Stoshingburg incident when I get back. Make the big guy take mass transit, it'll teach him a lesson. I think this is the third hover he crashed." Issam laughed. Both of us had a vision of the big 6' 6" detective slumping down on the subtrains. "I'll bet he won't give you a hard time about joining Martin." I saw Issam smile.

"Well, if you need me, get through on the police Jump line. I'm sure Consulate Borger will okay it. After all, remind him the FOI is here."

Issam laughed, "Got it."

"And tell Oleg congratulations." Then I hung up.

I rung off and told Hill about "good 'ole Phil" and Oleg news which brought a smile to her face. Oleg was all 4 ½ ft of pure muscle. No one messed with her despite her shortness. I had no doubt her 'about to be born daughter' would be the same. Hill looked up from her maps and shook her head. "I told you Phil was ruthless. This race track is quite a complex. It's very confusing."

I nodded, she'd understand better once she'd actually seen it in person. "Bill Connors, who Tony works for, he's my brother's teammate." I tried to explain how everything worked. "Monty, at the time he died, was Bill Connor's crew chief along with his brother Tony, who was his chief mechanic. Monty declined to be crew chief for my brother after my accident. Monty said he couldn't handle it. My Tohegian friend almost gave racing up after my accident but Ralph talked him into staying with his racing team and of course his brother, Tony, came as his shadow. Tony's a damn good mechanic. Julie could not have learned to be such a good mechanic with anyone better."

"Read Monty's autopsy," Hill pressed another button.

Monty had died of a single gunshot to the head. The coroner had determined it to be self-inflicted. Gun powder on Monty's hands and a suicide note confirmed it. The gun was found near him. It was an old Tohegian six shooter that was an antique from planet Casey's early pioneer days. I knew it, I'd seen it. He had taken me target practicing with it. It actually shot projectiles; an old carved bone handled six shooter that had been in his family for ages. The report was hard to read. Once again, his death almost overwhelmed me. I so regretted not having come back to see him.

Hill continued with her assessment, "He didn't have a formal published obituary that I could find. I gather that his brother had him quietly buried in St. Germaine's Mausoleum. He wasn't cremated. Most unusual." She brought up a police report showing the details.

"No, Tohegians don't believe in cremation. I know it sounds weird but they believe you should be brought home and buried on the Casey plains with no marker. They have special treaties, left from the early days of Casey's development that allows the bodies to go straight in the ground." I saw Hill shudder at the barbaric ritual. I ignored her, "The body returns to the spirit of their ground and renews itself. Monty's suicide would prevent his body being buried by the Tohegian Elders. It would be burying an impure soul into their holy grounds."

"He taught you all this?" she asked.

"Yeah. I was all ears. To an eleven year old boy, I soaked it all up. It helped ease the pain of my parents' death. I remember Killa would get so mad at him. She'd tell him that he was filling my head with garbage." I laughed at the memory of my tiny substitute parent pointing her finger at the tall Monty, lecturing him to not to tell me such things.

"Killa, if she was bonded to your mother, what happened when your mom died? Being a Ligi she would have to go onto someone with related Laositian high blood or die with her master within a Ligithian moon cycle which I believe is twenty Fed Regulated days.

I winced at the words, especially 'master', but chose to ignore it. "Uncle Jack was mom's brother. He took the bond and then gave Killa the job of taking care of us and his whole household. Giving the responsibility to raise Ray and I filled her bond-need and she gladly took charge of us. It really was just a continuation of what she'd been doing with my parents on the Moss space station. My parents were doctors there. Killa took as much of the burden of parenting us as she could. Parenting is rather alien to Ligithians as they don't have family ties, but she did well."

Hill nodded, "Ligis aren't allowed family ties. The High Bloods want no competition on their bonding. It's sad, really sad. The Laositians arrange Ligis' mating and take their children away at birth." Hill looked up, "Sorry, it's just what we call them in our sector."

I decided to ignore it, she hadn't meant it as an insult, "Killa also ran all the finances of Jack's racing career. He kept her busy. The key to understanding the blood bond is making sure that the person bonded has a feeling of fulfillment with the bondee. That's why they work so hard for their masters on Ligithia. It's born into them."

"She'd do anything he said. Is it true that the bond is so strong that if he told her to kill someone she would? During the Ligithian Wars, the bonded slaves fought against their own liberators because they were ordered to." The distaste of the bonding showed clearly on Hill's face.

I almost didn't answer her. Killa's bond was so personal in our family, that it wasn't something one shared. My parents had been killed by Ligithia high bloods, or Laositians as they called themselves; although it was never proven. The least people knew, the better. They thought Killa, my brother and I were killed with my parents. Hill looked at me, a serious look on her face. Her flashing t-shirt, glowing bell pants, hair tied back with flashing ribbons, somehow it didn't go together, it made me grin.

"It's not a laughing matter, Chief." She admonished me. "Two of my brothers fought on Ligithia. Then all those Ligithians were killed when they tried to free them. It was horrible. They have to remain slaves because we can't undo them from their bonds. Killing those pompous high bloods, killed their slaves too. The Feds had to leave them there, had to make peace with the Laositians. No one imagined that winning the war was really losing it. I think it was such a disaster it's not talked about, the Federation made a huge error."

"I'm not laughing at that. My parents were doctors. We lived on the Moss Space Station, the huge sector hospital. They were researching the Ligithian problem when they were murdered. Killa escaped and got us to Uncle Jack, who took on her bond. You're right, a Ligithian has only about twenty days before the bond will kill. They don't know if it's psychological or biological. When Jack died I was just finishing my law degree and really was not prepared to take on Killa's bond but Ray was just getting married and he traveled so much. So I reluctantly did. I keep her busy by being my superintendent. My apartment building is for the physically disabled. It keeps her time totally occupied. If there's one thing my mother taught us it is that you must keep them busy on something that is intrinsically important to you or they fall into a lethargic state. Responsibility helps fulfill their bond. And yes, she'll do anything, even kill for me."

"Oh, sorry, thought you were laughing......"

"No, I was looking at you. Do you realize how silly you look, Lieutenant?"

"It's all in the eye of beholder, Chief." She said indignantly.

"Exactly!" I laughed.

We were startled as the slider slid back and Phil dressed in a pair of jeans with an expensive leather jacket walked in. I had to admit, he looked good, but then he ruined it by knowing it.

"How the hell did you get in?" I snapped at him, getting up so quickly that my chair tipped backwards.

"Whoa, hold it chief. You didn't answer the door bell." He sat in one of the chairs, smiling at Hill. "Now aren't you a sight for sore eyes, literally!"

She stood up. I had to admire her. Despite the wild combination of colors, she had the body to pull off the outfit. "Phil, you are truly irritating me." She turned pointing at him. "I found out today, you commandeered the local governor's emergency Jump line. That is in violation of code 568. You could be in serious trouble if I reported you, which I am sorely thinking I will!"

"How did you find out?" For once he looked unsure of himself, "the dumb ass superintendent had no idea I have use of it."

"You forget, you taught me." She sneered at him. "You'd better explain, I already have my complaint written up ready to send to the sector Governor General's Office.

"Now Judy," he went over to her, putting his hand on her shoulder, trying to intimidate her, "I need that high speed Jump to contact home office, I just didn't have the time to get a court order."

I just watched. I had been right, if it was the FIO or Lt. Hill, she'd come out on top.

"Tell that to a judge." She walked away from him, heading to go back inside.

"Wait." He looked relieved when she turned back. "I think the police superintendent is also using it unbeknownst to the sector governor. If you report it, he'll know I'm on to him. The sup is on the take."

"My superintendent! Stan Holden!" I had met the man when he came to Fulton Station. He was on my weekly sector video meetings. He was a large, kind of a dopey looking guy but had seemed competent enough. I'd never gotten a complaint about him. I hadn't hired him, he'd been Nestor's Superintendent of police for almost eight years. He had come from off sector. I strained my brain, was he originally from over in the Pinwheel Sector? I'd never been back home to check personally on him. This was my fault. I'd been to every sector planet except this one as Chief. I had been afraid to come to Nestor, afraid of an attack. Coward, I chastised myself!

"You'd better have proof," I accused him. "It had better be good proof."

"Well, for one thing, he helped with that video of your brother." He could see my eyes widen. "And another thing is he's on Rosluke's take. We've been watching his bank transfers on that Jump line. He thinks he's safe from detecting since as Hill so aptly pointed out I'm not supposed to even look at it. It's strictly a data emergency line."

I was so mad, I saw red. My hand automatically went for a blue pill but again I realized I didn't need it. I had it under control. "I'm gonna kill the son of a bitch." I growled.

"Please, not until we get this solved first." He half smiled. "I have another problem. I need tickets to the races tonight. You'd think they were printed in gold. These fans have no respect for us Feds."

"Really?" I grinned back at the pompous ass. Felt good, although childish, that I could get something the damn FIO couldn't. "Is it worth a favor?"

"Depends." I told him what I needed. He agreed. I handed him two of the VIP tickets Ralph had given me.

"See you at the races," I told him as I watched him leave, wishing I could afford his jacket.

"Is that wise? I don't trust him." Hill sauntered back to the table reaching in my jacket pocket, retrieving another bug. She threw it over the balcony.

"Son of a bitch," I shook my head in disgust. "He can get me the profiles of each of the Rosluke's drivers faster and more thoroughly than I can. I need to see why they chose the drivers they did."

"Come on," she sashayed over to the doors, her pants swaying with her hips, each step roaring away, "we got some races to go to."

My ear cell rang. "Off Planet" lightly whispered in my ear. Crap I'd forgotten to check in with Killa. I was in for it now. Nothing worse than a worried, angry Ligithian.

Chapter 9

We walked out the back of the hotel. I didn't worry about reporters, they'd all be at the trials. I was right. Other than fans getting ready to leave for the races, the reception area was almost empty. The lobby and the walkway were thankfully void of the pushy racing news reporters. Although the news mongers were not permitted into the pits, they'd be mulling around the entrance to the cars hoping to get some scoops. They all had to depend on a pool of a few announcers that were allowed access to the teams near the actual cars during racing. Can you imagine the chaos if all those publicity vultures had been let into the pits? There would be no peace.

I used to hate even the few that were allowed. When your mind is on getting your car ready for going over 250 miles an hour, the last thing you want is to answer personal silly questions. Yet it was part of the package, being able to handle the press, I'd understood that even at seventeen. I'd been taught to smile, and make sure I mentioned our sponsors, to thank all the right people. The audience was billions, so it wasn't the time to screw up. I had been so young I hadn't realized the pressure of the attention. I had taken it all so much for granted, I'd been invincible with a beautiful young wife on my arm. Youth is wasted on the young.

Now I had trouble handling the small bit of news coverage I got back on Fulton. I wasn't popular with the press on Fulton Station, as I tended to growl at them. Yet they still hounded me, especially about dishonest politicians, which was the case with too many of our elected officials unfortunately. When I thought about how I'd handled the press at seventeen, it seemed like someone else.

Perhaps it was the bitterness at how I'd been handled after the accident. All the press could do was to sensationalize it. Thank goodness I'd done my treatments on M.O.S.S (Medical Operations Space Station) where access was strictly controlled. Still, I'll never forget one reporter who got in as a nurse and got a picture of me covered in bandages. I had been blind for close to a year so they kept the headlines from me but I saw it afterwards. *ROOKIE OF THE YEAR, GETTING WHAT HE DESERVES!* Although I'd been proven innocent of any wrong doing by the time I'd been released, it still had hurt, hurt badly and changed me. The innocent eighteen year old was quickly forgotten, gone, replaced by a tougher, cynical person.

The whole track was abuzz about the upcoming time trials. Race positioning is extremely important. The top ten spots were the most coveted. Getting into the top ten meant extra points and with the championship so close this year, they'd be fighting for those points. The first place pole was worth lots of money and prestige, so the drivers went all out to get the fastest time. Most of the time, it was decided by just a few seconds.

It was unusually quiet as we walked down the manicured, multi-colored flower lined pathway to the hotel's private entrance into the racetrack. The teams were in the outside pits getting ready. No one was on the track. It seemed eerie not to be surrounded by the engine roars. A rare moment on Nestor! We could actually hear the buzzing of the bees around the flowers. It was as if time was being suspended, the tension building. Even the fake roaring had been silenced as if it was the appropriate time to contemplate, time to get serious about the upcoming race.

It was all about the hoopla, getting the fans emotionally on a tensional high. I remembered how the stomach butterflies would begin for me. I'd be listening for the times as each racer finished. I'd be listening to Monty as he would describe how to tackle each part of the racetrack. On some of the tracks it was to keep the car high near the fence, some hit low near the inner island. Much depended on the time of day, the effect of the weather on the track. Monty knew it all, knew all the compositions and conditions of the track, with his brother Tony chiming in behind him. I felt my stomach knot as the memories just flooded my brain.

The little blue pills entered my thoughts but I held off, breathing deeply as Dr. Lily Issam had taught me. Hill jabbered away beside me, not aware of what it all meant to me. I concentrated on her words and they seemed to help bring me back to the here and now. I wasn't a driver, this wasn't happening to me. Breathe deeply, and it worked as I felt myself calm down, the chemicals in my brain returning to normal. Even the expert doctors on MOSS couldn't explain what had happened to my brain and they were the best experts in the entire humanoid sectors. The neurological experts "controlled" my episodes as best possible. Considering how damaged I had been, it seemed almost a miracle to me that I had gotten myself back together.

"Does your brother work on his own car?" Hill interrupted into my thoughts, "Are they a lot more complicated then hovers?"

"Yes, he helps Julie but also stays out of her way. She's very particular on the car's setup and meticulous about tweaking everything from the shocks to engine's torque ratio being just right. And yes, they are and aren't as complicated." She looked at me as if I was pulling her leg. "No, I mean it. They are combustible fuel engines," her eyes went wide, "but it's controllable combustion. They move, but they move differently than a hover. You'll see. You'll feel the rumble of the engines. There is nothing more exciting than that. As a matter of fact, people who are deaf will think they can hear because the engine rumble is so intense it feels like you're hearing. You'll see."

Although the crowd heading towards the entranceway was actually somewhat subdued, the anxiety could be felt in the way they jumped when the engine sounds started up again. Hill had been right, her getup fit right in. The walkway took on a colorful parade atmosphere; pinks mixed with bright greens, yellows competing with orange stripes. I tried to avoid the pulsating outfits. I had our tickets out. An old gentleman wearing a racing cap backwards with a worn jacket was taking the tickets and putting entrance bracelets on everyone's wrist. When I handed him ours, the special VIP passes caught his eye. He looked up and squinted. Recognition came into focus as he looked at me.

"Skip Brown?" he croaked out. "*The* Skip Brown?" he repeated. His face lite up, all his old wrinkles lifted with his smile.

I immediately recognized him. He'd been born and raised on Nestor. He seemed old even when I was a kid. He was a cemented part of the track. He had been a close pal of the track's old owner, Al Strom. The family that owned the race track had slowly over the generations built up the facility to the super track it now was. I wasn't at all surprised to see that the old guy, Bud Albright, was still here. He had been with Strom's racing facility from when he and Al were kids. He still hung around despite it being bought out by a huge conglomerate. "Hi, Bud." I shook his extended hand. "You look the same."

"Well, so do you." He grinned shaking my hand again. Despite his age and callused fingers, his grip was strong. "A little bit older and a little bit wider." I heard Hill huff, as if agreeing with him. I gave her my best scowl. He got off his stool and squeezed my arm. "So glad to see you, son, been awhile. Here to see your brother?" His voice was gruff, it had always been gruff as if a frog was in his throat croaking, but he was the nicest guy from the old school of racing. Racing was a fun sport for him not the big money business it had turned into.

"How's it been going?" I asked him, standing to the side letting him continue to put on ticket bracelets.

"Not the same as when you were here," his voice seemed a bit sad. "Cars too complicated now. All this DNA compatibility shit. What ever happened to good old fashioned racing? This your missus?"

I heard another huff from Hill. I elbowed her shutting her up. "No, had enough, one ex is enough, I'm not a glutton for punishment." Now I got the elbow from Hill.

"Ah, don't blame you. See her around, she's that big shot driver Hank Sims' wife now or he was until he changed to Rosluke." He leaned over to me, whispering, "Rich bitch. Don't have time for the lower echelons like me. She walks right by me as if I don't exist. I remember her when she was a nobody groupie, until you married her. She got a steward fired the other day. Didn't like the way he treated her."

"Yep, that's Charlene." I nodded at him. Hill pulled me along, heading down the walkway towards the racetrack proper. The back of the grandstands followed along with the path. There is nothing as ugly as the iron work of the back of a grandstand but nothing as beautiful either. It's like letting you get a peek at the track but just enough to hurry you along to get to the other side. It's like a hole in a fence. Someone was on the track, the whoosh as the car went by made everyone rush along. The trials would be starting soon.

"Did you know him well?" she asked, her bells swishing but at least she'd turned off the matching engine roars. I heard others though as they paraded down to the Midway. One couple was walking in tandem as their pants roared in unison. Only on Nestor!

"Everyone knows Old Bud." I told Hill. "He used to go everywhere with the owner of the track, Al Strom. The Strom family had owned the track for nearly two hundred years, almost from its conception. Al used to have this old gardening motor cart and always took Bud with him. They'd visit all the drivers, make sure all was set. There wasn't anything Al didn't take notice of; from the hotdog stands to the flower arrangements. Then the Strom family sold the track to Midplanet Bank Corp. Al died the next year. They say from a broken heart, but left his kids happily rich, by the way."

The walk way turned into a main drag; the Midway, a large area before the center entrance way into the grandstands. Here was every kind of racing paraphernalia imaginable. Every driver had a vendor truck set up with a life sized hologram of its driver, waving and smiling as if he could see the crowd. They were selling shirts, cups, flags, everything. Nothing was cheap either. Hill sauntered over to look at the ample range of personally driver signed bikini's. You could tout your driver at the beach and in his own handwriting too! She pointed at them, wanting my opinion. I was not going there!

Large screens are strategically placed to draw the crowds to spend money at the booths, playing the latest racing info. Interspersed were the hotdog, hamburg, fries and fried dough concessions. The smell of cotton candy made my mouth water. I always had a thing for the sweet pink stuff. Hill dragged me away as I was reaching into my pocket to buy some. "You don't need it," she grumbled. When had she become my mother?

We knew we were near the pits when an occasional roaring rumbling motor could be heard as they tested their engine's readiness. The actual visual aspect of the pits hadn't changed one bit since I'd left. I looked around, memories flooding me. My hand immediately went to my pocket for a blue pill but again I realized I didn't need it. I breathed deep, relief filling me. Perhaps I should have come sooner, I was actually relaxed. I felt at home. Hill must have seen my reaction, "You going to be all right?" she cautiously asked.

"Yeah, feeling great actually." I headed toward the fenced-in pit area, showing the gatekeeper our bright blue neon bracelets, giving us access. There was a time when he'd just nod me in, when everyone recognized me. Now, he just nodded at the bracelet. As I predicted the damn reporters were hanging around but weren't quick enough. By the time Merv realized it was me, we were inside. He yelled after me but I didn't turn around.

The different colorful cars were impressively powerful and sleek looking, covered in sponsor decals. Most had their hoods up, their crews working diligently if not furtively, making last minute adjustments. The adjusting of the engines was different for the trials than the races. Tomorrow the setups would be different for the actual race. Although, the car setups were strictly regulated, it was the small tweaks, like making the gasline mixture a fraction richer, or setting the shocks looser, putting more or less air in the tires, that could give the driver an edge.

Each car got a chance to go the fastest it could with no one else on the track. It was the loneliest feeling being on the racecourse all by yourself with an extremely expensive, highly complicated machine, but it was exhilarating. The focus was on speed with the control being on hugging the corners, taking the straightest shortest line. Tomorrow the actual race got very complicated with forty other cars vying for the same space, bumping and grinding towards victory. Speed obviously counted but so did skill and strategy of out-guessing the other crews and drivers.

My brother's trailer was in the middle with the three Attenson's driver spots. I saw Ralph running between the three. I saw his daughter Cally sitting in one of the open trailers looking bored. I stopped dead in my tracks, Hill bumping into me. Good 'ole Phil and a FIO cohort were talking with Julie. I saw red. I ran up grabbing his arm, turning him around to face me. He must have seen the rage in my face 'cause he backed up into the car getting alarmed yells from my brother's crew. No one touches the precious cars but the crew. I saw the alarm on Julie's face making me even madder.

I pulled him to me, grabbing his expensive leather jacket by the collar, "Leave her alone, I told you to leave her alone!"

Hill was pulling on my arm, "Chief, get a hold of yourself."

It was Julie pushing her way between us that calmed me. "Skip, please. It's alright."

"No, it's not!" I furiously told her. "You don't want to get involved!"

"But I do, Skip." She gently pushed me back, out of hearing range of anyone. "Why should you be the only one to help Ray? Why should you prevent me from my revenge?"

I looked at her. She was dressed in an orange and golden jumpsuit; my brother's colors. Her pregnancy was starting to show. The determination in her face was absolute. I wasn't going to change her mind. The best I could do was to protect her. "Fine, we'll talk about it later."

She smiled. "That sounds good. I never saw that famous temper before."

"Yeah, sorry." I know I sounded like a misbehaving kid caught by his teacher.

Julie went back to supervising the car's setup. Phil had disappeared. My brother was in the driver's seat listening to his wife's instructions. I waved to him. He nodded. I could tell he was totally concentrating. For the first time, I felt envy, felt the grief of having to give up something I so loved. I turned away. Hill was looking strangely at me.

"Are you all right?" she asked again.

"Stop worrying about me!" I growled. "Let's find Tip Stucksko."

Rosluke Racing had fancy large trailers and had managed to take up twice the space of the other teams. They were an intimidating bunch. Their three drivers, all three, had large body guards dressed in black suits. One of the goons stopped me.

"I'm here to see Tip." I told him, noticing the firearm the guy was carrying in a holster inside his jacket. I saw the look on Hill's face, she'd noticed too. She sidled up to the man.

"He promised me, I'd get to meet Tip." She alluringly touched the guard's arm. I noticed she'd shut off her outfit, my brother's number 15 no longer showed. Amazing!

"Sorry ma'am, can't let anyone near the cars." His voice was gruff and threatening.

"Oh, my mama is gonna be so disappointed if I don't get a picture with him. He's her favorite. She works for Salvaline. Works with the president. See I got VIP passes."

How Hill knew of Tip's main sponsor I had no idea.

The dumb ox looked uncertain now. I saw Tip, he was by his car. "Hey, Tip," I yelled, walking past the armed man, who Hill was still snuggling up to, strategically keeping him between her and me.

The other goon quickly stepped over to stop me but Tip yelled over. "Are you Skip Brown?" and the bodyguard stopped letting me advance to the young driver.

"Yeah, Ray's brother. Got a minute?" I asked him.

"Sure. Let him alone," He told the monkey in the black suit. "He's famous."

The guys backed off but kept within hearing distance. Damn. "Boy, these babies have come a long way since I raced." I circled his red car. "When you scheduled to go on?"

"Not until almost the end. At least I'll know what time I need to beat." He was young, maybe in his lower twenties. He was small boned with an almost under-fed look. Worry lines already graced his eyes. His red and green jump suit fit like a second skin, emphasizing his thin frame. His matching gloves and helmet lay on his seat.

"Looks fast," I prompted, hoping flattery would get him talking. Drivers were in love with their cars. It is like flattering a wife or better still, your lover.

"It could be faster." He said, looking over his shoulder at the two men. "It could be a lot faster."

It was Hill that gave us the chance I needed to talk to him. "Can I have a picture with you? My mama would be so pleased." She came waddling over, swinging her hips, a perfect bimbo imitation. God she was good. The bodyguards leered, watching her swaying hips below her revealing bare midriff taking their eyes off Tip and focusing on her flashing belly button.

"Sure," Tip agreed.

I took the camera. "Come on over by the side of the car. I want to get the whole car in." I took a picture of her as she hugged him to her.

"Let me get one of you, honey." She took the camera, letting me get next to Tip.

It was my chance. I didn't waste it. "Tip I need to talk to you about Caroline. Rosluke is blackmailing my brother. I can help you, if you're in trouble." I showed him my badge, keeping it in front of us out of sight.

He stared at it, his eyes lighting up, then at me. "I didn't know....."

"Very few people do, the Roslukes don't, let me help you." This was a crap shoot. If he wasn't in trouble he'd just have to turn to the goons and I'd be paper mache.

His eyes went thoughtful, squinting at Hill. "Can you meet me at the Lighthouse Parrot after the trials?" he whispered.

"I don't think I did this right. Let me take another one," Hill yelled over, giving me more time.

"Yes, midnight, OK? Please be careful." He nodded. I saw the flash of fear as he looked over his shoulder at the goons.

The body guards were nervous. "Hey, Tip, Walt wants you," They yelled past the blocking Hill, who had strategically placed herself between us.

"I'm coming," He yelled back. "Nice meeting you." He shook my hand and turned back, following the dumb brutes into their fancy trailer.

I started leaving when I noticed Hank Sims' sleek black and silver car in the next Rosluke's slip. It looked expensive and fast. He was sitting in the driver's seat talking to his crew chief. Behind the car stood a tall well shaped woman, dressed in the latest expensive designer high fashion. No bell pants for her! A small white fur wrap was draped over shoulders. Her platinum blonde hair was done up in cascading curls. A diamond necklace with matching earrings were the perfect accessory, and they weren't fake, I was sure. Charlene looked up, catching me with her gaze. For a moment she seemed surprised, then the old smile graced her face.

"Well, I'll be," She said crossing over to me. "Well how are you Skippy? Never thought I'd see you here."

"Just hunkie-dory Charlene, and you?" I tried to keep my voice casual, my eyes looking straight at her but it was hard. She'd always had a unnerving effect on me. Age only enhanced it. She'd lost the innocent look but gained a sophisticated beauty. My hand started for my pills but stopped, again to my relief I didn't need them. No tight neck or blurred vision. I was alright.

A black suited thug that came over, interrupting her, "Are you alright Mrs. Sims?" He asked, "is they bothering you?" The guy couldn't even get his grammar right.

"No!" she snapped. I was guessing they weren't her favorite people. She turned back to me, "What brings you to Nestor? Never thought..."

I interrupted her, she wasn't worth my time. "Seeing Ray. We're late." I grabbed Hill, who to her credit hugged close to me as if she was with me. Bless her little heart.

I heard Charlene's parting comment, "You never use to settle for the left over trash?" she flung at me.

"Yeah, he's stepping up," I heard Hill send back and had to smile when I heard Charlene gasp and swear.

As I headed back towards my brother, Hill snidely remarked, "Really Chief, really?"

"I was only seventeen for god's sake." She was pushing a raw nerve. I'd never gotten over Charlene dumping me. She had just stopped coming to the hospital. The day they took the first bandages off my eyes I was served the divorce papers.

"Well, let's hope you have better taste next time," she sarcastically remarked.

"They'll be no next time." I guess the bitterness showed as she shut up, thankfully dropping the subject. Hill turned her outfit back on as we headed toward the Attenson's cars.

I gave my brother the thumbs up. Hill was asking Julie about the cars when I went to retrieve her. "Those are stationary wheels, aren't they?" The lieutenant bent down touching them lightly.

"Yes, they aren't like hover's, they don't fold up," Julie was patiently explaining. "Unlike the hard synthetic wheels on hovers, these actually end up being used to move the cars. They are made of a softer synthetic material to handle the speed and hug the pavement. We have to change them several times during the race."

Hill shook her head. She actually shivered trying to imaging riding on *wheels*! I could tell she was totally confused. As we walked out of the pits, she asked. "Why gasline, is it because they want it to be more dangerous?"

"That's part of it," I honestly told her. "We try and pretend it's strictly for power and environmentally sound reasons, but yeah, it does perpetuate the idea of danger. But unlike the power cells we use in everyday hovers, these fuel powered engines can be exactly tuned to give the most control and power. In other words, it takes talent to drive and take care of these babies. In an earlier time, they started out racing hovers but the excitement was missing." I took her arm, "Come on I'll show you, we have a little time."

As we turned to leave, all the cars started up at once. The roar was overwhelming to someone not use to it. Hill just stopped. She felt the roar, her hand went to her chest. Her big eyes looked up at me. "Yeah, I know,' I told her, "I know." What a feeling, the feeling of power, tremendous power. It was what a driver lived for. It was what fed the fans their excitement.

We headed down the Midway towards the formal entranceway to the race track. It faced the city, all the underground trains and roads let out here. Massive parking garages could be seen, they were overloaded with fans streaming into the track's entrance. It was on this main boulevard leading to the Midway that the racing museum was housed in an impressive marble-faced building. I led Hill up the stairs, through the revolving doors.

We entered a three-sixty cinerama holograph. The cars whizzed by. I heard Hill laugh enjoying the sensation of speed. She ought to feel the real thing. A commentator was giving a running explanation of the track and its many features. I led her into a hallway that started the story of Strom's Super Raceway.

I pointed to some of the early photographs. For effect, they had kept this part of the museum primitive, no screens just old photographs, old movie projections. "This was taken shortly after when the planet was just finished being engineered and settlers were forming the cities, this was a primitive racetrack way back then." I showed her the small wooden grandstands. It showed drivers standing by simple hover crafts. In the background no city could be seen, just flat lands that would soon to become the capital city, Nes. There was a mock up display showing the first settlers in the crude hover crafts. They were dressed more like working farmers than drivers.

I took her down the hall. "See, there is Peteris Strom. He was the first to take the old track and start building it into something Nestor would come to be known for. He switched to the old fashioned racing cars that other sectors were already cultivating. It was soon discovered that the public was fascinated by these gasline cars. What really made it successful was the discovery of how easily Halka grass grows here. It's used to make modern gasline. It solidified Nestor as the center of the racing universe."

Hill seemed fascinated. "Look there is Johnny Peterson." She walked over to the life-like statue. He stood next to his "Blue Thunder" car, one of the first "cars". He had a crude helmet under his arm, smiling as he held one of the first trophies awarded.

We walked down the hallway, the holograms started appearing showing the track expanding, the cars evolving. A wall map showed the expansion of Nestor's racing influence over all the humanoid Federation sectors. We were into the modern era when Hill suddenly stopped. "Look, it's you. What a handsome devil you used to be."

I reached for my little blue pills. Perhaps now would be a good time to take one.

Chapter 10

In one of the corners stood a heliograph of my younger self. "The Super Rookie" was the title above the display. My image was standing next to my number 99 "Blue Horizon" car that was covered with the logos of all my sponsors. I never wanted for sponsors, Ralph even turned some down. My baby blue silver-striped sleek racing car was totally covered with decals but my big sponsor, *Attenson Financial Services,* took up the whole hood. It was a sign of Ralph's confidence in me that he'd been my biggest sponsor, had wanted his business logo on my hood. He hadn't ever done it again. No other racing car had been painted with his business logo since mine. He kept his business and racing hobby strictly separate. My brother told me that Ralph believed he'd jinxed me.

The three dimensional pictures on the museum's wall had me looking almost adolescent but extremely happy, with one of them having Charlene hanging onto my arm. My "rookie of the year" trophy was clutched in her other arm. The Championship trophy stood at her feet. Even back then she was decked out in the finest designer clothes and she stood there posing like a queen. Why hadn't I noticed her shallowness then? I had been so into racing that nothing else really registered. It wasn't until later years that I realized why the other wives hated her. It wasn't jealousy over her being married to me, it was how she flirted with their husbands and gave the women the cold shoulder. I hadn't even noticed how much money she had spent and it was a bundle.

A younger Ralph Attenson holding the owner championship trophy high was in one of the pictures with his small daughter by his side. Then there was the picture of the whole team. There was my Uncle Jack, in front of him was a young Ray who was looking up at me as only an adoring younger brother could. Everyone was smiling. The future had looked bright then, a frozen moment in time. Monty had his arm around my shoulders with his brother Tony peeking around from behind. It all seemed so distant, so alien almost like it had happened to someone else.

"It says you won thirty one races! In only two years! No one has ever done that. Not even come close." Hill was reading my biography up on the wall behind the display, it was scrolling slowly. Then she went silent. I knew she was reading about the accident.

She was reading how a ten car accident resulted in my finished career and the death of one of the other drivers, Ken Lonarer, leaving a widow and a young baby. "Oh my." Was all she said as the accident rolled out in front of her. Carnage on the track, the loud crunching of folding metal, sending debris all over the place. Ambulances taking me and several other drivers away.

"Yes, my car cut his car in half." I put a blue pill in my mouth. I walked over to my Blue Horizon replica, how ironic that it was the color of my pills. The original car had been smashed to pieces. I pointed to the nose. "See how my car comes to a pointed end. They don't make them like that anymore."

"It really is a dangerous sport." She looked at the mock-up of my car, paying special attention to the tapered front. I know she'd read that a criminal manslaughter charge had been brought against me, perpetrated by the accusations of the driver's widow who had accused me of having a vendetta against her husband, of crashing into him on purpose. The charges had been finally thrown out when racing tapes had been reviewed during my recovery. I had been pushed by the driver behind me. The back car had pushed me into Lonarer's number 11 car, right to the wall. His car cut like paper, right in half. Then I smashed into the wall, folding my car like an accordion.

Everything had been put on hold until I could stand trial. My recovery had taken over a year and by then the charges had been dropped. I had finished my secondary schooling at the hospital's space station and then I ran away to college and then on to law school, taking my blue pills with me. I had left my old life far behind, limping by on a damaged brain.

"No. It really was a fluke," I assured her, wanting to not think on it anymore. "We've only lost a couple of drivers over the years and since my days they've added even more safety features. Even the amateur small short tracks throughout the Federation have come a long way towards safety protections."

"You say you haven't kept up with racing but you know a lot for someone who's not interested anymore."

"Yeah," I admitted, "once it's in the blood it's hard to let it go. Killa leaves the racing magazines around. I've managed to read a few. She thinks she's so coy but I'm on to her." I laughed. I knew my old nursemaid kept up with Ray's career and made sure I did too.

"I think I like Killa," Hill interjected. "Of course anyone who would put up with you has to be a saint."

"Oh you're so funny." I remarked as we walked down the hall coming to the latest era. The room was full of active screens, showing the most recent drivers. It showed the bank corporation buying the track and making it the super modern track it was today. It showed all the tracks, twelve planets in six of the seven sectors throughout the humanoid Federation with the racing schedule. The Circuit, as the entire racing agenda was known, takes up three quarters of the common year and encompasses billions of fans.

"Wow, look at the new uniforms," she commented, reading the display. "The helmets are now DNA compatible with the drivers allowing direct flow of information to their brains. So each helmet is uniquely their own, made for only them. God, that must be expensive."

"Yes, that's the new thing. They are even working on uniforms that will match the helmets and will coordinate the driver's reaction times and their body temperature, everything that is unique to the driver. The suit will fit like a second skin. The rational for it is that it is the driver's own DNA so it is still "them" driving, still only capable of their skills. There is a lot of push back on it. Like anything else, we'll see what comes of it. Trying to keep racing '*pure*' as it is known, is a hard fight. Changes usually come slowly to the racing world. Many, like old Bud Albright, don't like any changes and even more important the fans don't like too many changes."

We didn't see much else as the sound of roaring engines was followed by the announcement over the museum's intercom that the trials were about to begin. All the cars would be taking one lap together around the track in the opening ceremonies. Time to get to the grandstands.

Leaving the museum, we were pushed along by the incoming wall to wall crowds forming long lines to get into the grandstands. There was no waiting in line for the VIP ticket holders, we got dirty looks as we bypassed everyone. We headed up the center escalator that led up to VIP seating. We went up and up and up to the very top of the middle grandstand, which was situated right over the start/finish line. Hill stepped out onto the back walkway, her eyes trying to take it all in. From the rear of the grandstand's top level, the capital city of Nes lay spread before us. The city went all the way to the horizon. The sun was setting and the city was highlighted in shadows. It was an amazing sight and gave you a good sense of how high the grandstands went. "VIP isn't down below?" she asked. "Geesh, you could get nosebleeds up here."

"The best seats are the higher ones. The higher they are, the more of the racing track you can see. The best seats are always on top." I pointed back out towards the main Midway which was way below us. It was still jammed packed with people. Lines of ant-like figures stretched almost down the entire avenue waiting for their turn to get into their seats. I pointed at the long lines, "They come from all over Nestor, from all over our sector and from all the other Federation humanoid sectors as well. The racetrack sells completely out when the tickets go on sale the first of the Fed year. You can tell the 'off sector' fans by the translators hooked in their ears. It is also being media Jumped to billions all around the Federation. It's become a huge business, worth a lot to a lot of people."

When we went thru the grandstand tunnels to the front seats overlooking the track, Hill gasped. Way down below lay the two mile track surrounded by the huge seating areas. "How many people can this arena hold?" she asked, her eyes trying to coordinate with her brain on the sheer size of the racetrack facility. The grandstands completely encircled the two mile track.

"300,000 people." I told her. Her eyes glazed over trying to take it all in. VIP's got a clubhouse built right on top of the grandstands, which we went into. Linen covered tables with cushioned chairs overlooked the raceway with a fully loaded bar in the back. A small kitchen for catering I knew lay in the back. Yet the favorite food still was hotdogs, hamburgs and fries. They had tried fancy food and it had bombed.

The clubhouse had its own private bathrooms, no waiting in line for us. Waiters and waitresses ran up and down the platforms bringing free drinks for owners and their patrons. Sponsors were wined and dined here. The room was still half empty. I guess it was fashionable to be late, but then you didn't have to wait in lines and could show up last minute. Huge screens lined the sides and back, giving every perspective view that was possible. I saw Cally over in the far corner talking with a tall, elegantly groomed young man. His haughty manner was evident even from this distance. Hill confirmed what I already suspected.

"That's Emanuel Rosluke," Hill softly said. "I recognize him from the pictures I got at the police files in Nes. The articles I read implied he is rather a spoiled rich bastard. Guess his father has gotten him out of quite a few scraps. He has an older brother who is the family business lawyer. The older son, Jared, is big in Nestor politics. Rumor has it he may try for the Dome Assembly. Emanuel, I gather, is the spoiled one of the two. Is that Ralph's daughter? She's prettier in person than the pictures they have on file of her, although she does some modeling."

"Yep, that's her with pretty boy. Well, they'll get along just fine, two peas in a pod." I watched as Cally, who was dressed very similar to Hill, except her top was just a bra leaving most of her midriff bare. Her bell pants were slit on the sides, showing those shapely legs. Hill noticed me looking.

"She has the body to pull it off," my lieutenant dryly commented while nudging me. "Stop staring unless you plan on taking up her father's offer." I glowered at Hill, still I noticed most of the men were also staring at Ralph's daughter. Little did they know.

We went to the gigantic floor to ceiling front windows. They offered binoculars for the VIP patrons and I grabbed a pair. Below the whole track became clearly visible with the car trailers in the middle and the painted car slots of the racing pit stops on an inner road. Each inner pit stop was marked quite clearly with the race car's number. All forty cars were lined up in their designated stops. While the federation anthem loudly played over the stadium's speakers each of the matching uniformed crew members stood at attention by their cars - hands over their hearts. It was important to be patriotic. Racing was a patriotic sport. Its fans were patriotic.

It was quite a sight. Since this was just the trials, no ceremony except a singular one lap ride showing off the cars was scheduled. Tomorrow, for the actual race, there would be a lot more hoopla. A lot more dignitaries would be participating. With billions watching you'd bet there would be no lack of participants.

The Federation President, Itika Titka, a Bassodian, would be present for the actual race, dragging his big lizard ass to the human ceremony. He'd wear a special atmospheric pressure suit, as their big scaly bodies were used to much lighter gravity and a much richer oxygen mixture. I had heard that the Bassodians actually liked our racing. The Bassodians were known as the master planet architects across the universe. Being such mechanical wizards themselves, the cars supposedly really interested them. If true, it was about all they liked about us. They were so alien, green scales came to mind, it made me shiver just to think about it. Yet they were supposedly the smartest of all the known species, one of the oldest. In reality they almost single-handedly ruled the Federation. Actually, they were pompous asses, treating us like a sub-species, like we were wayward children. They were the only ones to vote against us becoming part of the Federation Assembly. Yet here we are, thorns in their sides.

It was getting dark but the track was lit up like it was day. The whole stadium was brightened by large flood lights making very few shadows. Hover cameras were everywhere, sending the race over the high speed communication Jumps to all over the Federation, including some non-human sectors. Overhead were huge blimp screens hanging in the air, circling the track. Interviews, taped earlier, were being played of the top racers. It was ironically funny as each driver started out the same way, "I would like to thank our sponsors ..." Boy, did I know the drill. It was important to constantly mention the sponsors. The two moons of Nestor were already out, both on the wane but the sky was clear and the stars made a gorgeous background. "Wow," Hill exclaimed.

"Well, hello Skip," It was Cally. I hadn't seen her approach. "Wishing you were down there?"

"No," I simply replied hopeful she'd go away, but of course no luck.

"I don't think you've met Emanuel Rosluke." He was standing next to her, his arm draped across her shoulders. His face was one big smirk enhanced with small beady eyes and ears that stuck out at angles.

I shook his hand, it was weak, like a young kid. I fought the temptation to squeeze it hard. He'd probably whine like a baby.

"Emanuel, I'd like you to meet Chief Brown of Fulton Station." Cally completely ignored my companion. I didn't think Hill minded.

"Oh, government worker! How quaint. Must be thrilled to get VIP passes." Emanuel smiled, perfect teeth. I would have liked to knock them right out of his mouth. So much for Ralph's discretion, he must have told his daughter who I was. I just hoped he hadn't told Cally everything. I didn't think so, as her next comment confirmed it. She didn't seem to know the real reason I was here.

"He's here watching his brother Ray." She pressed against Emanuel, making promises she'd never keep. "I believe it's rumored Ray may be switching to you. You aren't making my daddy happy." Ralph's daughter smiled coyly up at Emanuel.

"We could only be so lucky, I've never seen your father upset," Rosluke's spoiled brat snidely remarked. "So what does *Chief* mean, as in Indian?" It was said in a sarcastic condescending tone. I saw Hill shudder, knowing my temper.

"I take smart-ass punks like you and I lock them up for a very long time. Now if you'll excuse me, my date and I want to watch the races outside." I took Hill's arm heading out to the VIP bleacher seats. I only got a quick glimpse of the pretty boy's shocked rage. I heard Cally's shallow giggle.

"Not good, Chief. You've made an enemy." Hill sat next to me, her ass fitting better on the cushioned bleacher type bench than mine.

"Yep," I answered, "but he'll be so mad, he won't concentrate on why I'm here. He'll think I'm a jerk and here just to see my brother. I doubt he can think much past himself anyway."

The bright neon pace vehicle headed the cars out of the inner island with its sides announcing in pulsating red: *"STROM SUPERSTAR RACE TRACK."* The pace hover craft stood out as it was decorated in bright incandescent orange and green stripes. It was a convertible with Ms. Crab Nebula waving and smiling from the back seat next to the president of Midplanet Bank Corp. The modern craft, unlike the racing cars, folded up its tires and started taking the cars for their once around the track parade, leading all forty-one racers out of pit row. The crowd went crazy as the drivers revved up their engines, gunning the cars from side to side, warming up the tires for the hard pavement track. The thunderous wild yelling of 300,000 people was quite exhilarating, overwhelming the track's sound system. Even Hill was yelling and clapping. For just a moment the universe was a wonderful place and all was well. Just for a moment.

Everything went smoothly. The drinks flowed, and despite all the catered hors d'oeuvres, everyone filled up on hamburgs, hotdogs and fries. The trial runs began. One driver after another took their turn. My brother was in second place having lost the pole to Sonny Jistin, who had raced in my day. I was glad to see an "oldster" still had it. There were only two drivers left. Tip Stucksko was up next. During the evening several of the VIP attendees came down to see me. News spread quickly that I was in attendance. "You remember him." I could hear it as they pointed down to us. Many shook my hand, took pictures. To Hill's surprise I was gracious to all, leftover manners from my racing days. To her astonishment I wasn't at all the barbaric "Chief" she was so used to.

Hill had gone to get something to eat when a gentleman, and I say that loosely, came down and sat next to me. He introduced himself as Walt Rosluke. He put his hand out but I kept my soda in one hand and my cotton candy in the other. He withdrew it. "I'd like to apologize to you about my son. His ignorance of who you are is no excuse for rudeness. Cally told me what a brute he was."

"I've already forgotten about it." I told him. I wanted to add, his son wasn't worth remembering but I bit my tongue.

"I'd hate to start on the wrong foot with you since your brother will be coming over to race for us." Then he added as an afterthought, "Ray never told me you'd joined the police force on Fulton. I thought you were off sector somewhere."

I played it safe, not wanting him to think I was here on Nestor for official business, "Well, I don't think Ray thought anything of it. It's just a job. I wanted to come back and see Ray take a championship."

"Well, hope he does. Your brother will do well under us. Perhaps I shouldn't have said anything, I don't know if he's told you he's going to race for me next year. I think he has a great future." Walt Rosluke was dressed in an expensive suit, he even smelled rich with an attitude that radiated his importance.

I decided to play ignorant, best not to rock the boat yet. "No, hasn't mentioned it to me. I am surprised, he's been with Ralph a long time."

"Well, we'll treat him right." He smiled, putting a pointed edge to his voice, "We'll treat you right too. We always like to be cooperative with our illustrious police force." He smiled again.

So, unlike his son, he knew who I was, knew what *Chief* meant. "I'm sure my brother will get along quite well."

"That's good, Skip. I look forward to working with you." He held his hand out again.

I didn't take it. My hand wouldn't move, he disgusted me too much. It was an awkward moment but he covered it up well, just nodding and walking back up to the club house.

My lieutenant came back with two hotdogs loaded and a chocolate milkshake. I looked incredulously at Ms. Healthfreak. She shrugged, "I'm just assimilating myself into the racing crowd. Just getting into the spirit of it." She childishly stuck her tongue out and swirled it around getting all the mustard off her lips. "Who was that?" Her head turned to the clubhouse watching my visitor through the large windows as he was handed a martini by one of the waiters.

"A jerk named Walt Rosluke." I saw her look back again, frowning.

"What did he want?" She put her hotdogs on her lap. "He's careful to stay out of police and newspaper files. He's the patriarch of the family, Emanuel's father and a top notch businessman. He owns most of the Halka farms. I gathered from the local cops, they're afraid of him. He wields a lot of influence and has no qualms about using it. Be careful of him, Chief."

"He wanted to apologize for his son and to hint at bribing me." I had dealt with plenty like him, Fulton Station had its tough important men, government centers always had their power hungry corrupt people. Yet, despite me not seeing eye to eye with my boss, the Consulate of Fulton, he was an honorable man, keeping those men in line and away from interfering with the enforcement of the law; which included Nestor and all the rest of the sector planets. Mr. Rosluke was about to feel my wrath and the long arm of Sector law. I just needed to solidly catch him, and I *would* catch him! He was an over-confident oaf despite his wealth, he thought himself untouchable. Those kinds always trip themselves up.

It came over the loud speaker that the last car, Adriana Buish, was having malfunctions which meant Tip Stucksko was the last one and it'd be a night. I pressed the left button on my cell, *22:35, Friday, 3rd month, 5th day, galactic standard time, location Strom*

Super Race Track, Nes, Nestor. I touched it off. "Looks like it won't be a real long evening," I said to Hill. She nodded, her mouth full of her second hotdog. I stuffed the last of my cotton candy in my mouth, letting it melt slowly on my tongue. I could feel the calories floating down my throat. My pants were going to get even tighter if I kept it up.

The overhead speakers blared Tip's statistics. The humongous aerial screens had the young racer's smiling picture. The announcer came over the loud speakers, "Tip is in the number 76 Salvaline car from Team Rosluke. Tip had a great year two years ago, finishing second. Last year he finished twelfth. This year, however, he's been struggling, with eighth place being his highest finish. He stands in eighteenth place. Let's all wish him the best!"

Tip came roaring out of pit row. He'd have two tries around the track to beat 263.75mph. My brother had missed it by three tenths of a second. The first time around Tip wasn't even close crossing the line at 261mph. His second go around, the overhead screen was showing 262mph. He could at least maybe break into the top ten. He'd taken the third turn when his car seemed to lose it. The front of his car hit the wall. He skidded along the wall and suddenly the whole car blew up. The crowd screamed, the flames reached high into the air. Hill grabbed my arm, saying "Oh no!" then I felt myself standing, my head felt like it was in an echo chamber, and   that   was   all   she   wrote...

Chapter 11

So, here I was outside the maintenance garage gulping air, trying to ignore smelling myself. I wondered what had happened to Hill? She obviously had me carried to that utility room table and then left me. I leaned against the side of the wall letting the door swing shut with a loud metallic bang.

I looked over at the track. I could barely see it through the iron laced bottom holding up the grandstand bleachers. Only the dim auxiliary lights were on. The events of the night were coming back to me in little pieces. The blue pill was working, the nauseousness had left me but I still sported a wicked thumping headache. I looked down the walkway, the maintenance shed was off on one side, the Midway wasn't far away, but it was all quiet now. I wondered what had happened to Tip Stucksko, but I knew. He was dead. No one survives a crash like that. Why hadn't the foam that was supposed to be released on impact not put out the fire before it consumed the car? That had been an explosion, not just a normal fire. It was supposed to be impossible; the safety precautions were almost overly redundant to prevent it from happening. The new systems did not allow the buildup of gasline fumes. The foam retardant by itself should have stopped it from happening. The sight of the huge flames reaching high into the air brought back the nauseousness, I slumped down, sitting on the still warm pavement.

I didn't think about it anymore as I was concentrating on two blurry figures coming down the walkway toward me from the Midway. A colorful mixture blended together. I knew it was Hill, the glowing lime green pants gave her away. "Chief?" She cautiously approached me, "What are you doing out here! I told that man to keep you safe until I got back." I saw her drawback from the smell.

"Are you alright Skip?" My brother leaned close to me. I saw him grimace when he smelled me, then frowned at the state my shirt and pants were in. He unconsciously took a step backwards.

"The guy in the orange jumpsuit fled." I told the swirl of colors. I tried to get up but slid down to the ground sitting with my back against the metal wall. "What happened?"

"I think you had one of your epileptic seizures." She was squatting down next to me. Her *Gasline Plus* perfume made my stomach flip but I didn't have anything left in my stomach to come up anyway. Hill saw my distress and leaned in closer, not helping any. "Do you need to go to the hospital? I was afraid to call the ambulance, I know how you like to keep things private."

"That's not what I meant, I'm fine." Although I knew I didn't look it, or smell it for that matter. "What happened after I blanked?" My voice came out weakly, it was an effort to get the words out properly.

"Oh." She seemed to hesitate, afraid to bring on another seizure.

"Tell me, I'm alright, I took a pill." I grabbed onto her arm, sliding back up to stand. "I should have been better prepared. I've been skimping on the pills thinking I could handle this."

"They got to him right away. The fire trucks and ambulances came. I'm afraid he's dead," my brother told me as he held onto me. I could tell seeing me like this bothered him. I'd always been the strong big brother.

"You're a mess." He took a firm hold on my arm, helping me stand straighter. "I thought you had these under control."

"I usually do," I tried to explain. "It was the accident." Hill waved him away, I saw the look she gave him to not bother me. It shut him up.

"Here, I ran back to the hotel and got you some clothes." Hill took my other arm. I felt my head clearing, the headache becoming a dull pain. She handed me the bag with the stuff she'd bought earlier. Just the glowing shirt made my stomach flip again.

"I'm not wearing those!" I growled, pushing the bag away. "Are you crazy?"

"I was in a hurry, I just grabbed the bag. It'll get you back to the hotel. You can't walk around like that!" Her nose scrunched up emphasizing her meaning. "I got your brother on the way back, he and Julie were worried sick about you. Now take the clothes and put them on! You look awful and you smell terrible! Stop being such a baby or I'll call an ambulance!"

"Fine!" I grumbled, nothing like a little humiliation to set me straight. Turning to open the maintenance door, I pulled the doorknob. It was locked! Great. I just peeled off my clothes right there. I probably would give the track security a good laugh in the morning when they reviewed the remote cameras or maybe they were watching now, who knew! With the help of Hill and Ray, I put the damn colorful outfit on. "One size fits all", yeah for skinny folk. The pants just barely fit, hugging my hips tightly. I had to roll my underwear down or I couldn't snap them. The shirt, however, was too big, which was good because it hung over my exposed hefty hips which bulged over the bell pants. I emptied my ruined pants pockets, attached my cellbutton to my bright red glowing collar and trashed my old clothes in the nearest garbage bin. I kept my socks and shoes and dumped the colorful sandals with my stinking clothes, getting a frown from Hill.

"Hey, those cost a lot!" She complained.

"Then take them out of the garbage!" I noticed she declined.

We walked down the silent Midway. All of a sudden my pants started to roar. I stopped dead, afraid to move. Hill reached over touching the button at the top of the pants. I scowled at her and tentatively took a step. Heavenly, thank goodness, silence.

"The officials are stunned. All racing has been suspended until an inquiry." My brother informed me, his voice was shaking. "This is horrible, Skip. How could this happen? This isn't supposed to happen anymore. It hasn't happened since your accident. Sure we've had injuries, but crap, no deaths!" He was upset, but I had no answers for him. He had been only twelve years old when I had my accident. Killa and Jack had kept most of the horror of it away from him. He had visited with Uncle Jack when I was recovering on Moss, but I had been mostly sedated and he hadn't realized the horror of it. He couldn't see my horrible burns through the bandages.

It was eerie walking down the raceway with no fans, no loud engine roars, nothing, not even the fake roars or buzzing crowds. When we arrived in the pits, almost everyone was gone, the trailers all closed up. The whole area was in dark shadows. Julie was standing by Ray's trailer. She ran to meet us. She looked strangely at me.

"This was Hill's idea." I sputtered, thankful of the darkness that hid my red face.

She smiled. "I think you look dapper," my sister in law said getting another scowl from me. I looked accusingly at Hill but she was ignoring me.

"Come on Skip, we'll take you home." Ray said.

"Hill?" I looked over at her. "What's on the menu?" Now that my head was clearing, my mind was returning to the investigation. We had plans made. Tony was supposed to meet Hill after the races.

"I have to meet Tony Monticutticu. I hope he's still here." Hill looked around. "It's seems everyone has left."

I looked at my brother. I hadn't seen Tony earlier when we'd visited my brother before the race in the outer pits.

"He was in the inner pits. If he's still here, that's where he'll be, at our garage trailer," Ray explained, getting a confirmed nod from Julie.

"Come on Hill, I'll take you." I was feeling better. The pills usually worked pretty well.

"I'll go with you too," Ray offered.

"No, take Julie home," I insisted. "Trust me Ray, I know how to do my job." Of course the pants took that time to start roaring again. I fumbled with the button. It was Hill who reached over and shut them off. "Damn," I swore, seeing Ray smile in amusement. Julie covered her smile with her hand.

It was Julie that grabbed Ray, "Come on, let's get home. I don't know if you're racing tomorrow but you'll need your sleep. I need to get to bed, I have a lot of sleep to catch up on." She punched Ray in the arm, smirking at him. "Just ring the bell when you get to the house, Skip."

"Don't worry, I have a room at the Checkered Flag, I'll see you tomorrow. Nice racing Ray." My brother just nodded. I could tell he was still thinking about Tip's death. When he looked at Julie, I could tell he was pondering their soon to be family. It wasn't all so cut and dry anymore. Death kinda puts everything in a different light. Priorities change.

I watched as Ray put his arm around Julie heading her toward their hover craft. For a moment, envy crept into my soul but I squashed it. I was happy for him, happy for both of them. It looked like they had patched things up. My niece or nephew, whatever it turned out to be, would be in good hands.

Hill followed me as I went to the beginning of the tunnel that led under the grandstand onto the track. "This is how the cars get to the inner pits for the races. They start out here and end up in the middle section you saw from the bleachers."

We were stopped by a questioning security guard, who although he saw our VIP bracelets wouldn't have let us go any further until both of us showed our badges. Then, after a security call, he let us go. I was grateful my pants didn't start roaring, he already had looked twice at our outfits.

We came into the center pits. For Hill it was breathtaking. For me, it was like being reminded of an old beautiful sweetheart that's left you and your heart still aches for her. The whole circle of the bleachers seen from the inner island was an awesome sight even if they did lie in shadows. There were no huge screens floating above, so the whole star lit night seemed something out of a fairy tale. Only a few lights were on. Dull lampposts just barely lit the area. Most of crews and maintenance people were gone. A lingering smell of burnt smoke from Tip's accident hung in the air reminding us why we were here.

"Come on. Let's find Attenson's area. Shouldn't be far. Their team standing is high. The higher points a team has, the better position on the inner island." We started looking, the inner pit road was to our right, beyond that the two mile track swung around. The huge trailers were on our left.

I was correct for a change. Attenson Racing banner was the third one we came to. A light was still on in the large semi that housed the mechanic's workshop, the ramp still down. The light filtered over the ramp that led into the trailer. Tony was Bill Connor's top mechanic, like my sister-in-law Julie was my brother's. I didn't know who Bill had gotten to replace Monty, his crew chief. If I remembered right, Bill was eighth in the standings. He drove the number 44 red Phillysteak car. Connors had been on the Ralph Attenson's team for five seasons.

I walked up the ramp of the trailer. In the back, Bill's car hood was opened and Tony was leaning over it, some tools in his hand. "I've been waiting on you," he said without looking up in that soft Tohegian voice I knew so well. He glanced up and almost hit his head on the hood as his eyes fell on me.

"Bobmista conga miea," he cried, dropping his tools and with two long strides came and embraced me with a big bear hug.

"Hillma conga miea," I replied returning the hug.

"Miea songa kia, Bobmista." He was crying. He looked so much like Monty; the short curly hair with the protruding thick Tohigian ears, the intense black eyes and the light brown complexion with his muscles bulging out of his rolled up t-shirt arms. It hurt, my throat felt tight as I held on to my old friend.

"What is being said?" Hill asked. "I don't have my translator module on."

"He was welcoming me. Both he and Monty called me Bobmista, which means "treasured little one." I could see in her eyes the amusement she took at 'little'.

"It's just an endearment, Hill," I told her in my most scorching voice. "Tony, this is Lieutenant Hill. She's come to inquire about Monty." He looked at me questioning my presence. "I never told you that I'm the Chief of Police for the Crab Sector." I showed him my badge, he stared at it for a long moment while letting the information seep in.

"Will you help me?" He looked at me in a new light. "Monty didn't commit suicide, you know this to be true, Bobmista." His shoulders slumped, tears filled his eyes. I could feel his hurt, his confusion. He had lost his world, the spunk that I remembered him for was completely gone.

"Yes, I do know. We need to get some information, Tony." He nodded his head. He went over and grabbed three folding chairs putting them around a work table.

As we took our seats, he put his head in his hands, "I don't know what to do. The Elders will not let me bring Monty home. I cannot bury him properly. His soul will suffer. We will not roam the Casey Plains together." He let out a sob but got himself under control, sitting up straight. "I will help you as much as I can."

"I know, Tony." I put my hand on his arm, I felt it shaking, "Tell me, when was the last time you saw Monty?"

"We came home from the race on Tilsi. All the cars came home because the next race on Mithuso is in heavier gravity, so we needed to retool before we headed out again." His hands were clutched tightly in front of him, "Monty was happy. Your brother, Ray, had won and Bill had come in fourth pushing him into eighth place. Even our third driver, Mark, had come in twelfth. Ralph was happy, everyone was happy. When I left Monty he was going over the setup plan and the racetrack strategy. He was fine. He planned to meet me in the morning to go over the car's final setup."

"Did he say anything about Caroline Waser?" I asked him. Seeing his head jerk up, from his eyes I knew he had.

"She was a good friend. I know what they say but Monty never had something going on with her. She was a Tohegian. When she first came to us, Caroline was a hojiti." He looked sadly over at Hill, perhaps hoping she'd understand being a woman.

I filled her in. "It means a lost soul, a female lost soul that has strayed from the tribe's teaching and is searching for a path back."

Tony nodded. "Monty helped her back to the light. The police came and told us she had driven over Canyon Clift drunk. Monty, he knew she didn't drink anymore, it wasn't an accident. He was upset, he didn't think the accident was right. Just like Monty, she was killed. They killed him Skip, but why? He'd never hurt anyone."

"Whoa," Hill interjected, "did he actually tell you that? What did he actually know? Did he know who'd kill her?" As cop detectives we were trained to be skeptical. She leaned forward. "People have gone off the wagon before, Tohegian or not! Woman or not! Redemption is only as good as the moment."

He turned to me, "Bobmista, tell her. Tell her of our ways."

"If he says she went back to the Tohegian ways, believe him. Tohegians do not lie and they do not exaggerate." I turned to Tony, "What did she know that would get her killed?"

"I don't know, but she was a smart girl. She was telling Monty about some DNA research she was doing. She often came and prayed with us."

"Did you know she was seeing Tip Stucksko?" My lieutenant looked up from her tab. The minute we had sat down Hill had turned on her tabloid, making a record of all this.

"I don't think it was serious. They were both young. I know, she was mad one day, that Emanuel, Rosluke's son had tried to hit on her. Tip wasn't happy about it, he had a fight with the son over it. The old man, he had to intervene. Caroline told Monty that she'd be going home to Casey as soon as her research was done. She said that Walt banned her from being near the cars. She was scared of the Roslukes. Do you think it was them? They cheat, you know."

"What research could she be doing, Chief? Do you think she told Monty?" Hill sounded exasperated. I had a bad feeling about all this. Someone was trying to cover something up and murdering to do it. But who and why? Was it the Rosluke's or the rebels? Did it have something to do with the FIO investigation? But surely, what could a recent university grad be involved in?

Hill was typing something into her tablet. When the screen changed, she looked at me. "She was a biochemical engineer. Her thesis that she had submitted to the University was titled *The Electrical Impulsive Connectors of RNA in the Humanoid Brain*. The files at University U show her as one of the top grad students and that is saying something for a human. She did an internship on M.O.S.S., the Medical Operation Space Station, spending a year there. She then worked with the major medical hospital in Nes. What could that have to do with the Roslukes?"

I shook my head, above my knowledge. I'd have to ask some expert or two. I'd have Hill find out from the hospital what she'd been working on.

Tony had gotten up and was nervously pacing the trailer. "They would not let me have his gun back. They told me they lost his suicide note when I asked to see it." Tony was pacing in front of us. "The head policeman, Holden, he threatened me if I go further. He wouldn't understand about bringing Monty home."

I saw red, "He threatened you?" I would definitely take care of my superintendent. There was nothing I hated more than a crooked cop. Nothing I hated more than a bullying cop.

"He told me to accept Monty's suicide or I could find myself deported. I couldn't leave Monty's body here. I had to clear his name. Ralph is the one who helped me file a sector complaint with the Federals. The police, they didn't want to anger Ralph. He's more important than I am, they can't threaten him."

Now it made sense. It was easy to push around a lowly Tohegian but not one of the most influential race car owners. I made a mental note to thank Ralph.

"What do you think happened tonight?" I asked Tony. He had been at ground level.

"Not much left of the car," he told me. "They hauled it away about an hour ago."

"I think we should go look at that wreck, Hill. Tony, are you free to come to the police station with me? I'd like your opinion..."

"The police station, why the police station?" He asked, puzzlement written all over his face.

"They'll take it to the impoundment yard for further investigation." I explained. "It's normal procedure. They always impound the vehicle when there has been a death."

"They didn't take it there. I saw the wrecker come, I was standing on the track. That head cop told them to take it to Rosluke's garage just outside of town."

"I'm going to have his head." I was beyond angry. "Let's go Hill, we gotta get there before they destroy all the evidence."

"They are playing it smart, Chief." Hill stood gathering her tabloid. "Once it's on Rosluke property, we can't go in without a warrant."

"I'll get one," I assured her. "Let's go find a cab."

"Wait, I'll take you," Tony offered. "If it will help clear Monty, I'll help all I can. Come, my craft is right behind the trailer."

We hurried. Tony's craft was an old model cruiser. He had souped it up and it came to life with a turbo roar unlike the silent hovers everyone else had. It had plenty of room, it could probably sit eight people. Hill looked skeptical, she was use to silent hovers with quiet silent motors. She climbed in though without a word, but I noticed she tightened her seat belt. We went up the tunnel and out of the racetrack in an amazingly short time. I had a feeling this thing could move!

"Can you tap into that private Jump line the FIO's been using?" I asked Hill.

She grabbed my cell tabloid bringing up a visible screen and typing into it. "Got it, Chief! Let's hope Phil isn't watching it right now."

"Call Issam! We don't have much choice." If I waited for a public Jump line it would take a lot longer. When I had placed a call to Killa earlier, it had taken more than half an hour to get through and that was using my special police ID. If I used the police official Jump line to Fulton, it would have been faster but Stan Holden, my Superintendent, would know of it. I definitely didn't want to alert him.

When Issam answered he was half asleep. "Chief?" When I told him what I needed he asked, "Do you know what time it is?" I heard Lily in the background asking if I was alright.

"Tell Lily, I'm fine." I didn't have time to tell her of my earlier seizure. She'd want to talk to me and I hadn't the time. I'd tell her when I got home.

I pressed my cellbutton, softly hearing in my ear, "2:05, Saturday morning, 3rd month, 6th day, galactic standard time..." I hit the button. That meant it was 3:05 in Fulton. "I don't care, call Judge Butten, she'll give it to you. She owes me. Send it to Hill's tab via this accelerated Jump line. She'll send you the info you'll need right now, and hurry!"

Hill leaned over from the back seat, "And why does Judge Butten owe you?"

I started to smile at the memory but quickly caught myself. "It is none of your business!"

She huffed and sat back, again tightening her seat belt as Tony stepped on the accelerator and it threw us back against our seats.

As we cleared the city, Tony hit the supercharge and we went speeding down one road after another. "We're here," he told me. We were in the country wooded outskirts of Nes. The facility was surrounded by thick forest with no neighbors to bother. I could see a test track in the back, half hidden by the huge garages. Unlike Fulton Station, Nestor had lots of land, lots of room for anyone with money. With Rosluke's riches they had plenty of private space. The Rosluke family didn't have a mansion on Racing Row. They had a friggin castle out here. I could see the huge stone structure in the distance, beyond the garage facility.

Besides having plenty of room, it was quite a modern facility, much more modern than Attenson Racing garages in back of Ralph's mansion. Huge car docks lay in a circle just inside a fenced in area. I looked at Hill, she shook her head, "not here yet." I swore under my breath, *come on Issam* I thought furtively. I could see lights moving in the yard. Every second lost meant they had time to cover up the evidence.

It took another few minutes and it came through. I had her transfer it to my cell tab. "Hill, stay here. I don't want them aware of you yet. Let them think you're my bimbo girlfriend."

"Gee, thanks Chief," she sarcastically answered me but slumped down out of sight.

We had parked outside their compound, across the street. With Tony at my heels, we headed toward the open gate. They obviously weren't worried about someone showing up and hadn't even locked up. The guard station at the gate was empty. They were all by Tip's mangled car. Spotlights made the area bright. When we cleared the gate, I could easily see the burnt out car sitting in the middle of the circular garage driveway. Several silhouettes were walking around it. I could see some of the guards carrying highly charged sub guns. They were illegal. Strike one, I thought.

"Everyone halt!" I yelled. Several heads turned our way. Then several guns, shining in the spotlights, were pointed at us. "Police! Put your guns down!" I yelled.

"Police!" I heard one man say, "You can't be the police, I'm the police!"

"Let me rephrase that, Chief of Sector Police, get those guns down NOW! And that includes you Superintendent Holden!"

Chapter 12

Stan Holden, in his Nes cop uniform, was standing next to Walt Rosluke. He had put his gun back in his holster but there were still several dark suited thugs with their large guns pointed at me. The young punk, Emanuel, was there and from the look of the man next to him, it looked like his older brother. That would be Jared. The older son looked like the high priced lawyer Hill had described. There is something about lawyers you can spot easily. It's not just the fancy suit, or the studious eyeglasses. It's their attitude, their superior cocky attitude; standing there with his arms crossed, his foot tapping, looking his nose down at us. How dare we interrupt. He made his pompous father seem tame. He was so sure he had us on trespassing. I couldn't wait to shove the court order down his throat.

An elderly woman leaning on a cane was also next to Walt Rosluke, her silver hair glistened in the heavy spot light's glow. She had a fierce scowl on her jowled face. It only accentuated her many wrinkles and small thin pouting mouth. The agitated senior citizen was yanking on Walt's arm, trying to get his attention but he was ignoring her. She even hit his leg with her jewel studded cane but he still ignored her.

They were all eerily silhouetted against the highly illuminated background as several large spotlights from the front garage had been pointed to highlight Tip's mangled car. There wasn't much left of it, you couldn't even see that it had been a red and green colored race car. The fire had burned it to raw metal. The flames had been so intense that the tires were melted on the scorch-marked rims. There couldn't have been much left of him. My hands clenched at the thought.

"Chief Brown!" Holden peered over at me, his palms up over his eyes trying to see me through the intense floodlights. "Put your guns down, please," my superintendent yelled at the ugly brutes, but they didn't put them down until Walt told them to. That put Stan in perspective, it was obviously Rosluke that held the power. I could tell right then and there that Agent Phil had been right, Stan Holden was Walt's puppet. I had to fight to keep my temper under control. I didn't want Walt to realize I knew that Nes's head cop was in his pocket. It wouldn't do me any good to lose my composure here. I'd need my wits to keep these vultures at bay or I'd end up another of their murder victims.

"Well, Skip. I see you've been at the races or were you at the circus?" Walt sarcastically commented. He was looking at my stupid flashy outfit, I swore under my breath. I'd forgotten I was dressed in the damn buffoon costume. I saw the goons snicker too, at least my Superintendent had the sense not to.

"Is he from the circus?" Gramma asked, her voice crackingly hoarse, confused at her son's comment.

"You might say that, Gramma." Emanuel laughed. "He's a government worker, same thing."

"Shut up!" Walt growled at his son. The head of the Rosluke family then looked over at Monty's brother, frowning, trying to piece the puzzle together. "Tony, what are you doing here?" He wrinkled his brow at the Tohegian, giving his disapproving eye to the well-known mechanic. "Don't you have enough to do? Does Ralph know you're here?" The threat was in his tone and manner. Tony looked over at me, uncertain if he should leave. I shook my head at him.

"Stay where you are." I told the Tohegian, then turned to Walt, "I brought him, got it!" I said harshly and left it at that, glaring at Rosluke daring him to say anything. I saw Walt's eyes angrily squint, he was not use to be contradicted or told in essence to shut up.

"Who are these damn men?" I heard the old woman snap in her high demanding voice, obviously she'd taught Walt everything he knew. "They have no right coming on my property." Her voice was high pitched and broke up at every other word. The voice of the old. "Tell them to get off my property! Shoot them!" Oh great, momma was mad, really mad like insane. Her eyes had that glow of the insane, but worse was the assurance in her voice that showed she was used to being in charge. Used to being obeyed! This is the woman that spawned all these morally deficient guys. No wonder they thought they owned the world, it was bred into them.

"It's alright, Mother," Walt grinned at the matriarch of the family. He raised his voice to make sure she heard him over her hearing aid. **"This is Chief Skip Brown of Fulton Station. The Big Important sector Chief of Police**. Besides a huge sector police force, he's known for his hard ass detective team of twenty strong. Known for their tough stance on crime? **Have I got that right Skip?"**

However it only irritated the old woman who screamed at him, "Don't shout at me! I don't care who the hell he is. Get him off my property! Now!"

But it wasn't his mother he had been talking to, it was me. So he had done some research, had he? I was now a known entity and he wanted me to know he knew exactly who I was and that he wasn't afraid of me or my police force. After all, he'd already gotten to one of my head cops.

"**Please step away from the car**." I talked just as loud, making sure the old hag got it, making sure he got it. I ignored his goading. I turned to my superintendent, sternly pointing at the mangled mess, "Stan, call the tow truck, get this car into the police impoundment area so a proper investigation can be done. You know the rules! What the hell were you thinking?" I growled and I can growl very well. I saw his startled expression as it dawned on him that perhaps I should be the one he should be afraid of. He looked over at the Roslukes, not so sure of himself.

"Why, Chief?" Walt was determined to get me angry, "it was a terrible accident, there is no need to upset everyone with false accusations. Remember what you went through when you had your accident. I'm sure we can come to some agreement." His smile made me sick. So he really had gotten info on me. I was glad I had popped a pill before I got out of the car. "After all, Chief Brown, this is my property. I have every right to it! I do believe you are trespassing. I do believe I have rights."

"You can have it back after it's been looked at by the police investigators and released by a judge. Like I said, step away from the car. Get that tow truck NOW!" I walked into the circle of light. They actually backed up a little. I gave Stan my scowl. He had to have heard I had a temper. I saw him reach for his cell button and speak into it softly.

"Get off my property!" The old woman screeched. "Emanuel, get him off my property! He has no rights on my property. Who does he think he is?" The old lady was waving her cane, hitting Walt's leg. He winced but didn't stop her. When he tried to take her arm she pulled away from him, hitting him right on the shins. I saw him cringe in pain.

"Mother!" he finally yelled at her, this time she backed up, but the scowl never left her wrinkled face.

She was one tough old bird, stamping her foot in frustration, shaking her finger in my direction as if I was some disobedient child. I got her even angrier by completely ignoring her.

"I agree with you, Gramma," I heard her younger grandson say to her. He nodded to the oversized bodyguards and the guns came out again.

I pressed my tabloid button, the warrant came on as a holographic screen in front of me. "Mr. Rosluke, this is a warrant signed by a sector Federal Judge. If you persist in this manner you'll all be under arrest. Stan, call in backup please, I want some cops here." I saw my superintendent's alarm, his hands fidgeted, not sure what to do. He looked at the Roslukes. Then his hand went to his cellbutton but Jared held up his hand.

"Please wait, Mr. Holden," using his best slick lawyer voice and looked to his father. "There is no need to call."

"Hold guys," Walt put up his hand. Everyone froze as he came over and examined the document. "He's right, how the hell did you get a warrant this quick? Jared, take a look at this."

The other young man came over. He looked like he'd just come from work. His dark expensive suit with his wing tipped shined shoes spoke of a high class professional. He probably wore the outfit to bed. He put on a pair of designer glasses peering at the official document. "It's authentic, dad. As your counselor, I have to tell you to obey the order. It's by a high level sector judge too. You don't want to ignore her."

In other words, he was telling his old man that it wasn't one of their "bought judges" and that he'd better not cause trouble.

"Now that that's settled, everyone away from the car." I ordered and was relieved to see everyone back up. Emmanuel took his grandmother's arm and got a cane across his leg. He yelped in pain. The old woman was upset. She glared at me, squinting from the spotlights high intensity.

"I don't know who you think you are, but my name is Cornelia Rosluke and I don't take lightly intrusion into what I own and I own most of Nes. Do you hear me!" The old woman looked like an old witch with her white hair blowing in the wind, being silhouetted against the bright light.

"Mother, please," Walt was trying to grab her, but for an old woman she was pretty spry, wiggling out of his grasp and heading toward me with her fancy cane threatening me. She had to be all of five feet tall. Her old lady flowered dress was flapping in the wind, her knee high stockings getting caught in the skirt. She looked like some tiny skinny crone skeleton. She surprised me lunging at me when she drew near.

She went to raise the cane against me and I took the damn thing away from her. Using my knee, I broke it in half. "Here ma'am, I think you'd better go inside now. I'd hate to put you in jail, they don't treat old ladies real nice there."

She gasped, looking incredulously at the two pieces of the broken cane. Walt took her by the shoulders leading her away. "Come on Mother. You should be inside. Emanuel, get your grandmother indoors. Better still, take her home."

I walked over to what use to be Tip's car bringing Tony with me. "Take a look. See quickly if anything is obvious." I tried to keep to the shadows caused by the high intensity lights. I preferred they not see what we were searching for.

We both looked at the burnt mutilated mess. Tony reached in under the seat, bringing out a tube that was half melted. He bent down, smelling the end. "Gasline," his eyes showing horrible astonishment.

"What?" I didn't know what he meant. I bent over, smelling it too.

"Air tube, filled with gasline." He reached over keeping his body close to mine and the interior out of the sight of the others. A big white tube lay almost melted into the side of the seat itself. He bent down smelling it also. "Gasline, I smell gasline in the foam tube. This didn't help him much. The poor guy hadn't a chance."

Then it hit me. Tip's oxygen line had been full of gasline and so had his anti-flammable foam tube." The horrifying picture of what had to have been sheer fear that must have flooded Tip's mind on the last moments when he was breathing oxygen and it flooded with gasline. I stood up, needing to get a fresh breath of air. Tony took my arm. I calmed, thankful for those self-sedating exercises the therapist had given me and for those little blue pills. I didn't want them to know we'd found anything. I have seen some brutal disgusting crimes but this had to be right up there with the worst.

I heard the tow truck pulling into the yard. I walked away from the car. Walt came up. "Did you find anything?" he couldn't keep the anxiety out of his voice.

"No. I think it's too damaged by fire to find anything but we'll let the crime unit at least look at it. We have to follow the law." I half smiled at him.

He smiled back, his eyes shining with delight. "Right. Right you are, Skip! I'm sure to mention to the sector governor how well you've done. We didn't mean to overstep your authority. I was just concerned about getting it off the track as soon as we could. Please forgive my mother, she's old, getting a little senile. This has been a terrible shock to her, to all of us, we were very fond of Tip."

I nodded, trying not to gag. Let him think I'd only done this to get my piece of the pie. It gnawed at my gut but if it meant I'd get him, I could play the great patsy until I put the handcuffs on him.

Walt walked back to the group. I heard his whiney son Emanuel, "Dad, you can't let him push us around. Doesn't he know who he's dealing with?"

"Shut up." His father took his arm, heading back towards the garage where Gramma supposedly awaited a ride home. The wicked witch returning to the castle.

The tow truck left with the mangled mess. Tony and I headed to his car. Hill was hiding in the back seat peering over the window with binoculars. I didn't want to point out her glowing outfit wasn't very good camouflage. She'd be spotted right off. "Where'd you find the binoculars?"

"In Tony's car," she answered. "I thought I was going to have to come to your rescue, especially when the old lady attacked you. Good defensive maneuvers, Chief. She's a pip." She laughed. "Find anything?"

I explained what we thought had happened. She was horrified. Give her a few years and nothing would surprise her. Being in sector homicide brought every kind of humanoid cruelty, every kind of animalistic greed, encompassing every kind of person. I almost envied her naivety.

I had called into the local police station, a sleepy cop answered and I made sure all was ready for the impoundment. I was assured all was, they were just waiting for the tow truck. I told them I'd be there in the morning to oversee further inspections. I was assured Stan had taken care of it. My superintendent was calling the track's officials, getting some mechanics to come in the morning, the yawning night shift cop told me. I buzzed off satisfied. I'd make sure Tony was included.

We rode back into the city in silence, listening to the rumble of Tony's hover. The night's horrors were getting to all of us, fatigue making it worse. Tony dropped us off at the Checkered Flag. The bus boys had stepped back when we came roaring up the circular drive and looked rather wearily at us when we got out. Of course, it didn't help that my pants started roaring and after fumbling to stop it, Hill reached over and shut them off. I was going to burn these clothes, just for the satisfaction of doing it.

We went into a somber late night lobby. So unlike earlier when all the screens were going full blast and the shops were blaring rumbling engine noises. The screens all showed pictures of Tip Stucksko. Soft music was playing and all the holograms in the hallways on the way to our room were just quiet subdued sad faced fan murals.

Hill pressed the fob to let us in, again no roaring engines, just quiet somber tunes. "I don't know which is worse, the roaring engines or this macabre music," she lamented.

The lights, however, were already on. Phil sat on the couch, a bunch of tabloids on the cocktail table in front of him.

"You know Phil, you are really, and I mean really, getting on my nerves." I looked at him, my worst scowl on my face.

"Well, you know Skip, I'd take you more seriously if you'd didn't look like you'd just come from the circus. I didn't know clown suits were in vogue. Is Hill rubbing off on you? How did you ever get the nerve to face down Rosluke looking like that?"

I had to give him his due, he got me and it didn't help that as I stepped toward him, my pants went off again. Hill automatically stepped forward and shut them off.

"Hey, I'll get myself a pair, if Judy will shut them off. Now I know why you're wearing them."

"PHIL!" we both yelled at him.

He put up his hands in submission. "My apologies. I have those files you wanted."

"I'm not going to even ask you how you got in here, or how you knew where I was tonight. Just give me the files and get the hell out." I couldn't keep the frustration and fatigue from my voice. It had been a long day.

"Not so fast." He grabbed the tabs and headed over to the table. "I think there are a few things we need to discuss." He motioned to two chairs, while taking a third seat for himself.

"I'll make us some java." My head was pounding and I needed a booster. I found the brewing maker and turned it on. After a few sips, I settled down across from him. It was now after four in the morning, not much sleep tonight.

"First, what did you find out at Rosluke's?" The FIO agent slid the files across to me.

"You mean you don't already know, there is something that you don't know?" I couldn't help ragging on him. I was dead tired and still feeling out of sorts. He just looked at me and smiled, making me want to kill him right there. I found solace in my hot cup of java.

I let Hill give him a recap of today's activities while I looked over the driver's files. Three files were there. I started with Tip Stucksko. His young face looked up at me, it was a good likeness, taken at a winning moment. He was smiling broadly, holding a bottle of champagne. My stomach ached. Too young to die, die like Lonarer. I shut my memories down, they wouldn't help me solve these senseless murders.

Up until two years ago Tip raced for Al Summers' team. Under Summers, he had come close to the championship his last year, his last year with them. He was 24 years old, born and raised on Nestor in their town of Chico, just above Nes. Started in racing when he was just a boy. Similar story to mine, but he'd come up through Nestor's amateur short tracks. Tip had been Nestor's junior champion at seventeen and had been picked up by Al and from all indications had been happy as part of the Summers' team. His teammates in interviews on the year he left were stunned that he had switched to Rosluke. Tip had said himself that he had expected greater opportunities with Walt. Yet, he had not done well under Rosluke; coming in the last two years in twelfth and eighteenth place. His income was way up there, though. His bank accounts showed a higher earning than most of the winning drivers, including last year's Champion.

I read Cab Tayler's file. He had left racing at the beginning of this year. Just up and left to go home, as was reported from Rosluke management people. It explained why Walt was down a driver, going after my brother. Tayler was from off sector, born on Lucis in the Pin Wheel Sector. Tayler had also come up with the amateur tracks and had been Lucis junior champion. He had started out with Sonny Fairbank's team. Again, like Tip he'd been a top contender. He was kind of a wild guy and all indications were that Sonny, who ran a tight ship, was glad to see Cab switch to Rosluke because he'd been hard to handle. I wondered what had happened to Cab. Did he really go home?

The last file was Hank Sims, my ex's present husband. Like Tip, he had also been an Al Summers' driver. He was champion two years running under Summers. Then he switched to Rosluke. Hadn't come in closer than seventh since. Again, like the other two, he was well paid. Now he was Rosluke's only driver. He really puzzled me. Had Rosluke blackmailed him like they had Ray? Or was it the extensive salary and gifts that Walt had showered him with? I knew Hank from my days of driving. He was thirty two years old. I was betting on the money. He was the perfect husband for Charlene, he lived the high life, the expensive high life.

Phil had asked me a question but my mind was deep into the files. He repeated it, with Hill kicking me under the table to get my attention. "Why do you think someone killed Tip Stucksko?" Phil asked as he picked up the young driver's tab file.

I shook my head. "He knew something. He was going to talk to me after the race, we were meeting at midnight. Someone got wind of it, or Rosluke knew Tip was scared and getting ready to jump ship. Tony showed me two melted lines, they were full of gasline and they weren't supposed to be. One was his oxygen line, the other was for the fire retardant foam line. With the car flooded in fuel, it would be easy to set off a spark. There was no foam to stop the fire. That's three murders that we know of. I have a bad feeling about Cab Tayler too. Hill, see if Cab ever showed up on Lucis. I'm betting he didn't. I'm betting he never got off Nestor.

She nodded, making an entry in her tabloid. "It will take a day or two, that's over a two day Jump."

She should know, it was beyond her former sector. We got interrupted by another Fed, who just waltzed in the room. "Does everyone have a key?" I snarled at him.

"Can I talk to you, boss?" He looked over at Phil, motioning him aside. I had a bad feeling about this. I noticed Hill straighten in her chair, something was wrong.

Phil came back to the table but he didn't sit. "John just told me, your tow driver's truck went over the cliff on Canyon Cliff Road. Luckily or maybe it was planned, he bailed out before the rig plunged. His rig and what was left of Tip's car is at the bottom of the ravine. Not much left of either. Says he had a flat tire on the curve."

Hill spoke first, "That's the same place Caroline Waser went over. They aren't too original, are they?" She banged her fist on the table. I was rubbing off on her.

"It's a treacherous patch of road. If he wasn't in on it, I would bet the tow driver wasn't supposed to take that way but found himself detoured there. We won't be able to prove it either way though." I knew, as a young teenager, we use to dare each other to drive that treacherous road full out. It was a dangerous foolish thing to do, but that's what youth does. I shuddered at the thought of how stupid we'd been.

"We won't be able to prove anything." Phil said. "They are good at covering their tracks."

I sat dejected, downing another cup of java. This investigation was turning into a disaster with bodies scattered everywhere. How could we prove anything with evidence being destroyed. A simple suicide investigation had blown up in our faces.

Phil had even more news. "They're racing tomorrow." Before I could say anything he continued, "They don't want to disappoint all the fans that have traveled here from all the sectors. They are dedicating the race to Tip."

"And they don't want to lose the revenue," I sarcastically blurted out, not even asking how he knew the races were going on as planned; FIO has their sources. "I suppose they are going to have a few moments of silence and then roar the engines!" I saw Phil nod. No, nothing ever changes. I wondered if my brother knew, probably not until morning when the Racing Foundation had a somber press conference sounding I'm sure as if they put the fans first. I looked up at Peterson plastered on the wall. Racing had changed since his #22 Blue Thunder had thrilled the fans. "What has been lost?" I silently asked him. Luckily he didn't answer me.

Phil, however wasn't done. "The race is tomorrow afternoon and then the cars are sent right away to Castor for the All Star Race."

I looked up, knowing something was coming. He didn't disappoint.

"The cars will be at the Jump Station awaiting the morning Jumps. I already talked to Julie, she's willing to help us take Rosluke's two cars apart - Hank Sim's main car and his backup. If there is something on the cars, it'll have to be there at the warehouse Jump terminal. With only one driver left, it's the only ones Rosluke is sending to Castor."

"Look Phil, bodies are everywhere. I'm not risking Julie, she's pregnant for god's sake!" There were already too many victims. I didn't want my sister-in-law to be the next. If the Roslukes got wind of it! I shuddered.

"It's not for you to decide. It's her decision. I'll have a team there to help her."

I was furious, Hill reached over tapping my arm. "He's right, Chief. You can't order Julie around. She needs to do this. Remember, she has a right to be mad at Ray's blackmailer. It could have ruined their lives as it did the others."

"Remember it has also killed others," I snapped.

"You'd better get a few hours sleep," Phil told me. "It's going to be a long day tomorrow. I'll let myself out. I'll check the lock on the way out."

"Why bother?" I sneered.

Chapter 13

I took a shower, the hot water took a long time to wash the previous night off me. I don't know which was worse, the smells of the seizure or the smell of Rosluke scum. It was almost dawn when I finally calmed my brain and laid down. I was asleep the minute my head hit the pillow but it seemed like only seconds when my cellbutton was screaming for me to awake, "Get up, GET up, GET UP, **GET UP NOW!**" I got up, crossing to the bedroom bureau and slapped the damn button just as it was starting the chant all over again. Enough! My brain screamed for more sleep. I used to keep my cellbutton by the bedside but I'd just slap it and go back to sleep. Making me get out of bed works better, but this morning was painful. My body ached from my epileptic episode of last night. My headache was a dull throb. The adrenaline high that the encounter with Rosluke's thugs created had worn off and a deep fatigue penetrated deeply into my bones.

I needed some caffeine. I needed a new body, that's what I needed! I heard Hill in the shower in the middle bathroom, good I'd have a few minutes to myself. She had the shower's media screen up high, listening to the racing news. She'd made herself right at home on Nestor. Pretty soon she'd be reciting racing statistics like everyone else here.

The glowing outfit I'd worn last night lay on the floor where I had just peeled them off. I reached down throwing them into the trash can. The pants started roaring. I kicked the container and it shut off.

Conservative clothes today, the most conservative things I could find.

It was 7:30 in the morning. I hardly remembered pushing the brewing button on the machine in the kitchenette. It took me three times to get it right. Finally, "Good Morning" it pleasantly said to me, giving me a loud engine roar. I grabbed a mug with Johnny Peterson's smiling face, glad someone was happy, and I took my java out to the patio.

The sun was hitting the porch full on. It felt great, so different from the searing heat of Fulton. Nestorites could actually spend lots of time outside without getting scorched. No suntan pills for them! I could hear just a few racing roars. It would be noon before the track got busy. The race was set for 14:00 that afternoon with a 250 lap race or 500 miles. That would take most of the rest of the day and possibly into early evening depending how many caution laps happened. The weather was gorgeous, so no rain delays expected.

I had dressed in my dark suit, shirt and regulation tie, dark socks and shoes. I was going on an official visit with Hank Sims, Rosluke's only driver left. I needed some answers. He must be worried. Too much had happened. It was under the radar for the fans but he had to realize he was an endangered species - it wasn't healthy to be on the Rosluke team.

Hill joined me, sipping her hot cup of healthy black tea. In her hand, she had a bowl of some special wholesome bran mixture. My stomach churned at the sight and smell of her breakfast. I turned my back to her, taking deep breaths by the patio's railings. After an episode, it would take the morning for my stomach to settle back down. The java would help. I took a big hot gulp, feeling my body relax.

The morning temperature was cool but promised to warm up; a bright sun and no clouds. "Nestor keeps this weather almost year round, doesn't it?" She asked me taking a deep breath of air while she munched on her damn breakfast. The air had a slight hint of gasline smell but she didn't seem to notice. It was amazing how quickly the smell assimilated into your senses.

"Yep." I explained further, "It's got stable mild weather patterns, this planet doesn't tip as much as most of the other sector spheres. A short winter followed by a short spring is about the only change. The rest of the year it's like this." Our planet miserably tips too much and not enough the other way, giving us constant hot weather. It was hard to imagine that Fulton Station shared the same sun, same orbit, just a quarter of an arc away. You'd never guess it, I thought.

Drinking up my caffeine, which I still desperately needed, I continued the lecture. It kept my mind off my own misery, "Most of this planet's livable land mass is in the northern hemisphere. Like most of our sector, there aren't many inhabitants, relative to the older more established sectors. The capital city is dead center, Nes City faces semi-direct sol rays most of the time, just a slight variance but the southern's large cap is always ice, so they keep a temperate temperature with cooler winds coming from the south. Goes to show how engineering could screw up a planet. Fulton Station was a model for engineering mistakes, hastily done. "Like all federation engineered planets, only one side is habitable and their days are the regulated twenty four hours, give or take a few micro seconds. It is why Nestor is only a two hour Jump from Fulton."

"At least they are only one hour behind Fulton City time-wise. It is better than Casey's capital, Hartdid, their 5 hours drag time kills me when I'm there."

I took a sip, enough chit chat. Time to face the unpleasant task. "I'm going to see Hank Sims. He'll be up early. He'll be home, he won't go to the track until late morning." I noticed she was dressed in her suit, matching regulation government tie, with her hair tied in a tight bun with no makeup, wearing black scholarly glasses. Only Hill strove to look plain. Such a different image from the bimbo look of last night. She obviously had anticipated my plans and was going with me. I hadn't the strength to argue with her. "We'll go pick up a hover at my brother's and head over to Sims' house."

We did just that, dodging Merv in the lobby, sneaking behind the lobby's big screens out of the reporters' sight. The racing atmosphere was slowly picking up; a few roars with only two screens showing track news, the other four display monitors were still pictures of Tip. I could tell it would be in full fan swing by race time. Fans were up, mulling around. Word had gotten out early that the race was back on. Within a couple of hours they'd be arguing again about their favorite racing team with only a few "poor Tip" comments.

When we got to my brother's place, Julie went to hand me Ray's hover keys but I opted for one of her utility cruisers. It went better with the suit. Hill, however, noticed the sleek silver bullet hover craft in the garage. "That's a Hundil, oh my god, I've never seen one up close. Can't we take that one?" She went over to it, running her hands over the beautiful smooth silver body. "I'd love to take this for a spin." She almost purred.

"Why Hill, you surprise me." I laughed loudly. "I never knew you had an adventurer's streak in any part of your body! That is the first frivolous thought I've known you to have."

"I like speed," she admitted. "I loved your turbocycle back at the apartment. If it hadn't been raining I would have asked to take it for a spin."

"How did you know it was mine?" I hadn't told her when she'd seen it in the Fulton garage.

"By the way you looked at it." Now it was her turn to laugh. "It was a dead giveaway. All you cycle hounds are the same. It's like your bikes are your soul mates. But, I must say I was a little surprised at you too, such an extravagance for someone who drives an Ant!"

How right she was! It had cost me plenty just in insurance alone but it was worth every bit. Fulton was a conservative pain in the ass society. Our illustrious city fathers frowned on such "radical vehicles". Like my brother on Nestor, the cops on Fulton Island knew my cycle and left me alone. Sundays were made to ride or any time I could get my ass on it.

We arrived at Sims' mansion close to nine thirty. It was a rambling building, twice the size of my brother's, almost rivaling Ralph's huge house but it wasn't as tastefully done. Huge white pillars graced the circular porch. Gigantic clay vases, filled with exotic plants lined the foyer. The high ceiling towered above with a stain glass dome interior. Money spent for the sake of spending money, the whole place reeked of money, of extravagance but not of taste.

The starched uniformed maid with Hank's number 63 on her little mini skirt had let us in. For some reason she thought we were expected. She had just taken one look at us and pointed down the hall. "He's in there, waiting for you."

Whoever Hank was waiting for, it was us he was getting. We hadn't gone half way down the long corridor when loud voices came drifting towards us. An argument was in full swing.

"I don't understand you, Charlene. You have everything you could want. Walt came through with all the money." It was Hank, annoyance dripping in his voice. "He saved our ass, we were in way over our head, thanks to you!"

"You just don't get it, you just don't get it!" My ex-wife was screaming at him, "We haven't been in the winning circle in three years. Not once! I married a winner, not some second rate racer!"

"Winning isn't everything." Hank's voice was shaking, almost pleading. "Look how we live. You spend faster than I can make it. Ralph gave us a good deal. I'm not complaining to him."

"Winning *is* everything!" She yelled at him, spitting out each word with extra forced vehemence. The sound of breaking glass resounded off the walls. "I've had it with you!"

My once upon a time wife came rushing out of the room. She was still in her nightdress, I guess you'd call it a negligee. It was all flowing pink with matching fluffy high heeled slippers. Yet, her makeup and hair were perfect. When she saw us, she stopped short. At first the anger in her eyes prevented us from registering in her brain. As she calmed down, she recognized me.

"Well, Skippy, I suppose you heard that bit of unpleasantness." Charlene always was one for understatement. I knew from long past experience it was better to say nothing. Her anger pouts were not controlled by reasoning. I had learned that early on in our marriage.

I just nodded. Hill stood stoically still, perhaps hoping not to be noticed.

"He just doesn't get it. You did though." She came over putting her hand on my cheek. "We had fun, didn't we? Over thirty one times, I stood next to you." Her eyes were somewhere focused in the past, not on the present me. The naive young racing driver was long gone, long gone.

"That's long ago, Charlene." I told her, removing her hand. "Is that all it was for you, standing next to me in the winner's circle?"

"For the most part, yes." Her sly smile graced her beautiful face. "For the most part, yes, but you did have your moments."

She walked past me, her eyes only taking in Hill as an afterthought. She almost said something, perhaps wondering why Hill was so familiar but the connection to the racetrack bimbo didn't come and she kept walking. She never even asked why I was there.

We walked into an expansively large living room. Again the ostentatiousness of the room ruined the attempt at decorating. The high ceiling, all window room was heavily embellished; the thick white carpet, the cherry walnut ornate carved furniture, the overabundance of naked marble statues. Hank was over by the double custom-made doors leading to extensive well-manicured gardens. More marble statues could be seen around a massive pool. Rosluke's star driver, their only driver, was kneeling, picking up some broken glass that probably had cost him plenty.

He looked up. "Skip Brown?" He froze, still kneeling, not grasping the here and now, probably still stuck in the recent argument. I noticed he'd cut his finger on the glass shards.

"Hi, Hank." I held out my hand, helping him up. "I'd like to ask you some questions. This is Lieutenant Hill." Hill took out her tabloid, stretching it to notepad size. She looked very efficient and very official. His eyes traveled from me to her and back.

"Questions? What kind of questions?" Time still hadn't caught up with his thoughts, he had the dumbest empty expression.

I took out my badge and showed him. "I'm looking into Tip's death."

"Tip?" He put the pieces of glass on one of the tables. His eyes became alert, that had woken him up. "I didn't know that you were investigating the accident. Are you from the racetrack? I'm expecting some of the officials to get my statement but didn't expect it to be you."

It made sense now. That's why the maid had let us in. "No, I'm Chief of Sector Police, I'm here from Fulton Station. We made the Jump yesterday. We're centralized out of Fulton City." God was it only yesterday, it seemed I'd been here forever.

"I don't understand, what is there for the police to investigate? Where's Stan Holden, he knows it was an accident. It was an accident!" He almost whined, as his hands went to steady himself on one of the overstuffed chairs. "It was an accident, a terrible accident." His eyes didn't match what he was telling me. His eyes held fear, he didn't believe it was an accident either.

"Was it?" I went over to him, the man was a wreck. "What happened to Cab?

It took him a few moments to remember who I was talking about. Hank always thought about Hank first, I wondered if Charlene even came in second. They made a good pair. He waved his hand at me, as if I was an overbearing fan pushing for an autograph. "He left. He was a wild man. Cab made Walt nervous. Never would do anything Walt told him to do. He just took off one day."

"Just took off one day?" I repeated putting as much doubt in my voice as humanly possible. "Didn't you ever suspect that Walt wanted him gone, so he was gone?"

"No! Walt pays us well, really well; there is no need to argue with him." Hank sat down, sinking into the deep cushioned chair. "If we do what we are told, he leaves us alone. Cab got the message that his obnoxious behavior wasn't acceptable and left."

"Did Tip argue with Walt or was it with Emanuel for hitting on his girlfriend?" I stood above Hank closing in on his space, making him uncomfortable and it worked.

The anger in his voice came to the fore, loosening his tongue. "Tip was a fool. That girl was too smart for him, she caused a lot of problems. Always getting in the way, making suggestions on how to set up his car, playing with his equipment upgrades. As for Emanuel, the man hits on everything, ask Charlene! Walt was more angry at that woman for interfering with our racing. He was really angry at that!"

Perhaps realizing he'd said too much, he clammed up. He wouldn't answer any more questions on Tip or Walt. Finally, exasperated he said, "I'm getting my solicitor, you can't come here and badger me. I don't care who you are."

"Chief..." Hill started to say but she didn't need to continue, I knew once they ask for a lawyer, we had to back off. I waved my hand at her, that I understood.

"Fine Hank, but if you need me, I'll leave my card, you can get in touch with me. For god's sake be careful. You don't want to end up dead like the rest of them."

He looked at me, desperation was in his eyes. "Walt didn't know you were a cop, did he?"

"No, my brother never made it publicly known." I wondered what he was getting at.

"No, I'm sure he didn't." He stood up shaking himself, trying to get a foothold on his crumbling world. "He'd never have gone after your brother."

The statement hit me like a ton of bricks. Walt must have gotten a real shock when he learned Ray had someone covering his back. Walt probably thought we were just a bunch of orphaned kids, that I had left Nestor a broken crippled driver and would pose no threat. I headed for the door.

Hank called over, "Tell your brother not to race for the Roslukes." I nodded that I understood. Then softly he said, "Do you ever miss her?"

I turned back. "No," I lied and left.

Hill never said anything all the way back to the hover. She sat there pretending to be busy on her tabloid not looking at me. I had a feeling she knew I had lied. All I said was, "I was young." She just gave me one of her looks and I shut up.

I pushed the car's dash computer and entered a name. I sat for a few seconds. My rookie detective looked questioningly at me. "I have one more stop and then we'll head back. We don't want to be late for the race." She nodded going back to her notes.

We left the racing mansion area and headed more toward Nes City proper. I took a street filled with good sized houses, not mansions but more upper class neighborhoods. Professionals who worked in the capital bought these houses. Good sized, nicely done family homes. I pulled up to one. "I'll be right back."

"You need me to go with you?" Hill asked quietly.

"Nope." I got out, walking up the asphalt driveway, taking the narrow cement walkway up the neat, nicely mowed lawn to a small porch. I rang the doorbell. No roaring engine, just a nice ding-dong sound. An inner door opened, leaving me with only a glass outer door, looking at a young boy, maybe four years old. His big eyes took me in and he held up what looked like some action figure. I nodded, he smiled.

"Tommy, get away from there." A woman's voice came from behind him. She came to the door, pushing him behind her. She looked up to see who had rung the bell.

"Hello, Marian." I had trouble getting it out, glad I had slipped a blue pill into my mouth walking up the driveway.

She wasn't older, just changed. She wore her hair short, she'd been a long haired flower child when she was married to Ken Lonarer. Same blue intense eyes yet the innocence of her earlier years was gone. She was a mature woman, self-assured, conservatively dressed in a pretty flowered frock. Her eyes were wide now, as recognition came.

"Skip? Skip Brown?" She stammered, standing up straight. "Well, I'll be. How are you? Didn't know you were on planet." Ken Lonarer's wife had only been twenty years old when the accident had happened. They had a three month old baby. We'd always gotten along when I saw her at the tracks. She wasn't a big racing fan just madly in love with her husband. She'd never gotten along with Charlene but few of the girlfriends and wives did.

"I would have come sooner, I just..." I started to say but she waved her hands at me.

"Come in. Please, do not apologize. Please come in." She opened the door, keeping one hand on the small, struggling to get free boy.

She must have seen the relief on my face as she smiled while letting me through the opened door. I wouldn't have been surprised if she had slammed the door in my face. I followed her with the young boy in tow to a good sized country kitchen with a large table. The center held a vase of white daises. Family pictures were scattered everywhere. The refrigerator was covered with memos and kids schedules.

"A cup of java?" She asked, "You always had a cup with you at the racetrack."

I laughed, "No thanks, I have only a few minutes, my associate is waiting in the hover, we have to make the race."

"Yes, your brother may take the championship this year," she commented. So, she did still follow the races. "He's come close for the last few years. Good driver." Yep, she still followed the races. Somehow it pleased me, it showed a lack of bitterness on her part.

"I hope he takes it." I commented then nervously continued, "I wanted to come and finally tell you how sorry I was. I didn't get a chance after it happened. It was awhile before I could even talk."

"Please Skip. It is I that should apologize. Your brother told me how you have epileptic seizures. He told me not to tell anyone and I haven't. I was a young girl, just out of my teens. I was overwhelmed with grief. I was wrong. I never should have accused you the way I did. I think I went a little crazy."

I went over and hugged her and she hugged me back. "I'm still sorry, Marian. I really liked Ken."

"I know and he liked you too. He always envied you. He thought you were the best driver that ever lived," she said stepping back but still holding onto my hands. She dropped them, walking over to the table arranging her white flowers. "I'm not saying I didn't have a bad time. It took me a lot of time to recover and a lot of therapy sessions." She sat at the kitchen table, as if the bad memories were too much. Then she looked up, her face was happy, her eyes bright again. "But I'm happy now, Skip. My husband is a doctor with a highly successful practice at White Memorial Regional Hospital. We do a lot of charity work. We've three wonderful children." Marian motioned behind her, two other boys stood in the kitchen doorway with the younger one I'd seen at the door, watching their mother talk to this stranger. I could see Ken in the oldest boy. "My life is full. I've moved on. I hold no grudges."

"Thank you for seeing me, Marian. I should have come earlier but this is my first time back. I was too afraid of having a seizure." I went to turn to go.

"What do you do?" She asked. When I told her I was a cop on Fulton, she laughed. "I bet you're a damn good one too. You'd be good at anything you tried. Good luck, Skip. If you ever come back I'd like you to meet my husband. He was a big fan of yours, likes your brother too. We'll be rooting for him today."

I didn't say anything more. I was overwhelmed with this woman's generosity. It was more than I could have ever expected. It was worth the trip to Nestor, no matter how everything else came out. She followed me to the door, her and the kids waving good bye to me as I walked back down the driveway.

I got back into the cruiser. Hill looked up, "You alright?"

I took a deep breath, and sat for a second, realizing how much weight had come off my shoulders. I took a few moments just to enjoy the feeling.

"Yes, I am. Let's drop off this hover and catch a ride with Julie and Ray back to the hotel and get ready for the race. They should be leaving shortly. Let's get to that race."

Time to move on, I thought, *time to move on*.

Chapter 14

After dropping off the hover, my brother had just enough time to get us back to the hotel before he headed to the race track to get ready. We headed to our now roaring room, the grandstands were shouting again, the door opened to the sounds of engines and Peterson's car raced once again around the dining table.

We quickly changed, this time into some casual pants and shirts. The lobby, as I figured it would be, was thundering again with every screen pulsating with racing's latest report cards, spitting out the newest driver stats. The hotel's retail shops were blaring their promotional racing sounds and the fans were all buzzing about the upcoming race as they hurried out the back. Maybe out of respect for Tip's accident, the majority seemed to be dressed more conservatively. Most just had t-shirts and caps with decals and matching colored pants.

The hotel was devoid of reporters as this was the big event and the action was at the track. The noise from the raceway was at a high pitch. Cameras floated everywhere trying to take it all in, with reporters down below trying to make sense of it all to the billions of off-world viewers. Tip, unfortunately, was just a sad memory.

I saw one screen with Walt Rosluke almost crying about how he'd come to think of Tip as a son. His lawyer son Jared, who was obviously there to make sure his father didn't say anything wrong, put his arm around his father's shoulders and drew him sorrowfully away. Such a fake woeful picture, I wanted to puke.

Then the announcer turned to Hank Sims with Charlene holding on to his arm, the picture of beauty and sad grace, and asks the only Rosluke driver left how he feels. Hank, with tears in his eyes, matched only by his own wife's, tells the audience how *he's racing this race for Tip*. Again my stomach turned over. I threw my cotton candy in the trash, the sweetness only left a bitter taste in my mouth.

Julie had given me driver's passes. I hadn't time to get some VIP tickets from Ralph but then I wasn't sure I wanted to cope with the Roslukes. I'd deal with them later. Only owners got to give out VIP passes, so no clubhouse for us. Our seats were high up though; right near where the clubhouse was situated. We would get a good view of the race. The driver's passes also got us into the outer pits and I got to wish my brother good luck as he and the crew headed into the inner island. I saw Tony with Bill Connors, working frantically on his number 44 Hansin's Soap yellow striped car. Bill was intensely listening to the Tohegian's last minute advice, just like I use to. It was all so familiar it hurt. We watched as the last of the cars headed into the tunnel for the inner island. The sound of the roaring engines echoing in the enclosed tunnel was exhilarating, the rumbling filling the air with excitement. I could see the suspense building in Hill's face as she grabbed me to head for the grandstands.

Earlier, Julie had taken me aside, "If we don't see you after the race, I'll see you tonight." She had squeezed my arm when she saw me frown. "It's important I do this Skip. Wish us luck!" I could feel her anticipation; they had worked hard all year for this championship chance.

I had just reluctantly nodded. It wasn't the time to think of tonight, when the cars would be at the Jump stations awaiting transport, where we'd meet the Federal

Investigative Operation agents to go over Rosluke's cars. The idea didn't thrill me. I wished Julie would understand the danger of getting involved. Her anger at what they had done to my brother overshadowed her reasoning. My brother didn't say anything. I think he was still too embarrassed to argue with his wife. I could tell that he wasn't thrilled with the idea but he had a championship to win. I could tell he was blanking everything else out, concentrating on what strategy Julie was going over one more time with him.

"Come on," Hill's novice exhilaration pulled me along, "I don't want to miss anything." Boy oh boy, it didn't take long to get her hooked. She talked my ear off, giving me her opinion of each of the drivers. She believed my brother would take the Championship. I wish I had her confidence. At least now he was totally focused on winning. The difference in him was amazing. He looked his young self again, his concentration had returned. He might just pull it off. He just might.

We had to wait in line this time to take the public escalators up. Unlike the private VIP escalator, it took two different escalators to get us to our high seats and then to walk up and over near the center. I have to admit, I was huffing and puffing as I walked up the bleachers to our upper location. Of course, Hill had to comment on my being out of shape as she bounced up the steps.

To our right, we could see our VIP seats of the night before and the clubhouse behind them. I had Tony's binoculars. I could see the clubhouse was full. Watching out the clubhouse windows was Emanuel. He didn't look happy but then he always looked like he had bees up his ass.

I was surprised to see Cally next to him. Was Ralph trying to get Emanuel to marry her? I shuddered at the thought. Of course, they'd make a good pair. "I now pronounce Spoiled Child One and Spoiled Child Two as man and wife." The thought rolled around in my head. I would bet that Ralph had no idea that his daughter was seeing a Rosluke. He thought the Roslukes to be crass cheaters. I would bet this was his daughter's way of defying him. Oh, the tangled webs we weave. Cally was playing with fire and she'd get burnt bad. I suspected Emanuel was a little touched in the head. Probably got it from his grandmother's genes!

We had watched as each driver was brought to their car by going once around the track in open hovers. Each waved, giving their best smiles to the crowd. My brother was in one of the last cars as the hovers brought each driver, from least qualified to first, into the pit stops. Ray's car had been placed second just behind the Sonny Jistin's first pole car. Everything looked grand as each of their matching uniformed crew stood awaiting to get them settled once the anthem had been played. With my binoculars I could see Julie, smiling from ear to ear as Ray got down from the open hover. He hugged her and stood proudly next to his orange and silver striped car, hand over heart as the band played our Federation Anthem.

Hill had grabbed my arm, pointing down the track. A stage had been erected at the finish/start line. The whole stadium was standing as the loudspeakers were blaring the band's rendition of the federal ode, emphasizing it with patriotic red and green laser lights shot into the air. They had been tinted just right for daytime viewing, pulsating with the music.

Then the show was followed by a few choice words from the Nestor Racing President and then the Federation's Chancellor had to say a few words. The importance of this spectacle was evident as the pompous lizards weren't overly fond of humans but felt compelled to attend this event. A couple of billion of those impetuous uncontrollably emotional humanoids did add up, especially as potential customers. If the Bassodians were anything, they were the universe's sharpest business entrepreneurs.

The Chancellor was a big bubba, even for a Bassodian. He must have had a hard time in this gravity even with the cushioned lifting suit and boots. He carried an oxygen pack, as they need more air than we do. Although he was far below us, the huge lizard looked like a giant, his long tail sticking out of his formal Federation outfit. From what I heard the Bassodians could not understand human behavior, found us frivolous and stupid. They mostly ignored us, especially in the Federation Council, driving our representatives crazy when they ignored our votes. They often even forgot to include us in the roll call.

Bassodians were one of the oldest of the known races and they were also excellent scientific cosmos engineers. Most of the planets to be engineered had been brought into the sectors by them. They also manufactured the huge space crafts needed to pull them. I'd heard a rumor that they enjoyed our circuit racing because of the mechanical engineering of the cars but I found it hard to believe they could be interested in anything we did. Still, I was impressed that the Chancellor had come. His guttural words were being translated over the speakers, "Welcome to this fine race. Good luck to everyone. Praise be to our Federation!" Everyone gave a huge cheer that echoed around the arena and crescendoed as the drivers climbed into their autos.

As they disassembled the stage, the forty cars stood in pit road waiting. The screens overhead were constantly changing, profiling one driver after another. Then over the loud speaker the Bassodian yelled through a translator, "DRIVERS, START YOUR ENGINES."

Forty cars came alive, thunderous noise, even this high up you could feel it push on your body as the power behind the noise hit and grew in intensity. 300,000 fans added to the excitement. I looked over at Hill, she was mesmerized by it all. Her eyes followed the cars as they left pit row, two by two behind the hover pace car. The tension was mounting as the cars followed the official Strom Hover Craft once around the track; the sides of the hover with its neon pulsating lights radiating the word CHAMPIONSHIP RACE.

"Get ready racing fans! Get ready!" came over the loud speaker. Loud music with a lively beat got everyone swaying. No one was sitting, they were standing as the cars made the final turn and the pace car exited off the track. A deafening ROAR, ROAR. The cars took off. I found myself flooded with memories, the adrenaline starts to flow - it's you and the car against the best drivers in the cosmos. All the work your crew has put into the car is now put in your hands. The responsibility is overwhelming but the high is *so* high.

Hill was silent, she looked over at me. "You going to be all right?" Her eyes were full of concern.

"So far, so good," I ventured. I wasn't going to spend my life in fear. "I've taken my pill. It's time I faced this. Besides, I have you to take me down to the maintenance garage. You know the way now."

"Funny, Chief, real funny." Hill shook her head, "I think I'll get a hotdog."

"You're gonna get fat." I warned her, patting my own stomach. "While you're at it get me a cotton candy."

She laughed. "We come home fat or should I say in your case, fatter, Issam's gonna kill us. We will get lectured until our ears fall off."

I spent the afternoon explaining the race to Hill. It fascinated her to see the crew running around the car every time the driver needed to "pit". I explained how they changed the tires, filled the car with gasline, even cleaned the window shield. The crew raced against time, trying to get their car out of the pits as fast as they could. "In some ways the pit crew is just as important as the driver. It can make the difference obetween winning or losing." Hill listened intently, checking with her program as each driver raced by.

We were hoarse from yelling for my brother. We held our breath as he passed and got bumped, only to recover the car and race ahead. The last fifty laps were excruciatingly tense as one driver after another kept taking the lead. My brother needed to finish at least third to get the championship. He was in fifth going into the last ten laps. Stan Linkis, who drove for the Fairbank's team in the number 12 Tinner Pharmaceutical car, was just ahead of him. Ray also needed to beat Stan, who was ten points ahead of him in the overall standing. It was nerve wracking.

Then it happened. The front car driven by Sonny Jisten spun out, hitting Johnny Liliarnst the second car. Then they collided with the Marina Kikar number 20 Tunson Candies car, spinning into the wall. Chaos, as everyone scrambled to get out of the way. Most didn't make it. Smoke was billowing up along with dust from the cars going on the grass surrounding the track. The sound of bending metal and squealing tires was grating on the ears.

Hill took hold of my arm. "Where's your brother?"

I popped another blue pill in my mouth just in case, although I didn't feel the tension I get just before a seizure. I wasn't taking the chance. Hill, again shouted, "Where's your brother?"

I didn't know. Then I saw his number 15 bright orange car come speeding out of the cloud, along with several others. Relief flooded me. They switched the track from black to yellow. The whole track's center line went from black pavement to blinking yellow, meaning caution.

"How do they do that?" Hill asked.

"I don't know the particulars, but it's chemical," I answered her as all the cars slowed and the pace car came out again. Only twenty two cars remained. It took a while to clear the track. Then the pace car took one last lap, the cars roared behind it. My brother was now second but Stan Linkis, who despite being bumped, had survived the wreck and was first. "Here they come, folks. Last turn. They'll have one last lap 'til they get the white checkered flag and then it's a go to the finish. *HERE THEY COME*!" The announcer screamed in our ears. The crowd screamed all around us

I had kept track of how many times Ray had hit the pits. He had passed up a chance to get more gasline before the accident. He was gambling that he had enough fuel to see him to the finish line. He couldn't go in to pit now, it was his only way to keep up with Linkis.

Hill grabbed my arm as the pace car left the track and the cars roared ahead. My brother's golden Number 15 flew by us right on the tail of Linkis. "Go, Ray, Go," I screamed silently, praying he had enough fuel. I would bet his wife, Julie, was saying the same prayer.

He got ahead but Stan passed him again on the back stretch. They both came around the last turn screaming tires. Neck and neck they headed toward that checkered flag. I couldn't breathe. Just before the start/finish line Ray surged ahead! He'd done it! He'd not only won the race but he'd won the championship. Best of all, I saw him do it. I had my own victory this afternoon.

Hill was jumping up and down, screaming. I watched as Ray did swirls with his car. I watched as my brother's car went into victory lane where his crew awaited him with champagne and flowers. I saw him grab his wife, giving her a hard embrace. Ralph was there, shaking everyone's hand, the proud owner.

"What now?" Hill asked after they'd given him the trophy and the speeches were done. "Can we go see him?"

"No, he'll be busy. They have to inspect his car. After the race, the officials go over the top three cars to make sure everything is legal. He'll be awhile." I looked up at the screens. Hank Sims had come in tenth.

We grabbed a hamburg and a soda on the way out. "Hill, you're getting some bad eating habits," I sarcastically taunted my usually health-nut lieutenant. "Good thing you don't live here."

"Well, if you don't tell Capt. Issam, I won't tell him about the cotton candy," she countered.

Phil Ober came walking toward us. He looked great in his designer casual clothes that looked perfect on his work-out body. I'd bet no popcorn, hotdogs or cotton candy for him.

"Congratulations are in order on your brother's win," he patted my arm as if we were friendly acquaintances, which we were not! I let it slide, it wasn't worth the effort to be annoyed.

"Thank you. What's up?" I knew he wasn't here for no purpose. He had something on his mind, which I was sure wasn't going to make me happy.

"We're all set for tonight. Make sure you're there by midnight. We have it set up with the Jump station's management to have them put Rosluke's cars in station five. I'll see that Mrs. Brown gets there."

I threw my hamburg away, suddenly I didn't have an appetite anymore. If Phil was around more, I'd probably be thin.

Phil wasn't done, "Oh, and by the way, Hill, don't bother to check on Cab Tayler. He never made it home. I would bet he never made it off this planet. I ran an official inquiry on him. No one has heard from him since he quit. No draws on his accounts, no family or friend contact yet his place in Nes City was cleaned out and sold."

Hill looked at me for a reaction. I had none, not in front of "ole Phil" here.

"Hey Hill, how about some supper?" He winked at her. "Got a restaurant here that highlights local specialties. Come on, we have a few hours. Like old times."

"No thank you." Her voice was cold. "There was no good old time. I'm not interested."

He shrugged. "I sure thought there was."

"You would," she snipped at him and walked away.

I caught up with her. She looked at me, "I was young."

I didn't say a word.

We went over the files while waiting to leave for the station. It just didn't make sense. Nothing pointed to any real pattern. Were all the drivers involved? If they were smuggling in information for the arms dealers, were all the Roslukes involved? Why hadn't the FIOs found anything? Would Julie be able to find something they couldn't?

"I would bet it started three years ago," I commented. "That's when they started with Hank and Cab. They got both of them away from other teams either by blackmailing or giving them lots of money. Don't know which. If you look at the records, they never paid their drivers that much until first Hank then Cab and then Tip. Why pay them top dollar when they hardly break the top ten?"

"I agree." Hill flipped through the three files. "Also Emanuel never traveled with the teams before then. He was too busy leading the playboy style life, leaving the racing business to his father and lawyer brother. All of a sudden, he's interested? I don't think it was to please Gramma."

I couldn't figure it out, but it was getting late. We met Tony outside the Checkered Hotel. I brought him along to help Julie. He was a top mechanic and he had a stake in this too. My bet was Monty was just another Rosluke victim. We parked and met Phil outside Jump station five. It was an industrial Jump station, where cargo and goods were shipped. The whole area was in shadows being deserted at this time of night.

Phil took in Tony, "Good evening, Mr. Monticutticu, glad you could give us a hand," as if he'd been expecting the Tohegian. Roll with the punches, that was Phil.

We went in a back doorway. We entered a hanger type facility. The Rosluke cars were at one end. Two of Rosluke's goons were lying unconscious by the door. That was another point, no one but the Roslukes had bodyguards at the Jumps. Everyone else just depended on the station's security. Phil pointed to the black suited car's escorts, "They won't remember a thing. Their cellbuttons are being monitored, if they get a call we can handle it. We have five hours before they'll wake up. Can you do a complete scan in that time, Mrs. Brown?"

"Let's get going and see." Julie was there dressed in her mechanic's jumpsuit. My brother was with her. I should have guessed he wouldn't have let her come alone. I went up and congratulated him. He should have been out celebrating, not here. He looked like a new confident man, championships will do that for you. It's a confirmation of your skill and the celebration of your team. My chest tightened as I remembered mine. They had sent my second championship trophy to the hospital since I'd won despite the accident. The doctors and nurses had a little celebration for me. It had even meant something to me through the pain of recovery.

I looked over at my sister-in-law, worried this was too much for her. Julie, however, was in her element. She took charge, ordering the FIO mechanics as if she'd worked with them all along. They brought over the Xray machines, the hoists and the mechanical robots. Tony worked right by her side. They slowly methodically took the cars apart. She had the engines down to nuts and bolts. Every piece was examined and X rayed.

Phil had also brought along body shop experts. They took off the doors, took apart the seats. Every light, every fixture was taken apart. Ray and I helped where we could. The clock ticked and the goons slept the night away.

"What exactly are you looking for?" I asked Phil. Hill had gone to get us some java. The FIO had a supply cruiser out by the door and had set up a type of make shift canteen. Leave it to the Feds, they had all the comforts.

"It will look like a circuit module. We are guessing probably the size of your thumb. It will contain data on the drop locations for the weaponry and account numbers to pay for them. The Roslukes, we figure, are just the intermediaries; the means to get this info out to carriers. We don't think they're actually involved in the weapon selling themselves. The info modules give out a low, very low energy pulse. We have scanners but so far nothing. They should stand out, but so far nothing."

I just shook my head. The war seemed far away, on the other side of our Universe. Our sector was insignificant, sparsely populated. We hardly got noticed by the Federation. Humans were too new to the picture. Perhaps that made us attractive to smugglers. Perhaps they'd leave us alone if we could expose this.

At four thirty, the cars were completely put back together. They had found nothing. The cars were clean. Julie looked tired and discouraged. Ray had his arm around her, "I need to get you home," he told her.

"Julie, you did your best. If there is nothing, there is nothing," I tried to console her. "It happens all the time in investigations. It helps to eliminate one more part of the puzzle."

Phil was over making sure everything was cleaned up. He had his medical team checking on Rosluke's guards. I almost felt sorry for him, almost, his shoulders slouched in discouragement.

Julie wasn't happy either. "They are high powered engines. Even in some sense better than Rays but they're not set up right." She quietly told me, a frown gracing her small petite face. "I'll tell you one thing, Skip, they won't win with them."

"How so?" She'd gotten my full attention.

"They have regulators on the gasline flow valves. The car will experience first too rich a flow then be cut off, slowing it down but at times seeming to be fast."

"Wouldn't the track officials see that?" I asked, skeptical despite knowing Julie was an expert, it just didn't make sense.

"Why would they ever see it?" she pointed out. "They aren't going to be in the top three. Not set up like that and the regulators aren't illegal, even if they did. They won't make the cars win!"

Hill had been listening. "Something is wrong here." An understatement, but we shut up as Phil had returned.

"Thank you, Mrs. Brown. I will just advise you again, that this is Federation business and will not ever be discussed without our permission. Do you fully understand?"

Julie nodded, "I'm sorry we did not find anything."

Phil just nodded. We all left, heading back to our hovers.

"Get some sleep," I told my pregnant sister-in-law.

"I'll be able to sleep on the Jump out of Nestor. We leave early tomorrow." She corrected herself, "I mean today," realizing the new day was upon us. "In just a few hours, to be exact. Give Killa our best. We'll visit soon. The season will be over with the All Star Race."

I hugged her and my brother. I watched them leave. The sun would be up soon. We took Tony out to breakfast. We made a sad tired threesome at a local diner I was glad to see still existed. It had been a favorite haunt of mine.

"Chief, we need to think this through. Even I understand what Julie was telling you. You don't set up a car to lose."

"They don't want the officials to inspect the cars," Tony speculated. His eyes were tired. "Why wouldn't they want the officials inspecting them if there is nothing wrong with them? The regulators aren't illegal, stupid but not illegal. We didn't find anything else. Why pay top dollar for top drivers to lose?"

I shook my head in dismay. We weren't getting something. The sun was full up when Tony left us at the hotel's entrance. The lobby was full of people checking out. I couldn't think of anything more. It was time to go home. Perhaps we could regroup with the rest of my detectives, maybe a fresh look was needed.

We headed up to our room. "Hill, get us a Jump ticket as soon as you can."

She nodded, "I can't help but feel we're missing something obvious. It can't be the drivers, they are screened." She pressed the fob to open the door. The lights were on, the screen blaring away. We walked into two guns pointed at us. Emanuel was there also. Cally was whimpering on our couch sporting a bloody nose and a swollen lip.

"About time you got your asses back here," Emanuel smirked. "Celebrating the win?"

"You know, I'm going to have to contact hotel management. They have lousy security in this place. The scum that gets in." I pointed my finger at him.

For my sarcasm I got a punch in my gut. That boy could not take a joke.

Chapter 15

Hill went to grab me as I fell but Emanuel reached over and slapped her hard, sending her reeling back. "Don't interfere you cheap whore," he snarled at her. I was gonna kill him. That coward.

Hill staggered back catching herself on the large projection screen that lay on the back wall. Through my pain, I saw her reach around the rear of the televiewer. She was getting the bug she'd put there, getting it away from the noise the video of the replay of the race was making. It went into her pant's pocket and she moved closer to me until one of the goons pointed his gun at her. I was hoping someone was listening. I had no idea if the federal agents were also packing to go home. It would be just our luck that Phil wouldn't be eavesdropping.

"You're a bastard," I yelled at Emanuel, getting him to take his attention off Hill. The guard that had been pointing his gun at Hill switched it to me. The other muscle guy came over and reached in and got my gun. They didn't even consider Hill would have one. Stupid idiots, thank god.

"Now is that nice language for the Chief of Police?" the spoiled idiot son taunted me. "No matter what my father says, you're just a low life government worker. At least Stan Holden knows enough to be bought," he snickered. I needed to get him talking. Punks like him usually were so stuck on themselves that bragging came natural to them. Perhaps I could find out the truth and stall for time. Please be listening, Phil.

"At least I'm not a spoiled little boy," I backed up as I said it, just missing his fist. Emanuel's eyes were glistening, the look of the insane. The hate he had for me shown right through his cold stare. I'd seen the same eyes on other murderers. Their lack of empathy and their self-centered personality made them immune to any type of morals or of any type of reasoning with. I had no doubt he planned to murder me. I was just an annoyance, an insect to be stepped on.

"You're just a stupid low paid government worker, like I said." He looked over a Cally who was whining. "Shut up you conniving bitch or I'll have them hit you again."

I was so mad, I had trouble not to just charge him despite the goons pointing their guns at me. "Why are you doing that to her?" I yelled at him. "Ralph will kill you."

"*Ralph, Ralph*, you sound like my father." He walked over to Cally pulling her head up by her hair. "You were playing me, weren't you, sweetheart. You were working with the Chief here. Were you hoping he'd get me to give him your videos? Not to show your father?" His laughter washed over the scared girl, who cowered even further into the couch.

"She isn't," I told him, but he wasn't listening. A one-track mind, with no regard for what was out of his realm of thinking. Nothing I was going to say would sink in to his thick dumbbell brain. He slapped Cally across the face again. I took a step towards him and felt the guard's gun in my ribs. I stopped but glared at Emanuel, who wickedly grinned at me.

"She's so stupid. Caught her in my office going through my desk." He was totally insane. "I don't like being played for a patsy." He patted her cheek, then slapped her hard again.

"I wasn't going through your desk," she pleaded., sobbing uncontrollably. "I was looking for something to write on."

I didn't believe her, she'd probably been after something. I wondered if he was blackmailing her with that video he had mentioned. It made sense, he had some kind of hold over her. What video was he talking about? Blackmail seemed to be his expertise, his modus operandi. *The weapon of feeble cowards.* He didn't believe Cally was innocent of looking for a piece of paper either, smacking her across the face again.

I tried to keep calm, having a seizure would not be good. I felt myself relax. I'd been in numerous police situations, some really brutal and if I could handle those, I could manage here. He was nothing but a dumb spoiled brat, but a dangerous one I reminded myself. A murderer.

"Hey, boss, we need to get going, you got to meet your father at the station soon. The Jump's gonna leave." The goon was nervously fidgeting, shifting from one foot to the other. It was a sign that Emanuel wasn't in charge, that daddy Walt scared them more.

"Yeh, right." He looked at me, the smile was so evil, I felt the hair stand up on the back of my neck. "You see Chief, you all are going to join poor ole Cab. You are all going to be dump fodder." He cackled as if he was picturing the whole thing in his sick mind. He'd probably tortured animals in his youth, he fit the profile.

"You're going to shoot us, here!" I almost laughed, "I don't think even you're that stupid. Although with you, it might be about right. If you're smart, you'll leave us alone and run to daddy."

"I not stupid!" He was going to come over and punch me again but the goon interfered.

"Come on," our nervous guard complained. "Mr. Rosluke don't like us to be late. If we miss the Jump again. Remember his warning! He was real mad last time. It ain't good to make him mad."

"Alright!" He turned back to Cally pointing at the terrified girl, "Make sure your gun is on optimal stun and shoot her first, then these two. Put them in those three crates. Make sure the tops are closed tight. We'll get rid of them at the dump. I brought the key to the crusher." I hadn't notice the good sized storage crates that were stashed by the table. They had wheels, easy to roll out of the hotel. No questions asked.

I took a wild guess, "Your father doesn't know what you're doing does he? He won't like you killing Ralph's daughter." I figured Walt could care less about me, he'd taken care of cops before, he would just get my superintendent, Stan Holden, to cover for him. I was just an inconvenience. Hill, collateral damage. Walt would know, however, of Ralph's influence on Nestor. He hadn't been able to stop Tony's police complaint when Attenson had backed him. Ralph's panic over his daughter wouldn't be something Walt would dare stir up."

"My father," Emanuel's eyes again glassed over, "he's an old man. He gets upset then realizes it's for the best. My Gramma has more balls than him. Like that Waser girl, caused so much problems. What could I do? She was too nosy. The bitch, she was going to ruin everything. Got Tip all upset."

So Cab was the first followed by Caroline Waser, I thought. It gets easier, especially when you don't get caught. "Why Monty?" I asked, "he wasn't a threat to you."

"Please," he dismissed me with his hand. "He complained to Stan. He came over to the police department demanding an investigation. Claimed that she didn't drink. Claimed she was a "good" girl. Please! There is no such thing." Emanuel looked at Cally,

"Right? You bitch!" he demanded of her. She only sobbed. He smirked, "Monty told Stan what a good Tohegian Caroline was. A true Tohegian. Then he came over to our garage and got Tip all upset. If he'd kept his nose clean, I wouldn't have killed him. Tip wouldn't let it go either. He was going to tell you everything! Like that smart university bitch was worth it!"

"You're just lucky your father could cover your tracks." I pointed a finger at him, "you're sloppy but daddy got the police to lose the evidence or say there was evidence when there wasn't. There was no suicide note, was there?"

"Oh, such a smart cop!" He actually chuckled. His beady little eyes sparkled thinking himself so intelligent. He puckered his lips, blowing me a goodbye kiss. "Soon to be a dead cop, that no one can find. Where are the pictures you took of Tip's car? Give me your tablet, Stan says you haven't sent any pics over the lines. Give or you'll watch me torture your girlfriend. I know your kind, do-gooders, tough cop aren't you? We'll see how tough you really are. The garbage crusher doesn't care who you are or how tough you are! Bones are bones."

I knew he would think nothing of torturing Hill. They might discover her gun before she'd get a chance to use it. Better to stall for time. I didn't take any pictures, though I wish I had. I thought I'd have plenty of time at the police impoundment area later. I knew he wouldn't believe me anyway. Just like Cally, the truth would get me nowhere. So I lied, "Don't touch her, it's in my bedroom." I must have been convincing, putting as much whining in my voice as I could. Let the punk think he scared me.

"Go with him. Get them. Hurry up!" He motioned to one of the brutes to go with me. Pointing at the other guy, he said, "Shoot her!"

I saw him point the stun gun at Cally. She went to scream but slouched down on the couch as the electro charge hit her. No one was paying attention to bimbo Hill. I saw the look she gave me, it was now or never. She reached for her gun as the bruiser turned to her. I spun around and plowed into my escort. We both went down. I heard Hill's gun go off. I heard a cry on my way down. I fell on top of my attacker.

My thug hit the floor hard. I butt headed his arm, watching him let go of his gun. At the same time, I took my elbow and hit him square in the windpipe. His eyes rolled back, he went slumping into oblivion. I jumped up grabbing his gun.

Hill had both of the others covered. Emanuel was screaming at the wounded bodyguard to charge her, even though the man was bleeding from his shoulder where Hill had shot him. The door exploded inward ending all conversations as FIO agents swarmed into the room.

"About time," I moaned. Every inch of my body ached, my lip was bleeding or maybe it was my nose. Phil handed me a cloth.

"I couldn't count on both those assholes having their guns on stun. I couldn't break it down in time to shoot them before they shot you." Phil put his gun back in its holster, letting the other agents take the three into custody and he called an ambulance for Cally.

"Do you know who I am?" Emanuel screamed, struggling as the agents put him in handcuffs. I thought they looked very good on him, went well with his expensive clothes.

"Yeah, pretty boy. Someone who's going to jail." Phil smirked, infuriating Emanuel even more. Suddenly, I liked Phil.

When they'd taken them out. I turned and thanked him, even though the words didn't want to come out. Hill pointed to the large screen. "Look, it's your brother. He's at the Jump station with Julie, what's his name is interviewing them."

Sure enough, Merv had cornered my brother. "So, how did it feel to have your brother see you win? I don't know if our viewers know, his brother is Skip Brown. The greatest rookie ever to race!"

Well I'd have to thank Merv for that plug. My brother, the current champion, was beaming, "It was the best having him here. He's my biggest inspiration."

I reached into my pocket and got a blue pill. Too many emotions were bubbling up.

Hill pointed to the screen. "Your brother is carrying his helmet, is that a backup helmet that Julie is holding? Why don't they just ship them with the cars?"

"Yeah, those are his helmets. They have to carry them themselves," I told her, "they're too valuable. Each one matches his DNA, very hard to replace. Then it hit us both at the same time. "That's it!"

"What's it!" Phil threw himself between us. "What!"

"The helmets! The chip is in the helmet. That's why they need the drivers, they'd need their DNA brain waves to download. They wouldn't want them to win because the track checks the car while the driver has his helmet on! The track inspectors might have noticed an extra chip. God, I feel stupid!"

"Let me guess. Because of who they are, the helmets aren't scanned at the Jump stations. That's why they get top drivers, no one questions their integrity." Phil had gotten the idea.

"Even if the helmets were scanned, which they probably aren't, the helmets are too complicated. The track official may see something different but not your Jump scanners. It would look just like part of the helmet's electronics. That's why he killed Caroline. She was a biochemist. She knew when she played with Tip's helmet. She knew!"

"Rosluke is leaving." Hill urgently interjected. "If he finds out Emanuel has been arrested, especially since they aren't going to show up, he'll destroy Hank's helmets."

"Let's go." Phil headed for the door. We ran after him. He was speaking in his cell, giving instructions to his agents. "They'll meet us at the station. We have a blackout, we don't want to alert your superintendent Stan."

We ran out the front. There was a long line waiting for taxis. People were going home. Phil ran to the head of the line waving his FIO badge. "Sorry, folks. Federal agents, urgent business." The crowd didn't care, they started yelling and shoving us.

We heard a loud beep. A taxi cab had pulled in front of the disputed cab. We saw the driver waving. Hill ran over dragging Phil and me along with her. We jumped into the cab. Phil took out his badge and started waving it. "Federal Business..." he started to blurt out but Hill shut him down with her hand. "There's no need, we know this guy."

I couldn't believe it. Our first cab driver, Ni Li, turned around. "Race fans not friendly when you cut the line," his smile as big as ever. "You need quick ride pretty lady?"

Phil again pushed his badge in his face, he didn't like his former student stealing his thunder, "Federal Investigative Operative business, step on it, fast, to Nes' Jump station."

Ni looked at us. "How many are there of you? Hey, congrats on your brother's win." I nodded my thanks.

"Just get us there, hurry!" Hill loudly urged him.

The hover screeched, we were thrown back against the seat. Ni's unrealized racing career was forging to the fore. Phil talked into his cell. "I'm clearing the way. Don't worry about being stopped." Ni Li smiled even wider. Only the FIO, I thought. I saw the racing glow on Ni's face in the front mirror as he stepped on it. He probably imagined himself on Strom Racetrack. He was really pushing it. I noticed Hill close her eyes and grab onto her seat belt, bracing for an accident. To Li Ni's credit, we didn't hit anything as we traversed the crowded Nes streets. Maybe I'd introduce him to Ralph Attenson.

We got to the station in short order. We rushed out. "Hey!" came from the cab, "don't forget to pay me!"

Hill rushed back, giving him his fare plus. She caught up with us. "Thanks, Hill." Phil commented. "We'll reimburse you."

"Sure, Phil, just like old times. I won't hold my breath," my sarcastic rookie lieutenant dryly commented getting a frown from the agent but getting a smile from me.

"They tell me they're on platform 22. It's a private class cabin on the back of a loaded regular Jump. It is scheduled to leave in ten minutes, I've got a hold on it but I'm afraid Walt's going to get nervous. We've been blocking all calls into him. If he hears from Emanuel, he'll know. The Jump officials are also giving me a hard time. It's a complicated Jump to Castor, they don't want to miss their window connection.

We reached the entrance to the platform. We could see they'd already closed the inner doors. We stood just outside the Jump cabin. I could hear Walt as they hadn't locked it air tight yet. He was nervous and annoyed. "Where the hell are they? He's going to miss the Jump again. I've had it with that boy."

"Dad, we really have to get going." It was the Jared, the lawyer boy. "We have to make that deadline, they get angry if we aren't there on time. Can't you get the pilot to get us hooked up?"

It was Hank Sims' voice, "Do you really need me to go with you?" He was half whining. "I don't care for them. They scare me. I can wait for Emanuel and we can catch a later Jump. It's only the All Star Race. My wife has a later Jump."

"Shut up, Hank," It was Walt. "Don't go sounding like Cab. You know we need you to help download, so suck it up like a man."

Phil looked at me. "Ready?"

"Yup." Hank spoke into his cell. The inner doors flew open. They were all there, grumpy Gramma too. The two bodyguards were reading a newspaper and were taken completely by surprise.

"Federal Agents. You're all under arrest." Phil had his gun pointed at the guards. They immediately put up their hands. The goons weren't supposed to be able to carry their guns on through security, but I could tell that they had from the bulge in their jackets. Still, fighting armed FIO agents was not an option.

"Shoot them!" Gramma yelled waving her goddamn cane. "Help! Help! Security." God I wanted to shoot her. She started to stand but I shoved her back into the seat. Her face was full of outrage.

It was the lawyer who brought out a small handgun. I realized it was Monty's antique Tohegian gun. They hadn't recognized it in the security Jump scanners as a weapon. He pointed it not at us but at Hank. Without Hank it would be almost impossible to access the helmet. Hank saw it, a look of pure horror crossed his face. He started to put up his hands. Hill lunged across the compartment just as the gun fired. He got two quick shots off. They hit her square in the chest. I heard her gasp and collapse.

Phil lasered the son before I could even get a shot off. I saw a burn hole appear in Jared's chest. I rushed over to Hill. Other agents came flooding in. I heard Phil call for assistance as I rushed over to my wounded detective. "Hill," I moaned, as I knelt next to her. Her eyes were closed as if she was in pain. "Hold on, help is coming, we'll get you to the hospital." I knew it had to be bad, the bullets had hit her square in the chest at fairly close range.

It was Phil, who was kneeling next to me with a first aid kit in his hand that said, "Where did she get hit?"

I pointed to her chest but there wasn't any blood, just holes. Phil reached over ripping her blouse. She was wearing a police protective vest! A damn bullet proof vest. He laughed. Her eyes slowly opened. I helped her sit up. She'd be sore tomorrow but she's alive today.

"God that hurt," she exclaimed, gasping for breath. I gathered they didn't teach you that in the academy. The vests were really built for a regular gun's burst of energy, absorbing a lot of it. Thank goodness they also stopped projectiles.

"Yeah, it hurts." I knew, I'd been shot a few times. It's the ones that the vest doesn't stop that hurt even more. "Whatever were you wearing a vest for? Did you wear that all night at the warehouse?"

"It's regulations, Chief!" the old Hill was back, annoyed as all hell at me. "I didn't have time to take it off before going back to the room." She was gasping, talking between breathes.

"Right!" I smiled. "Right you are, Hill." I would have hugged her, but I knew it would hurt, her chest was going to be very sore tomorrow.

We ended up at the hospital. It was also regulations that once shot you get checked out, vest or not. As usual it was a long time waiting as they needed all her information and that needed to come from Fulton. I finally tapped into the private line and speeded things up. Phil noted my rule breaking but said not a word..

I was waiting for Hill in the outer reception area when I saw Ralph. He had aged in the few hours since I'd seen him. He'd been crying, his eyes red, his nose running. "Did you see her?" he asked me, grabbing onto my arm to steady himself. "Did you see what he did to her?"

"Yes. They say she'll fully recover," I tried to reassure him. He looked like he was going to collapse. Gone was the self-assured owner, replaced by the worried father.

"That son of a bitch," his anger came swarming out. "I'll see him dead. I'll kill him myself with my bare hands!" His face flushed red, his eyes were bulging in anger.

"Ralph, the police will take care of it." I sat him down, how many victim's relatives had I said that to. "Concentrate on Cally. She needs you. The law will prosecute him and his family to the fullest. The Federals are involved, Walt won't be able to buy his way out of this."

"Promise me Skip, promise me he'll pay, pay dearly." He was clutching my arm.

"We'll do everything to make sure he never does it to anyone else." I firmly assured him and I meant it. He saw that I did and nodded.

Marcie came walking in. She wasn't in much better shape than Ralph. She'd been crying. Cally's lover looked haggard, a real mess of worry. She didn't even recognize who I was, her eyes went unseeing right past me to settle on Ralph.

To my surprise Ralph went over and let her cry on his shoulder. "Don't worry, she's going to be fine. I blame myself. I'll leave you two alone. I know when I'm wrong. I've been a goddamn old fool. The doctors say she'll be able to come home tomorrow. I'll let you take care of her, I'll be heading out to join my drivers on Castor."

Marcie just cried harder, clinging to Ralph.

Hill was finally ready. They had given her some pain pills so it wasn't hurting too bad. She'd be sporting a huge purple chest bruise tomorrow. We rode in silence through the capital city. Racing banners still covered the skies, roaring engines could still be heard from the amateur drivers whose turn it was to use the track. The circuit drivers would be practicing on Castor for the All Star Race. Hank Sims would not be one of them. I wondered if Charlene would be there, would she stick with Hank or dump him like she did me? I was betting on the later.

We didn't put the windows down, but I knew the smell of gasline was still permeating the air. This time my Lieutenant didn't even notice the antics of the city. She didn't look out the windows. Her thoughts were far away. Give her a few years in homicide and it wouldn't bother her so much. Wrong or right, she'd become somewhat immune to the stupidity and brutality of the villains we sought to stop and put away. The victims would all get clouded in together. You never stopped caring, but a numbness would set in or you'd go crazy.

I dropped her off at the hotel. "Our Jump is tonight. I have some things I have to take care of before we leave. Can you manage to get our stuff to the station? I'll meet you there. I'm meeting Phil at the police station and we're arresting Stan. I should be present." I was dreading it but I had to be there.

"I'm fine. Just a little sore and the doctors gave me something for the pain," she assured me. "Good luck. See you later, I'll send Issam and Killa notes that we are heading home." That was my efficient rookie, Hill was back to normal. I noticed she was moving slow though, the aches and pains of being a cop.

I heard the sound of engines roaring as the busboy opened the lobby door for her. She looked back, smiled and shrugged. I waved. After all this was Nestor.

Chapter 16

The rest of the morning went better than I had anticipated, or dreaded really. It's the worst scenario for a cop to find another cop is the crook. Stan Holden acted almost relieved that he'd been caught, which just confirmed my feeling that he found himself in a web of deceit and the more he twisted the more he got tangled. His awe of the Rosluke family, one of the oldest and most powerful racing families on Nestor, had blinded him to their faults and before he knew it he was involved in a murder. His comment of "I didn't sign on for murder but they had me and I didn't know what to do," confirmed what I thought. He originally had only been involved with the transmitting of illegal information, of abetting the illegal arms deals. The feds would take it from here; it was a federation offense, local sector law took a back seat. It was out of my hands. Even the murders were being handled by the Feds.

I had been right, there had been no suicide note. Monty, who always kept his unloaded pistol in a glass case behind his desk, gave Emanuel the idea to shoot him with his own gun. Phil assured me that they were searching the son's computer record for purchase of the antique ammo. I had no doubt they'd find the record. Emanuel thought he'd have nothing to worry about, so I'm sure he hadn't hidden his computer purchases. At any rate, he wasn't that smart, it had been Walt who'd cover his son's tracks. I doubted the father thought about the bullets being ordered by his stupid spoiled son.

Emanuel had no idea the gun was worth anything. But Jared was a different story. I guess the lawyer son, Jared, couldn't resist the valuable antique gun. After all, who would ever know, especially after the deportation of Tony that Stan was arranging. Holden had admitted that he forged Caroline Waser's lab results. She didn't have alcohol in her system, she had drugs pumped into her and been pushed over the cliff. They even had the sense to remove the guard rails and put them back, looking like she'd sailed over them.

Tip's car was rigged. The FIO agents were looking for the mechanics that did it, probably brought from off sector. The rebels had deep pockets and deep influence. Phil assured us they'd find them. I sure hoped so, Tip didn't deserve what was done to him. Everyone involved should be brought to justice.

Hank Sims was waiting on his lawyer. He was shook up though, he realized how close he'd come to being another dead Rosluke driver. He'd promised to cooperate. Hank had acted shocked that it was weapon smuggling that the Roslukes were into. He hadn't asked Rosluke what it was all about and hadn't wanted to know what was actually going on. I wondered how much of a plea bargain Phil would cut with him.

Phil Ober actually thanked me. He walked me out of the Nes' police station, which, by the way, is far more modern than Fulton Station. Such is life.

Emanuel was telling the FIO all they needed to know. The pampered spoiled youngest Rosluke son had not held up well under interrogation even with a lawyer present. His father, Walt, had been harder to crack but had eventually broken down, especially after learning that his oldest son had died of his gun wounds. Phil also told me they had recovered the tow truck and Tip's burnt up car. They had their forensic experts going over it. It looked promising that they would be able to retrieve some of the evidence of tampering with the car. He'd send me the report including what they found in the helmets; though not the specifics he admitted.

Grumpy Gramma was given the option of a nursing home or jail. She's at Country Manor and I'd make sure she remained there. I wasn't the least bit surprised to find out she helped Emanuel plan everything. Being old doesn't excuse culpability. Although their lawyers claimed senility, I knew better. The woman was evil!

"I hope we can work together again," Phil commented, slapping me on the back. "And of course, Hill too!" He smiled.

"No," I quite simply said. He just smiled again. Damn cocky FIO.

"Well maybe I'll see you on Fulton sometime." He held his hand out to shake.

I hoped not. Being a diplomat, Hill would have been surprised at me, I shook his hand and walked away without comment. I took the underground to the outskirts of Nes listening the whole while to the recap of the race. They had some nice pictures of my brother and even Julie was being praised. Glad to see that. Too often the mechanics and crew are forgotten.

It wasn't a long walk to St. Germaine's monastery. I enjoyed the fresh air. I went through the gates up to the huge castle type stone building. I walked up the granite wide steps through to the church which lay in the front. They actually had a saint for racing, this was Nestor after all, and Saint Germaine took center stage in back of the altar. The marble statue was dressed like an old fashioned racer. He looked down on a myriad of children sitting at his feet.

When I had been young and come here with my uncle, I had pictured one of the children as me. Racing had been the salvation for the pain of my parent's death and I was grateful that I'd had it and my Uncle Jack. He had continued what our parents had always stressed; honesty and hard work. He had taught me the principles for being a good racer but he'd also taught me the principles of being a good cop. My mother would have been proud of her brother. She had been smuggled out with him and their mother when they were both young. Killa had been with them, the four running away from my Laositian grandfather. Running away from the horror of human slavery.

The brown robed monk who'd been lighting the candles came over, seeing me looking at the statue. "Can I help you?" he asked, his modest sandals clicking on the stone floor.

"You already have, you already have," I admitted, thinking of the comparison of Stan Holden and myself. The monk smiled and went back to lighting the candles.

I walked through to the back where there was another building; a large mausoleum. It had a circular driveway coming to its side. There was a hearse there loading a casket into it. I walked up seeing Tony talking to the driver.

"Bombista conga miea," he came over and embraced me. "I so glad you came. I'm taking him home now. He will be buried on the Tohegian plains and join our ancestors."

"That is a good thing," I told him. "Are you staying on Casey?"

"Yes, I don't belong here without him." He already looked better, the lines of worry had already left his face. Sadness still hung about him, but now there was also a sense of peace.

I handed him a package. "This belongs to your family. The police don't need it, they have enough evidence." It was Monty's antique Tohegian pistol. He unwrapped it, holding the old fashioned rare bone handle, looking long and hard before a tear fell on his cheek. He put it back in the case, wrapping it up carefully to go home. I didn't mention that the shooter had died so they didn't have to use it to prosecute him.

"My humble thanks." He hugged me one more time before getting in the hearse and I watched him leave.

I walked into the mausoleum. It was huge. It wasn't far to my parents' markers. I stood in front of "*James and Helen Masters*" which lay about half way up the wall. My Uncle Jack's ashes lay next to them, "*John Brown*". It was the first time I had been here to see his ashes. I belonged to both names, belonged to both the heritages they had left me.

"So this is where they were buried?" Hill was standing behind me. "You took your uncle's name?"

"Yes, it was a name he had taken and he needed to hide us. So we became *Brown*. By the way, what are you doing here?" I turned giving her my most famous angry stare, "How did you know where to find me?"

She reached into my jacket pocket. A small metal disc lay in her hand. "You really need to be more diligent." She was lecturing me! "You also forgot your Jump pills." She held out her hand, giving me a bottle of water to take them with. I took them. "I figured I better find you, the pills have to be taken at least a couple of hours before we Jump. Got your other pills?" Was Killa giving her lessons?

She also handed me a small memory chip. "This is your brother's original tape before they doctored it. It shows him running from the girl. This is everything. I wiped out all records of the incident. I don't know if your brother would like it or not. Or you can just destroy it."

"How did you...." I started to say.

"He owes me," she embarrassingly grinned. "Let us leave it at that."

We looked at each other, both saying at the same time, "We were young!"

She walked over to the far wall. Half way up the wall was Johnny Peterson's marker. Just like my parents it was unpretentious and simple. No indication of his famous racing stature. "No matter how great we are, we all end up the same." She handed me my small overnight bag. "Let's get home."

****

The All Star Race was just finishing. Ray had come in third. It was early morning. They were racing on Castor Speedway. It was a late afternoon race there, Castor was one of the planets that had been engineered within an asteroid belt and hadn't been totally matched to Federation Time. Still, the inconvenience of having to get up early on my day off was well worth it. I could have disked it but there was something about seeing the race as it was happening. It was the closest I could come to sharing it with Ray.

Killa was in the kitchen. She had come up to watch the race with me and then had disappeared into the galley. I heard the bell buzz. Someone was at the elevator cellbutton, probably a resident or vendor. She'd handle it.

The dogs suddenly picked up their ears and raced out of the room. Someone was coming up. Crap. I was in my sweats. I headed toward the bedroom when I heard, "Hi guys, brought you something."

"Hill, what are you doing here?" I walked over, she was standing in front of the elevators with several packages.

"I read that eating lots of protein, along with lots of fiber, helps epileptics. Keeping the body in balance is important." Before I could say anything she continued, "I talked to Killa..."

"You talked to Killa!" This was getting much worse.

"And I brought over some eggs and green veggies." She handed a bag to Killa.

"I don't like eggs," but I might as well not have said anything because I was ignored.

"It will be good for you. A nice vegetable omelet for lunch." Killa headed back into the kitchen.

"Wait...." I yelled after her but Hill wasn't done.

"I also brought the dogs two nice big bones. And I brought you these."

She handed me the bag with the neon blinking clothes. She had even included the damn sandals! So she had gotten them out of the garbage! "Why the hell did you get these?" I demanded.

"It'll remind you of Nestor." She laughed as she held them up for Killa to see. "He looked really dashing in these."

Killa looked at me. "You wore those?" Her face lite up with laughter and I couldn't help but laugh too.

"Yeah, I was really dashing," I told my old nursemaid. I hadn't seen her laugh in a long time. Looking at the dog bones, "they only get dry food," I exasperatingly told Hill. "Hibernia Hounds have finicky stomachs. Of course, if you're willing to pick up the mess. Last time it kept the dumpster busy for a week..."

"They are not real bones!" she explained. "They're specially made. The vet said it would do their teeth good, the bones are made for preventing stomach ailments." She smiled at me, "They can have it right after their walk."

"Walk? No don't say that!" It was too late, the dogs know that word. They started bouncing around. When I say bouncing, it means knocking over furniture, sliding into walls, knocking me on my keister. "Hill!" I growled bringing them to a halt, they know that tone of voice, it means trouble. They immediately sat, but their eyes were following me, their tails swishing frantically on the ground behind them. Their heads tilted at me. Walks were not to be denied.

"I want to see that jogging, I mean walking path." She followed the dogs over to where their harnesses hung. They were all excited. "Come on, Chief, get into your sneakers. I do presume you have jogging sneakers?"

"I have sneakers, whether they jog or not, I don't know," I growled at her. The dogs were so energized, they were going on a walk!

She got them into their harnesses. "Are these remote harnesses fully charged?" She was looking at the gauges on the leash holder. "Are these new?"

"No, but they were expensive. I just haven't had time to use them." Why was I feeling so guilty, the dogs had their run up on the roof.

Killa was in on the conspiracy. "I'll have lunch ready when you come back," she smiled the same conspiratorial grin Hill had. Killa's light purple eyes sparkled mischievously, her ears twitched.

If looks could kill, they'd both be dead. I got my shoes on as the dogs jumped all around me. I showed Hill the harness controls, "you press the button and it lets the dogs go. Don't let it get out of range because you'll never catch them. Got it?"

"Sure. See ya Killa." Hill waved as the four of us got in the elevator. The dogs sat obediently as I had taught them. In the small area, if they stood, the wagging of their tails could hurt. They were big dogs with big tails. I knew from experience. So I was strict on elevator obedience.

"You could have ordered Killa not to make the omelets," Hill scratched the dogs' ears as we descended to the lobby.

"I know." The doors opened and the dogs bounded out. "I don't order Killa, ever."

Hill just nodded, "You're a good guy, Chief."

We went through my garage. My poor little Ant looked rather shabby after my brother's supercharged Hundil. We passed my cycle. Hill went up to it and jumped in the seat. Her look told me everything. "NO you are not riding my bike, EVER!"

She got off but I knew what she was thinking. *NO NEVER*, I thought but somehow I knew, I knew she'd finagle a way to try it. I just knew!

Good guy or not, I watched as Hill started on the track. She'd taken Hoover, not Bear. Bear could never let Hoover take the lead. I felt my Hibernia Hound pull me hard chasing after his brother. "Wait," I yelled as I rushed after her. Damn, she'd done this on purpose. "Hill, wait up!!

Thank you for taking time to read Murder on Nestor, the first book in the Space Detective - A Skip Brown Adventure series.

If you enjoyed it, please consider telling your friends or posting a short review. Word of mouth is any author's best friend and is much appreciated.

The adventure continues

www.ingramcontent.com/pod-product-compliance
Lightning Source LLC
Chambersburg PA
CBHW022006170626
46808CB00001B/314